LITTLE (99 DADDIES BOOK 5)

CASEY COX

SYNOPSIS

Little: (adjective)
Small in size, not big, not large, tiny.
See also: Addison "Big Brother" Mark.

A big boy who wants to be a little.
A little who can't find a Daddy.
A Daddy who will do anything for his boy...s.

Nick Macklin doesn't do "normal" or "typical." So when this loud, out and proud big boy explores being a little, things don't exactly go according to plan. Despite feeling a deep pull that draws him to age play, there's something that's...off. Something is holding him back and he has no idea what it is.

Neither does his Daddy, Steel Crawford. And it's driving him crazy not being able to give his boy what he needs. Steel begins to question himself and starts doubting whether he's the right Daddy for his boy.

Until one day, fate brings Addison Mark into their lives. He's smart, sexy, and has the cutest Australian accent Nick and Steel have ever heard. Could he be the missing piece that Nick and Steel didn't even realize they were looking for?

LITTLE

Little is a Daddy-lite age play MMM romance featuring a big boy who wants to be a little, a little struggling to find a Daddy, and a silver fox Daddy who is about to have his hands very, *very* full.

Come along for the ride and enjoy some crazy/sexy/cool shenanigans involving questionable beauty treatments, some light age play (no ABDL, but it is discussed), spontaneous singing, creative uses of kitchen countertops, an unforgettable hottest daddy contest, a crew of sassy friends, lots of LOLs, and all the feels on the way to a heartwarming HEA... Actually, wait, stop.
That's not entirely true. Every single Daddy (and their boy) in the *99 Daddies* series will return for an EPIC round of happily ever afters!

Little is the fifth–and final!–book in the *99 Daddies* series. Each book in the series will contain overlapping characters and storylines, so you may enjoy them more by reading them in order.

99 DADDIES

99 Daddies is a hilarious, entertaining, and heartwarming contemporary/new adult Daddy-lite MM romance series.

Escape to Daylesford, the (fictional) Daddy capital of America. If you love steamy and complex Daddy/boy dynamics, May-December gay romances with a twist, sweet and sassy MM age gap romances—and chasing those guaranteed HEAs—you'll love it here.

So come along and meet the 99 Daddies of Daylesford. Who will be YOUR favorite?

CHAPTER ONE

NICK

I know, I know. The sequel is never as good as the original. Well, at least that's true most of the time, right?

I mean, watching Keanu and Sandra stopping a bomb from exploding on a bus full of people was super cute that one time back in the old days of VCRs, fax machines, and phones that were stuck to the wall for some reason. Did the world really need to see it happen again...on a boat?

Or those movies with Liam Neeson, where his family members keep getting themselves kidnapped. Seriously, by the third movie you really gotta ask yourself: why am I even watching this?

There are reasons why most movies, books, and fairytales stop once they reach the *happily ever after* part. Part of it is that as soon as we've seen magic strike once, it's almost a little redundant to be expected to believe that it can happen again...and again...and again.

But the main reason that most sequels don't work is that, as much as we like the idea of a happily ever after—the chase, the drama, and the fantasy of it once it actually does arrive—we aren't actually interested in all the gritty little details.

Yes, we want to see the main characters end up together, but how do you go from watching a grand romantic gesture unfolding—like, say, a totally fab-u-lous flashmob throwback to an epic '90s music video—to seeing the couple having fights about stupid things like whose turn it is to do the laundry and paying bills?

It's romance we're chasing, after all—not reality.

Luckily for me, I got both with Steel Crawford, and my happily ever after is super fucking amazing.

A lot changed in my life over the past eighteen months.

I was no longer a slashie. I'd had to give up being a naked butler *slash* go-go dancer *slash* erotic cake-sitter *slash* magician *slash* every other crazy side hustle I had going on. I was solely focused on creating a bakery empire.

The business was going well. I had to hire more staff which was a little scary, but awesome. I learned that a spreadsheet is not an obscure dance craze from the '80s. And I worked my sassy big boy magic on social media and built up quite the cult following. In news that will surprise absolutely no one, everyone loved me online. I was quotable, meme-able, and oh so gif-able.

What can I say? Being an out, proud, and loud plus-sized boy who gives zero fucks inspired people to sprinkle some of that big boy energy into their own lives, like fairy dust icing on cake...or something like that. Hey, I had bakers who baked, I was the face—and booty—of the business.

The bakery still required a lot of hard work and ridiculously early starts. That, like my waist size, hadn't changed... And I couldn't be happier (about both things). I'd always been a hard worker, so there was no way I was going to slack off after Steel bought me the bakery. And while I had turned things around and started to make a modest profit, I still had a long way to go before I achieved my ultimate business goal: nothing too fancy or out there—just total world domination.

Speaking of the world, my grandparents were still living their best lives, traveling around Europe. Who knew that there were so many countries over there? When they left, I thought they'd be back in a few weeks once they'd seen everything. The Eiffel Tower, a few bridges, some castles. What else was there, really?

I knew of the UK, France, Italy, and Spain. Maybe a few islands floating around the edges, but that was pretty much all there was there. Or so I thought. We video called every week, and each time we talked, they mentioned new places they'd visited, and there were always plenty more on their bucket list. They were fast approaching their eighties, yet they were giving off major young and carefree vibes. I couldn't have been happier for them.

And then there was big ol' me.

I got my happily ever after with Steel, and let me tell ya, the reality was just as good as the fantasy. Our path to true love wasn't a smooth one, but hey, I was *so* worth it. I'd landed the best Daddy in the world—and I was prepared to jelly wrestle anyone who dared to challenge me on that.

Steel was beyond amazing. He was the most thoughtful, kind, smart, and sexy man I had ever met. He was strong and looked after me in a way that filled something inside of me I'd never known needed filling. For the first time in my almost twenty-six years of life, he made me feel the one thing I hadn't truly felt before—safe.

He was just the right amount of patient, observant—and when needed, controlling. He absolutely needed to be, with a boy like me. In that good way. In that *Daddy needs to set the rules and I need to be a good boy and listen* way. Which, spoiler alert, I didn't always do. That was why him being so patient and knowing me so well came in handy.

I knew I wasn't a typical boy and could be a handful. I wasn't a pushover and I didn't do anything just because someone told me to. I was strong-willed and not afraid to share my opinions. The best thing was, he knew all of that...and he loved me anyway. In fact, I think part of the reason he loved me so much was because I was who I was.

In the same way that he gave me something I'd never known I needed, I think I did the same thing for him. Steel was so used to boys being impressed by his looks, his money, his high-powered career, that they didn't look any further to see the brilliant man that he was underneath all of that.

But I did. I saw through all of that surface-level stuff to the heart of who he really was. And I knew that it meant a lot to him, that I loved him for who he *was*—not for what he *had*.

So yeah, we deffers had a pretty perfect relationship. Everything was going great. We were in love, living together in his gorgeous penthouse in the clouds, having the most mind-blowing amazing sex I'd ever had. Everything was just like my fine ass— peachy as fuck.

Um...

It's just, what....

Well, you see...

Here's the thing...

This big boy has got one little problem.

Emphasis being on *little*.

Emphasis being on...me.

As much as I wanted to, and as much as I had really and truly tried, there was just something blocking me from—something standing in my way of—becoming a little. Or at least, being a little in the way I saw it in my head and felt in my heart. It was like there was a line in front of me that I just couldn't seem to cross. A barrier I couldn't overcome.

But I damn well wanted to, and I was determined to give it my best shot. Because, and I had no idea how I knew this, I could feel it there within me. I knew it was something that I wanted. I could feel it there just under the surface. It was so close I could almost touch it.

Almost.

"How are you feeling?" Steel's voice stirred me back into reality.

"Good. I feel good." I smiled and looked down at the brightly colored plate filled with chicken salad.

I could feel the heat of Steel's gaze on me. Out of the corner of my eye, I saw Steel's hand reaching across the table. His fingers met mine and it sent a warm rush through me. As always. He wrapped his smooth fingers around my hand. His presence, his touch, always managed to make me feel both calm and excited at the same time.

I looked up. A shadow of doubt flickered across his face, but it quickly disappeared. "I'm glad to hear it. So, you liked the bath, then?"

I nodded enthusiastically. "Yes, I did."

That part—right before we had sat down for the dinner we were having—I had really enjoyed. I'd had so much fun splashing around in the warm bubbly water. Steel had bought every bath animal toy known to humankind. I loved playing with them all, rearranging them around me in the bath. All lined up neatly, taking them from one side to the other, and then back again. It was a silly game I had made up, but it really helped me to get out of my own head, and closer to what I imagined a little headspace felt like.

Tonight, Mr. Ducky'd had a fight with Herman, the giant pink octopus. It was a long-standing issue between them both, which had finally come to a head. Mr. Ducky accused Herman of hogging my attention. He may have had a point there. The giant squishy octopus had become my new favorite bathtime toy; his long tentacles were so much fun to swirl around the water. But that didn't give Herman the right to splash water at Mr. Ducky like he had done, even if it was, literally, water off a duck's back.

So, I had given them both a stern talking to and a time-out at separate corners of the bath. They each needed to think about what they'd said and what they'd done. Tomorrow, they would make up and become best friends forever. What could I say? I was an eternal optimist who didn't mind some basic-bitch drama along the way.

"So, what's wrong?" Steel's light blue eyes narrowed.

I pushed the plate away, suddenly losing my appetite. That was never a good sign. My heart started beating faster and I felt the first signs of panic coming on.

Steel's fingers escaped from my hand. He stood up. "Let's go."

"Where?" I asked, getting up and following him before he even had the chance to answer.

"To the room." His voice was flat and firm.

I smiled, placed my hand in his and we walked silently from the kitchen, across the living room, until we reached the very end of the corridor. He opened the door to the very last room and flicked the light on. The nursery came to life. I always felt comfortable here, like I had loosened a really tight belt and could finally breathe for the first time.

I sat down on the fluffy white rug by the large window overlooking the skyscrapers of Daylesford as Steel padded around the room, switching on the assortment of lamps. He knew how much I liked them. When they were all turned on, he walked back over to the door and turned the bright overhead light off.

The only light in the room was coming from the lamps. No two were the same, but they all had pretty stained glass lamp shades that threw subtle hues of orange, red, blue, and green light all around the nursery. It made me feel as if I were in a fairytale. I guess, in a way, I was.

I blew out a noisy breath. Steel sat down beside me and crossed his legs. "How are you feeling *now*, baby?"

My heart swelled. He knew me so well. He could tell that I wasn't feeling right at the dinner table, so he'd changed the setting to one that he knew would soothe me. He was so good like that. That perfect blend—patient, observant, and exercising just that bit of control that I needed.

I flicked a glance at him. The gentle lights danced across his beautiful face, lighting up his thick gray head of hair in shades of blue and orange. He was staring at me, making me feel like I was the only boy in the world, the only thing that mattered to him.

I wanted to tell him. I did. But that would have meant that I first needed to know what was going on with me. And I didn't. I had no freaking idea of that myself.

Why was I so comfortable being a little in the bath, so free and joyous splashing around in the water, but when I got to the table and saw the sippy cup, the colorful plate and children's utensils Steel had laid out for dinner, that block within me returned, feeling like it was going to suffocate me? It was like I could only get to a certain point, do certain things, but not go a single step further. I had no idea what any of that was about.

We had talked about this before—many times—but it still didn't stop my insides from filling with shame. As if I had let my Daddy down. Like there was something wrong and broken with me, and before too long he'd see it too, and my whole fairytale life would come crashing down around me...kinda like Paris Hilton's fame.

I had spent countless hours online, reading everything I could possibly find about how other littles got into their little headspace. From what I could tell, Steel and I were doing everything right. Steel was the most out-of-this-world amazing Daddy when it came to creating an environment for me to access that part of myself. I had a big beautiful nursery, and every single accessory and toy that a little could possibly want, and still, I couldn't *get there*.

Which meant that the problem wasn't with him.

It was with me.

I sucked my lower lip in between my teeth, hoping it would hold back the tears that were threatening to burst through. I felt embarrassed. Exposed. Like an idiot. But worst of all, I felt like I was letting down the man who loved me so much—and who I loved in return, more than anything else in the world.

A single tear fell down my cheek.

"Oh, Daddy." I closed my eyes, praying that the dam wall of tears wasn't about to break.

Before I knew what was happening, Steel's strong arms were wrapped around me. He was holding me tight, bringing me into his warmth. His safety. His love. He stroked the back of my head before he wove his fingers into my shoulder-length tangled hair, playing with it the way he knew I liked.

"Oh, my sweet boy." His voice was deep and smooth like velvet. "I've got you, Nick. You are so precious to me."

And with that, I sank deeper into the hug, wiggling myself closer into his body, as wave after wave of confusion and shame rolled through me.

Why wasn't this easy for me?

What was wrong with me?

Why was I blocked like this?

I didn't know what I had done to deserve Steel's love, but as he held me in his tender embrace, I hoped that he would be able to forgive me for not being the boy he wanted me to be.

Like a defective toy, I silently prayed that he wouldn't take me back to the store and return me.

CHAPTER TWO

STEEL

"Remind me again why we're hanging out at my place and not at your bar, Steel?"

I looked over at Porter, still dressed from the day, looking all important and mayor-like in his expensive suit. He had let his ashy blond hair grow out a little longer. It was styled neatly to the side.

"Because I want to talk," I replied, glancing around his sunken living room. "And Deffers is way too busy. Even on a Tuesday night."

My eyes briefly met Stirling's. He was sitting on an armchair, across from the couch Porter and I were seated on. Stirling scrubbed a hand across his stubbled jaw. He looked like he needed to talk too, and by the sour look on his face, the private location suited him as much as it did me.

"Mikey, Nick, and Declan are at my place, Stirling's water pipe has broken"—I heard a grumble escape Stirling's lips at the mention of that—"and Hudson's out of town, which only leaves your place, my friend."

Porter *hmpfed* theatrically, but I could tell it was only for effect.

"Well, I guess when you put it like that." He tapped his fingers excitedly along the edge of the coffee table as he tipped his head at the glass he had given me. "Anyway, what do you think of the drink? I think it's good enough to be added to the drinks menu at Deffers. I won't even charge you a licencing fee."

I ignored Porter's comment as I lifted the frosted margarita glass to my mouth and took a sip. Stirling did the same.

"Holy shit," I exclaimed as the drink burned through my tongue. At least, that was what it felt like it was doing.

Stirling looked like he had swallowed a squirrel.

"What is that?" he said, putting the drink down on the coffee table, shaking his head.

"It's a jalapeno margarita. Pretty good, right?" Porter was looking way too happy with himself for me to bring him down.

"It's...got some kick to it," I said diplomatically.

Porter's eyes widened as he looked at us. "Is it *too* hot?"

"Maybe a little," Stirling said as his face flushed a red hue. He wiped the sweat forming across the top of his forehead with the back of his hand.

"Well, you can always take the jalapenos out." Porter pointed to the little green pieces floating around in our drinks, before quickly adding, "Just use a spoon, not your fingers."

I looked at him curiously. "Why?"

Porter's lips curled into his customary devilish smile. "When I was making the drinks before you two arrived, I was cutting the jalapenos, when I had to go to the bathroom."

"Oh." For the first time, a sparkle returned to Stirling's eyes, as if he knew where Porter was going with his story. I still had no idea.

"Yeah..." Porter dropped back onto the couch. "Let's just say that taking a whiz after touching jalapenos can be quite... painful."

The three of us roared with laughter.

"Ouch," I said.

"Yeah, one big motherfucking ouch," Porter said, still laughing. "I think I might even be out of action for a night or two."

I laughed so hard my cheeks started to hurt. "Poor Declan."

"Indeed." Porter's face lit up as he shuffled forward on the couch. "Did I tell you guys what crazy-ass position we got into over the weekend?"

"No." Stirling's voice was firm, as if he were speaking for the both of us. Because he was. "And we don't need to know either, Porter."

Porter rolled his eyes. "Fine."

"It's nice to see that not even being happily in love can change your predisposition for oversharing," I said, giving his knee a friendly slap.

"I like being open about my sex life. I have nothing to hide, especially now that the whole world knows pretty much everything about what I do and what I'm into. And besides, I refuse——"

"—to apologize for it," the three of us said in unison. We'd all heard Porter's mini-rant so many times over the years, it had permanently etched itself in our group memory.

Porter looked taken aback, but I wanted to make it clear we weren't mocking him. I squeezed his knee.

"Hey, I'm glad you're happy with Declan. I really am. And I am thrilled that you're able to be your true, authentic self. I don't think you can ask for too much more in life."

"I'm happy for you too, Porter," Stirling added.

We all lifted our glasses and clinked them noisily together. Stirling and I both took smaller sips this time, while Porter practically threw his back. If his throat was on fire, I certainly couldn't tell by the neutral expression on his face.

He turned to look at me. "Well, anyway, think about serving this drink at Deffers. The customers would love it, and it would be a great drink to have for the upcoming *Daylesford's Most Eligible Daddy* contest you guys are hosting soon."

I shook my head and couldn't help but smile. Porter Jones really was something else. After knowing the guy for over half my life, what else could I expect from him though? He might have been weird, and annoying, and an oversharer, but I still loved him like a brother.

"So, you and Declan are all good," I said after a moment as I turned my attention to Stirling, hoping to avoid addressing Porter's suggestion. "How are things with you and Mikey going? Any news on the baby front?"

"Specifically, any news on the baby *making* front you'd care to share?" Porter added jokingly, but his smile died on his lips as we both saw the change in Stirling's expression.

The lightness was gone, replaced by the dark, stormy clouds that had covered his face since he and I had arrived at Porter's place.

He cleared his throat. "Mikey and I have put our names down with a couple of adoption agencies."

"That's great, Stirling," I said with a cautious optimism. I could tell there was more to the story.

He nodded, taking his time to summon the words. That was the great thing about him. Even though he had opened up so much since he had gotten together with Mikey, the slow and stoic Stirling was still very much there. I loved him like a brother too.

"It is." He cast a smile in my direction. "It's just that, well, did you guys know that it can take years to adopt a child?"

"Yeah, I've heard that," Porter said. "It's a big, complicated system, unfortunately. But Daylesford does have some of the most successful adoption agencies in the country."

More nodding from Stirling.

There was something else going on with him, but he was building up to it. Porter and I exchanged a brief glance. We both knew when Stirling needed some space, and this was one of those times.

"We actually spoke with a potential surrogate last week." His words hung heavily in the air. It was clear by his tone that things hadn't gone well.

"What happened?" Porter asked softly, before adding, "And if you'd rather not tell us about it, that's fine too, Stirling."

I was impressed. The man was maturing.

"It all started off fine," Stirling began. "Until she realized that there was no *Mrs.* Bishop."

"Oh, shit." I felt so bad for my best friend. "I'm sorry, Stirling. That's a terrible thing to go through."

"Thanks, Steel." Stirling's spirit seemed to lift a little, as if talking to us was unburdening him.

"How did Mikey handle it?" Porter asked, a worried look firmly planted on his face.

"Remarkably well, actually. I mean, not that I should be surprised. He's one of the strongest and most resilient people I have ever met."

Porter and I murmured our agreement.

"It's funny, but it seems to have hit me harder for some reason." Stirling's face was twisted in pain.

I wanted to do something to fix it, but I was powerless. There was nothing I could do to make it better.

"Are you okay?" I asked, racking my brain trying to come up with some sort of solution.

Stirling considered my question.

"I am," he said. "We're getting through it together. Talking helps a lot."

"It does," Porter agreed. "It's such a cliche, but communication really is the key to a healthy relationship."

My face must have contorted strangely at that remark, because both men skewed their heads in my direction. Porter's light green eyes zoomed in on me.

"And what about you, Mr. Crawford? How's the age play thing with Nick coming along?"

I folded my arms across my chest. "It isn't."

I loved Nick with everything I had in me, and I was so proud of the progress we had made. We'd come so close to not even getting our relationship off the ground because of miscommunication. Then, when we took our first steps, our mutual inability to talk about things jeopardized our future. If going through all of that had taught me anything, it was how much we needed to talk—about everything.

It was just that talking was a lot easier said than done. Some things were easy to bring up and discuss. Silly things like how my biggest pet peeve was a certain someone leaving four or five wet towels on the bathroom floor...after every one of his three daily showers. That topic I could raise, and we resolved it quickly and easily.

Even some sexy topics were manageable. Like sharing with him that despite being a top, I secretly loved having my ass eaten out. Sure, that conversation might have been a little awkward for me at first, but I pushed through it. And now, I had my legs swinging in the air, with Nick's tongue lapping at my hole, practically every other night. So in other words—totally fucking worth it.

But our forays into age play were in an entirely different stratosphere compared to anything else we had encountered as a couple. And even though we'd promised each other we would talk about everything—no matter how hard, or weird, or uncomfortable—this was...different.

I was failing my boy.

I was doing something wrong and because of that, Nick couldn't reach the headspace he needed to in order to fully become a little. I had tried everything, bought everything I could to try and help him, but it was pretty obvious that it wasn't working.

That *I* wasn't able to make it work.

My chest felt heavy as it sank with the realization that maybe I wasn't the right Daddy for Nick. Here I was with the most beautiful, wonderful boy in the world, and I couldn't step up and be the Daddy he needed me to be.

I didn't deserve him.

And soon enough, I was sure he would see it himself. Heck, maybe he already had and that's why we were having these issues. The darkness I was spiralling into for the millionth time was interrupted by Porter's unnervingly calm voice.

"Do you want to talk about things, Steel?"

I looked up and saw his and Stirling's tight faces looking at me. They were both studying me carefully, their eyes filled with genuine concern. I took a deep breath and nodded.

"On the one hand, things are going really well with us. We're madly in love, and I'm over the moon about it. I can't even find words that express how much I love him. I've never felt anything like it before. He sets my soul on fire, and I just burn for him, you know?"

"Whoa, very poetic," Porter said with a lighthearted chortle. "But yeah, what you guys have is totally amazing."

"I can see it," Stirling chimed in. "When I look at you together, there's such a strong chemistry there, Steel. A real connection."

My friends' words were reassuring. It was nice hearing that they could tell what Nick and I had was real. But then the heaviness returned to my chest as I continued talking.

"But on the other hand, there's this...thing."

"The age play thing, you mean?" Stirling asked.

"Yeah. That. It's not going very well. I've tried everything I could possibly do—"

"And you guys are talking, right?" Porter interrupted. "Because you know that was a key part of my patented three-point plan—"

"Oh my god," I groaned.

Thankfully, Stirling found a pillow and aimed it precisely at Porter's head, knocking him backward onto the couch.

"Thank you," I said with a smirk, looking over at Porter as he straightened himself. "Yes, we're talking. A lot, even."

I stopped, unsure of what to say next or even how to say it.

How do you find the words to admit that you're fucking up the best thing that's ever happened to you?

"I must be doing something wrong."

Stirling leaned in closer. "What do you mean by that, Steel?"

"Well, Nick knows this is what he wants to do. And he knows that I'm all in. Even though I've never explored this lifestyle with anyone else, I had a freaking nursery ready to go before I even met him. So, it's something we're both keen to explore, and it's not working, so...that's on me. My lack of experience is messing this up. I can't give my boy what he wants."

My voice cracked on those last few words. I reached for the jalapeno margarita and took a massive gulp. The liquid ignited my throat, but funnily, it made me feel better this time. Like it was knocking some sense into me.

As my closest friends were just about to.

"This isn't your fault, Steel." Stirling kept his voice low and deep. "Just because you're new at something doesn't mean you're bad at it. I mean, look at me with Mikey. I'd never been a Daddy before I met him, and yes, there was a learning curve, but I got there. Heck, I'm still getting there. You never stop learning or growing, especially in a relationship."

"Exactly." Porter raised a finger sharply into the air. "You and Nick are in a relationship *together*. If something is happening within the relationship, you both have a part to play. It takes two to tango..."

Stirling and I looked over at Porter. He had almost lifted off the couch in excitement. He definitely wasn't done talking yet.

"And sometimes...it takes more than just two."

I looked across at Stirling, then back to Porter. "What on earth are you talking about, Porter?"

A smirk tugged at his lips. "Well, by the sound of things, you and Nick are solid as a couple in every other area but this. So, why not get a little help?"

Stirling lifted an eyebrow. "I'm still confused."

"Yeah, me too. Use better words."

Porter sighed. "Have you considered the idea of opening your relationship up? You can bring in a co-Daddy—which is a copyrighted Porter Jones original term by the way—to help you guys get through this."

"People do that?" I asked. I still wasn't fully clear on how what he was suggesting would work, but I was a little surprised to find myself not outright rejecting it either.

Porter gave a firm nod. "It is. I have some friends who have just done something similar. They're both tops, which made their sex life a little...complicated, shall we say. So, they brought in a third. It started off as just a weekly sex thing, but over time, they've all developed feelings for each other, so now they're seeing where things go."

I could see Stirling mulling the idea over. I was doing the same. It wasn't the stupidest thing that Porter had ever said, and believe me, the man had said plenty of dumb-ass things over the years.

But his words did hit upon one raw nerve. Was bringing someone else into the relationship an acknowledgement of my failure as a Daddy? And how would Nick react, even to the suggestion of it? We'd been doing a lot of talking, but this topic had never come up.

"Just think about it," Porter suggested, shooting me a delicate smile. "And once you have, talk to your boy about it. Who knows, it could be the very thing that you both need."

CHAPTER THREE

ADDISON

"Are you sure this is safe, Kymmy?"

I cast a nervous look at my best friend, who was standing just a few feet away from the treatment chair I found myself lying in. Because of her. This was all her idea.

"Why are you asking me that?" Kym's high-pitched voice echoed in the small room. "Is it because you think I'm some crazy Asian bitch?"

"What? No. Oh my god, Kymmy, you know I don't think that. Why would you even say that? What—what are you talking ab—"

Kym's head flung back as she erupted in her customary cackle.

"Oh, it's too easy to wind you up, Addy." Her eyes were filled with tears of evil joy. Pure evil joy.

She may have been my best friend for the last five years, but Kym Lee still knew how to push all of my buttons.

"What can I say?" she said, giving a casual shrug. "I like making white people squirm. It's a guilty pleasure of mine."

"Well, please don't." I was already feeling nervous about the treatment, I didn't need her adding anything else to the mix to put me even more on edge.

"Relax, I'm Korean. I can make a joke like that."

"Yeah, well, I'm a white Aussie gay dude," I shot back. "And I can't laugh at a joke like that. And you very well know that."

A knowing smirk stretched her lips before dissolving. "I'm sorry, Addy. I won't do it again...today."

I shook my head, trying my best not to smile. Kym's lack of a filter was one of my favorite things about her. It was just that right now, I had other things on my mind. Gross, slimy things, to be precise. I began to wonder why I hadn't opted for a more conventional beauty treatment, preferably one that involved me being slathered in a dreamy cream filled with something decadent like Essence d'Escargot.

Before I could ask Kym for any more details about what I was about to put myself through, the door swung wide open. A perky blonde woman, who looked like she was just out of beauty school—no wait, make that high school—entered.

"Hello. I'm Emma. You must be Addison Mark?" I gave a quick nod. "I'll be your technician today."

Technician? Geez, that sounded so...serious. Like it involved heavy machinery or something. Oh god, did it? I swallowed and smiled as normally as I could. Even though there was nothing normal about what was about to happen.

Emma stood near me, her head briefly shielding me from the bright white lights of the treatment room.

"How are you feeling?" Her eyes were a deep blue and they were friendly.

So, I guessed that was a good thing.

"I'm...okay, I guess."

Emma's eyes lit up. "Ooh, I love your accent. Whereabouts in England are you from?"

Kymmy let out a cough and I swore I could have heard a

muffled *idiot* coming from her direction. I looked up at Emma. It wasn't her fault that Americans always seemed to get my accent so wrong. Like, *different country that's on the opposite side of the world* wrong.

"Actually, I'm from Australia," I explained, summoning my inner Hugh Jackman friendliness. Or what I imagined a friendly Hugh Jackman would sound like. Or what I imagined I would sound like with Hugh Jackman inside of me. Alright, I needed to stop stressing about this, it was clearly scrambling my thoughts like an omelette.

Emma gave a wide smile. Her voice went dreamy.

"Oh, I love Australia. I really want to go. But that flight though. It's so long."

"Not a huge fan of flying?" I asked.

She shook her head. "Nope... It's very drying for the skin."

A suppressed giggle filled the air. I glanced over at Kymmy who had positioned herself in the corner of the small room. She made her *she's an idiot and I can't wait to bitch about her the second she leaves the room* face at me.

"Also," Emma continued, "I hate, hate, *hate* snakes. Ew, and spiders, too."

A shudder spread through her entire body at the thought.

"But snails you're alright with, I take it?"

She let out a sweet-sounding laugh.

"Yes, snails are fine." Her face turned slightly more serious as she looked at me. "So, can I ask your reason for doing this? It's just that we don't have many men coming in for this sort of treatment."

"I'm gay," I said, hoping that would somehow explain why I was about to do something totally wacky, vain, and completely self-indulgent all for the sake of trying to reclaim some of my recently departed twenties looks.

She nodded her head.

"Ah, I see." Yep, she got it. "Well, you've come to the right place. This will completely revitalize your face, Addison."

Great. Because if I was going to sink to the desperate depths that I had to in order to hold onto my looks at the age of thirty-two, an empty promise from a teenage-looking technician was just the assurance I needed. I let out a noisy, sad sigh.

"Are you just visiting Daylesford or have you moved here?" Emma asked as she busied herself, getting her workstation ready.

"I moved here when I turned eighteen. I got a scholarship at Daylesford University. I fell in love with the place—and with someone who lived here—and almost fifteen years later, I'm still here."

A knowing grin spread across her face. "Yeah, Daylesford is a pretty amazing place. Why would you want to live anywhere else? If you'll excuse me, I just need to get one more thing. I'll be back in a moment."

As Emma disappeared out of the room, Kym practically leaped at me. "Oh my God? Did you see her? She's like a fucking tweenager."

I frowned. "You're not helping, Kymmy."

"Relax, it'll be fine. It's not a complicated treatment." She waved her long fingers in the air, her brightly painted red nails catching my eye. "It's so easy...even a twelve-year-old could do it."

"Why *am* I even doing this?" I asked Kym, but really, I was asking myself.

I felt her hand brushing lightly against my forearm. "You don't have to do this if you don't want to, Addy."

Another sad sigh, this one more for dramatic effect than anything else, really. The truth was, I had no choice. I did have to do it.

In GayWorld (which is kinda like Disney World but with more magic and glitter, and fewer carbs in the restaurants), I was in no man's land. And believe me, that wasn't a good place to be. I'd gone from being a lean party boy twink in my early twenties, to a filled out (body-wise) and settled down (relationship-wise) twunk in my late twenties, to...whatever the hell I was now in my early thirties.

So basically the stereotypical gay lifecycle: I went from a twink, to a twunk...to a 'twas.

I was expired, like an old coupon. On the verge of becoming invisible. Ignorable. Unloveable. It was hard to lose your identity simply because the number of candles on your birthday cake kept going up.

In so many ways, I was still the same person I had always been. I still loved Godney (commonly referred to by non-stans as Britney Spears), I still had the same levels of energy I'd had when I was in my twenties, and most importantly of all, I still wanted to find a Daddy.

But that was getting increasingly hard—no, wait, borderline impossible—as I was approaching the gates of Daddyhood myself. At least, in terms of age. There was no switch in my brain that could ever shift me from boy mode to Daddy-ville. Not in a million years.

No. Even though my age was starting to work against me, I was as much of a boy now as I ever had been. I needed to be looked after. I wanted the surrender. I wanted to be...loved like that. Taken care of. Completely and totally.

Kym's fingers lifted off me and she made her way back to the seat in the corner as Emma returned to the treatment room. She was holding a tray, which she carefully placed on the workstation beside me. She flashed me a wide smile, revealing two rows of perfectly bleached white teeth.

"Are you ready, Addison?"

I gulped. "Ready as I'll ever be. This might be a stupid question, but it doesn't hurt, does it?"

Her blue eyes shone brightly. "No, it won't hurt. It might feel a little wet and maybe even a little icky, but there's no pain. I promise."

Something about her youthful optimism reassured me.

"Alright, let's do it," I said, glancing over at Kymmy who flashed me an over-exaggerated smile with two thumbs up.

Or in other words, her totally geeky selfie-pose for whenever we were traveling and taking photos in front of cheesy tourist traps. Something about her familiar dorkiness reassured me.

It seemed like I was in need of a lot of reassurance.

"You may want to close your eyes," Emma suggested.

So I did. There was no way in hell I wanted to actually see what was going on.

I held my breath as I felt the first touch on my forehead. She was right. It was wet...and icky. Then, I could feel her placing more of them across my cheeks and on my chin. Then I heard the sound of a photo being taken.

"Kymmy," I growled.

"What?" She giggled. "When else am I ever going to have the chance to see my best friend's face covered with snails?"

"Keep still," Emma said, interrupting my attempt to come up with a suitable retort to fire back at Kym.

"Just don't post them online," I muttered, trying to keep my lips from moving too much. I peeked one eye open and could see Emma frowning at me. "Sorry, I won't say anything else. Promise."

"Good. You need to keep still." The twelve-year-old could be bossy when she needed to be.

I took another breath as Emma placed the sixth and final snail on my face.

"There," Emma said, her voice filled with pride. "Just relax, Addison. Stay as still as you can. No talking"—that part was as much directed at Kym as it was at me—"and now we just let the magic unfold."

"Uh, how long does the magic unfolding part last?" Kym asked from the corner of the room.

"We recommend about ten minutes for your first treatment—"

"First treatment?" I interrupted as the slimy critters slowly slid all over my face. "You mean I need to do this again?"

"Please stop moving, Addison," Emma reprimanded me. "Your

skin needs to be still so that the snails' secretions can penetrate through."

Secretions.

That was just a fancy word for mucus.

She was right though, in that it wasn't a painful experience. It was just gross. Sticky, slimy, and...so fucking gross.

"I don't think I can do this," I said.

I started to feel sick as a snail made its way over my nostril, blocking my breathing while I felt another one leaving a sticky trail of slime as it wandered over my lower lip.

"Can you take them off, please?" I spat the words out.

"We just need a few more minutes for the hyaluronic acid that the snails secrete to really seep in. Can you wait a bit longer, Addison?"

I shook my head and a snail slid its way down my cheek at the movement.

"No. Please take them off. I've had enough," I said through gritted teeth.

Emma adeptly pulled them away and wiped my slime-ridden face with a wet wipe in a panicked frenzy.

I opened my eyes and sat up. "I'm sorry. I just couldn't do it anymore."

"There's no need to apologize," Emma said as she placed the snails back onto the tray she'd brought them in on.

"I guess there's a reason why this treatment isn't more popular with men. They have impossibly low pain, or ickiness, thresholds," Kymmy added from the corner, completely unhelpfully.

Emma pursed her lips, suppressing a grin. "Take your time leaving, Addison. I'll meet you in the reception area, just to make sure you're okay. You did well."

It was an unconvincing lie.

She left the room and right on cue, Kym and I burst out laughing.

"Holy shit, you should have seen your face," Kym said in between fits of giggles.

"Of all your crazy suggestions over the years, Kymmy, I think this one takes the cake."

I ran my fingers over my skin. It still felt a little damp.

"I'll meet you out front," Kymmy said, leaving the room and closing the door behind her.

"Okay."

I walked over to the mirror, hoping to do a double take in disbelief at how many years it had shaved off me. But no such luck. My face looked exactly the same. Same dark brown eyes, same solid nose, same shoulder-length deep brown hair. I tilted my head to the side and let my gaze soften.

Faces fascinated me. Not my own, obviously. Just like some people didn't like hearing their own voice, I didn't necessarily like seeing my own face. That was why I felt a lot more comfortable behind the camera, shooting other people's faces, rather than in front of it.

I was a photographer for a reason. I felt safe behind the lens, looking out at the world in front of me. I also felt in control, as if I could in some way sculpt reality to fit into my lens. If only my life were as easily manipulated.

I had just finished doing some photography work for a community-funded senior citizens' project. The campaign was designed to highlight the advice seniors had for younger people, gleaned over a lifetime of trials and tribulations. The photos I took were pretty standard black-and-white portraits.

The skin of people in their seventies, eighties, and nineties was such an interesting thing to look at close up. In so many ways, it looked what we'd think of as bad. It was dry, wrinkled, sun damaged. All the things I was desperately trying to avoid, myself.

And yet, I also saw a deep beauty in their faces. Every line, every spot, every patch of folded skin told a story. And as Daylesford's favorite senior citizen, Mrs. Langley, told me once the shoot had wrapped up, "When you get to this age, you don't have time to waste on things that don't matter."

She was right, of course. But she was a hundred and two years old, not thirty-two like me. And at this age, it did matter. Especially if I wanted to find someone who could love a boy of my age. I sighed, pulled my hair into a low ponytail, and slipped my baseball cap back on.

I walked out and met Kym in the reception area.

"Let me pay for this and let's go get insanely drunk. How much is this so-called beauty treatment going to cost me, anyway?"

Kym's eyes widened for a moment, before she put on her classic over-the-top smile. "Five hundred and thirty dollars."

She made a beeline for the front door before I could throttle her.

"Are you kidding me?" I yelled after her.

"I'll buy drinks," she said over her shoulder as she disappeared out the front door.

I paid for the treatment and stepped outside, where she was waiting for me.

"I can't believe you talked me into this."

She looped her arm around my waist. "Yeah, my bad on this one. But you still love me?"

I smiled even though I didn't want to. She was my best friend, after all.

"I do."

"And are you ready to get insanely drunk with me?"

"Yeppers," I replied loudly with a massive grin.

"Ah, I love you my crazy Aussie friend."

"And I love you my crazy...Kymmy."

CHAPTER FOUR

NICK

The good thing about talking when you're in a relationship is that it cuts out a lot of unnecessary bullshit and drama. But as I looked up and down Steel's muscular, tanned, and very naked body lying on the bed in front of me, I didn't give a shit about any of that.

Because the good thing about Steel telling me he loved getting his ass eaten out was that it meant I had just discovered my newest, favoritest thing to do in the world. A talent I didn't even know I had—world-class rimjob giver.

My eyes traveled up and down the most splendid specimen of silver fox that had ever existed. After all this time he could still take my breath away. His abs were a field of hard ridges, the veins in his biceps popped with every slight movement, and his skin was so gloriously smooth and supple, it made me commit to never forgetting to moisturize after showering ever again.

I licked my lips hungrily. His light blue eyes landed on me and I smiled.

"Are you ready for your tongue bath, Mr. Crawford?" I asked, putting on my most serious, professional voice.

He laughed at my silliness. It made his eyes sparkle and his whole body shake. I liked being able to have that sort of an effect on him, but right then, I wanted to make his body shake for other reasons.

"Assume the position," I said, switching to a Southern drawl for some reason.

His face stayed fixed in that beautiful smile of his. "God, I love you so much."

"Well, don't be shy," I said as I gently grazed my fingers up and down his strong thighs. "Tell me why?"

Now, I had morphed into poetic mode.

"Because, my beautiful boy," Steel said as he raised his legs into the air, cupping the back of his knees in his hands, "there is no one in the world like you."

"Well, duh." I tried to give off a casual smile, but his words ricocheted in my chest...and it felt wonderful.

With his legs in position, I scooted my body down so I was lying on my stomach, my mouth inches away from his tantalizing pink hole. I smacked my lips again.

"And now, my boy," Steel's voice was imbued with the sweetest need, "eat Daddy out."

He didn't have to tell me twice. I jammed my face into his meaty ass and began slurping away, filling the room with the filthiest, sloppiest sounds. I liked to approach rimming the same way I approached kissing, or an all-you-can-eat breakfast buffet—I went all in.

There was something so hot about the vulnerability it had taken for Steel to tell me how much he liked this. How much he wanted me to do this. Even though I hadn't really had a lot of experience with rimming before, I became a pro in no time.

"Oh god, that feels good." Steel dragged his fingers through my long messy hair, gently pressing my head even closer to his ass. He *really* liked it when I got all up in there.

My tongue was swirling about like crazy. I was savoring his woodsy scent, his tantalizing taste. I reached my hands around to each of his solid ass cheeks, and gently pulled them apart, making his sweet hole gape further open. I wanted to be as deep inside him as my tongue could possibly reach.

His body rocked and heaved about on the bed as I drove my tongue farther into him, lapping furiously. Greedily. As if my life depended on it. As if I loved him with all of my heart and soul. Because I did. I really, truly did. And I wanted to show him that in everything I did for him.

Including this.

Including being a little.

That thought quickly got pushed out of my head as I felt Steel's ass clench around my mouth.

"Oh, fuck. I'm coming, I'm coming, baby."

I peered upward. I had been so engrossed in what I was doing that I hadn't even noticed Steel had begun to jerk himself off. Soon, sticky ropes of cum landed on his belly while I kept my tongue gliding around between his cheeks, just enough so that he could still feel it, but backing off slightly too. I knew how sensitive he got down there after he came.

"Oh, my beautiful baby," Steel exclaimed when his intense orgasm finally subsided. I crawled up the bed and lay down beside him. "That was fantastic. Thank you."

I threw a cheeky smile at him. "I'm the one who should be thanking you. That's, like, the best dessert ever."

He let out a sweet laugh as he pulled me into his arms. My head rested on his chest and I could feel his heart beating like a freight train.

"You know what we should do now?" he said, still a little breathless.

"What?" I said, happy that it was taking him a while to recover from my expert rimjob.

"We should go online. I've been looking and I've found some little clothes that I want to show you."

"Oh, okay."

I got up and walked over to the desk where Steel usually left his laptop. I turned around and he patted the bed, motioning for me to sit down next to him. I tried to keep my face as normal-looking as possible, but inside, a familiar tightness was gripping my chest.

Just go with it, just go with it...

Of course, it would have been a hell of a lot easier if I knew exactly what I was meant to just be going with. I still had no freaking idea why I was experiencing this—whatever the fuck this was—any time the topic turned to anything little-related.

I sat myself down on the bed next to Steel and handed him the laptop.

"You know, you don't have to buy me any more things. You've spent too much already. I don't think there's anything left to buy...Daddy."

His lips tugged upward at that word.

Daddy.

It was just the smallest of small movements, barely more than a twitch, really, but it happened.

Every.

Single.

Time.

I guess I had made it hard for him to get me, so the man had well and truly earned the right to be called Daddy. And it was rolling off my tongue so much easier as more time went on. Especially when my tongue was still laced with the lingering deliciousness of his hole.

Steel flicked the laptop open and the screen filled with rows of brightly colored onesies.

"See, I've been thinking, baby," he said as he scrolled down the seemingly never-ending array of clothes, "we've got a great setup with the nursery. It's filled with lots and lots of toys. And you have such a great time when you're having a bath, and we have plenty of toys for that too. So maybe the one thing that we're missing is...clothes?"

We both turned our heads and looked at each other. I tried to match my smile to his, but he seemed confident. As if he were on the right track. That all of my problems and issues could be resolved by wearing the right type of baby clothes.

I mean, maybe he was right. Every fiber of my being was hoping he was right. I just didn't know for sure. And that scared me. Could a few onesies and pajamas fix everything that was wrong and broken within me?

"Okay, let's have a look. Show me what you've found." I turned my gaze back to the screen, determined to give this a proper, decent chance. I trusted Steel, and I knew that everything he did came from a good place.

"See, look at this piece." With a few excited clicks, Steel opened up a short-sleeved safari onesie. It was white and covered with cute monkeys, giraffes, and elephants, all designed in a cartoon style.

I felt the tightness in my chest loosen a bit.

"I like it," I said. And I did. "It's super cute."

Steel's eyes were scanning the product description. "It's made of five percent spandex, so it has a good amount of stretch. It comes in a wide range of sizes, oh, and it's also available in black. That might be nice." His eyes drifted over to me, then back to the screen. "Ooh, and look, baby, it keeps diapers in place without sagging or shifting."

Fuck.

There it was.

The tightness was back around my chest.

That word.

Diapers.

An oppressive heat was now clawing its way up my neck.

Steel's fingers tapped away at the trackpad until he found what it was he was looking for. Even with only the nightstand lamps lighting the room, I could see the excitement written all across his face.

"Look, Nick," he said, tugging my arm gently. "These blue diapers are covered in balloons and airplanes. Don't they look like fun?"

My heart stopped, and not in the good, *ohmyGod Britney just announced another residency in Vegas* kinda way, but in the *I am seriously freaking out and about to lose my shit* kinda way.

Silence filled the room. I closed my eyes, trying to calm myself down and answer what was a very simple question. Did I like the diapers or not? Any other normal person wouldn't have had any problem with answering either yes or no. But just in case I needed any more evidence—I clearly wasn't normal.

I heard the sound of a laptop being placed on the bedside table, and then I felt Steel's arms wrap around me. I kept my eyes closed as I snuggled into his body.

"I'm sorry, Steel," I whispered into his chest. "I don't know what's wrong with me."

"Hey," he said, stroking my hair. "There is nothing wrong with you, my beautiful boy. Did the diapers freak you out a bit?"

I nodded and Steel kissed the top of my head. I breathed in his scent and allowed myself to be held by him. I didn't know how or why he was being so patient with me—or how long it would be before he moved on from a boy like me who couldn't give him what he wanted—but right now, I let myself sink into the safety he was offering.

"There's only one thing that I want in this world, Nick."

I peeled myself off him so I could see him as he spoke to me. He looked worried, burdened. A pang of guilt pummeled into me for making him feel so bad. Any other boy would have been jumping for joy in my position.

A crazy-hot silver fox daddy? Check.

A crazy-hot silver fox daddy who adored having his sweet pink hole rimmed? Check.

A crazy-hot silver fox daddy who was loving and kind and generous and patient and every single sort of amaze-a-balls? Check.

The man couldn't be more perfect, and here I was on the brink of fucking it all up. Until, of course, Steel Crawford took even the most perfect of perfections and raised it to new heights.

"The only thing I want, baby, is to make you happy."

His words sent a shock of warmth across my entire body. I pressed my lips into his, kissing him with even more force than I had rimmed him with earlier. I knew I would never be able to say it, so I wanted to show him just how much his love and faith in me meant. Our tongues wrestled as Steel's hands caressed my body, sliding over my big belly, across my hard ass, and down my hairy legs. He was just as hungry for me as I was for him.

When I eventually pulled away, his eyes were filled with love. True love. I swallowed around the lump that had formed in my throat.

"I really liked the onesie," I said.

Steel stared at me with wide eyes. "Are you sure, Nick? I don't want you to feel like you're under any pressure. Because you're not. If you didn't like anything, or if you don't want to wear these types of clothes, please know that you don't have to."

I took a moment and considered his words. "I know."

"I don't want you to ever do anything just for me, okay? I love you unconditionally, not because you do what you think I want you to do."

"What about the towel-on-the-bathroom-floor situation?" I joked, and Steel's face broke into a wide grin.

"That's different." He lightly traced his finger across the bridge of my nose. "That's the only exception."

"Thank you, Daddy. You make me feel so safe and so loved."

"I'm glad, Nick. Because you are both of those things. You are safe and you are loved. So much."

"I do want that onesie. It'll really make my booty pop." I giggled.

"Okay, as long as you're sure." Steel leaned over and picked the laptop up. I snuggled in beside him as he rested it on his knees and opened it up.

"Can you go back?" I asked. "There was another onesie that I liked on the previous screen."

"Sure, baby." Steel tapped away and brought up the entire range. He started to scroll down slowly. I became slightly dizzy trying to take them all in.

"That one." I pointed to an orange onesie that was covered with illustrations of trucks and cars.

"You like it?" Steel asked.

I nodded firmly. "Deffers. I like the trucks on it."

"Then I will get you one in every single color." After a few more clicks, he shut the laptop and placed it on the nightstand. "Done. It'll arrive in two days."

I looked up adoringly at Steel. "Thank you."

A wrinkle formed on his forehead. "For buying you a onesie?"

"No," I replied. "For being the bestest Daddy in the whole wide world. I love you so much."

CHAPTER FIVE

STEEL

"It's here," I shouted excitedly as I kicked the front door shut with my foot.

The package had just been delivered downstairs and the doorman had brought it up the second it did like I had asked him to. The last two days had stretched out for what felt like an eternity. But it had finally arrived and I was so fucking...aroused. Just holding the damn box was making my cock twitch.

"Nick," I yelled again as I placed the box on the kitchen countertop.

"I'm coming," he hollered from the direction of the bedroom. "Please don't hurry me. You can't rush the perfect grand entrance I plan on making."

I laughed to myself as I grabbed some scissors, delicately slicing through the tape to open the box.

I didn't know why I hadn't thought of it earlier. Nick and I had spoken about it before. I knew that being a little wasn't coming as easily for him as he'd hoped it would. Heck, it wasn't exactly flowing for me either.

I'd always assumed that when I found the right boy, things would just click into place automatically. I *had* found the right boy, I was soul-level certain of that. I trusted my feelings for Nick more than anything else in my life, and I knew he felt the same about me. But despite that—with things feeling so right between us in every other aspect of our relationship— it felt like there was a missing piece, or something just a tad askew, when it came to this.

I opened the box and carefully took out the onesies one at a time, laying them out on the white marble countertop. I looked at them and smiled, imagining Nick's body snugly wrapped up in them. Don't get me wrong, I wasn't expecting the clothes to be the solution to whatever was going on for both of us, but it was definitely a step in the right direction. I could feel it.

My boy liked to strut around for me, parading the findings of his latest thrift store shopping spree. And I loved nothing more than watching him do it. The way his face would beam, his lips curling into the most inviting smile I had ever seen. How his body would bounce as he walked around, transforming whatever room we were in into his own personal catwalk. The looks he gave me—sexy, pouty, silly, funny, smoking-fucking-hot—as he snapped his head and popped his shoulders back, channelling the long lost days of the true supermodels. It was all the things I loved about him wrapped up in one.

But the diaper thing?

That was a step too far for him...and for me too, if I was being entirely honest. I'd only suggested it the other night because I thought it might have been something that he wanted to explore. And if he had been willing and open to it, I would have gone along with it as well. There wasn't anything I wouldn't do for him, and that included expanding my horizons beyond my current comfort zone.

But his reaction when I opened up the diaper section of the

website told me everything I needed to know. He wasn't into it at all. And that was totally alright. The thing that I was very quickly learning about the age play lifestyle was that there was no one-size-fits-all approach.

Just like being a Daddy, there were at least ninety-nine different ways to approach how people wanted to experience age play. Some people liked diapers, and that was great. Others didn't, and that was fine too.

There was no right or wrong way to do any of this, other than keeping lines of communication open, having trust, breaking through any barriers that came up along the way, and being in love. And it filled my heart with so much pure joy that Nick and I had all of those things. The important things, the stuff that truly mattered.

We might not have figured out all the little details just yet, but we were on the right track. Stirling and Porter were right, the connection Nick and I had was real. They could see it. I could feel it. And I knew that whatever roadblocks we were facing, we would be able to get through them...together.

I was just about to let out a groan as I realized how my thinking had taken an unexpected turn down Cliché Avenue, when my eyes were pulled like magnets to the other end of the kitchen.

Standing there, completely naked, was the most gorgeous boy in the entire universe.

"Oh, hello," he said casually, lifting his hand and giving an innocent-looking wave. "What have we here?"

He lazily wandered over to where I was standing, his fingers running along the countertop.

My eyes were transfixed on him. I couldn't look away. His lure was irresistible. His tan skin was glowing. His tousled hair fell gently over his shoulders. His brown eyes shone brightly in the late afternoon sun and his beautiful, meaty cock dangled between his legs, bouncing softly from side to side with every step he took.

"I could ask you the same question." I was surprised I had enough blood left in my brain to even respond.

Nick bit down seductively on his bottom lip as his fingers traced over the onesies I had laid out on the countertop. "Which one of these would you like to see me in first, Daddy?"

I loved how he lowered his voice and put more breathiness into that word.

Daddy.

I squared my shoulders. I always tried my best to hide it, but it made me all sorts of hot and bothered hearing him say that word, and hearing him say it *that way*.

Every.

Single.

Time.

I looked down at the onesies I had laid out. I'd ordered five in total. They all sported the same print of trucks and cars, but they came in different colored backgrounds—white, black, brown, orange, and blue.

I picked up the brown one. "This one."

Nick smiled. "Good choice."

He took it from me and our fingers touched. Just that minor touch was enough to give me a massive hard-on, my cock straining against my briefs. God, how was he still able to do this to me after all this time? Not that I was complaining in the slightest. I was perfectly fine with being this responsive to my boy for the rest of my life.

"Is there any particular reason you like this one so much?" he asked as his eyes flickered with playful mischief.

I looked at it again. "I like it because it reminds me a bit of that shirt you wore when you did the flashmob for me."

His eyes lit up at the memory of that memorable night.

"I can see that." He placed it over the front of his body and looked up at me. "How does this look, Daddy?"

"So beautiful," I said without a second's delay. "Would you..."

My breath caught in my throat, but I quickly cleared it. "Would you like me to help you put it on, my boy?"

Nick's eyes widened. "Ooh, yes please."

I planted a gentle kiss on his forehead. He gave me the onesie, then placed both hands on my shoulders. The firmness of his pressure felt... different this time. Normally his touch, any touch, no matter how small, excited me. This time, it didn't. At least not in a sexual way.

This time, his touch ignited another part of me. The protective, Daddy side of me. Even though he was standing before me, completely naked, the energy between us was changing. It was going from being purely sexual to us slipping into him being a little and me being his Daddy.

Holy hell, it was happening. It was really happening.

My eyes met his and he gave me the slightest nod, as if he were thinking the exact same thing that I was. My heart beat hard, knocking about in my chest as I continued unlocking the deep primal instincts within me.

I gently took Nick's hands off my shoulders and placed them by the sides of his body. Then, I pulled the onesie over his head and helped him push his arms through. The material fell down his chest and landed at the tops of his thighs.

His face was relaxed, his eyes soft. "How do I look, Daddy?" There was such tenderness in his voice that I thought it would make me snap in two.

"You look stunning, baby." He really was a sight to behold. The material stretched out beautifully over his body, clinging to him just enough to give him the right amount of support, while having enough give which would hopefully make it comfortable for him to move and play about as a little.

"But more importantly, how does it feel?" I asked, tracing my fingers along the stitching in the shoulder area. "Is it too tight? Not tight enough? Does anything feel scratchy or not right?"

He moved closer. "It feels amazing, Daddy. I feel—I feel..."

I picked up a loose strand of hair that had fallen across his face and wrapped it back around his ear. "What is it, baby?"

"I feel like I'm becoming...a little."

"Oh baby, that's so good." A heady mixture of relief and elation washed over me. "Let me just button you up and we can go into the nursery and you can play with some of your toys, if you like?"

"Okay, that sounds good, Daddy."

"Here, put your hand on my shoulder again."

Nick obeyed as I lowered myself until my knees touched the floor. With his hands leaning on me for support, I pressed into place the three buttons located in the crotch area of the onesie.

Even though I was at eye-level with his cock, my body was filled with all sorts of warm, protective feelings and not the usual sexual desire I was used to. Being a Daddy—in this particular way—was something I had wanted for so long, and now to be here with Nick, actually doing it, was blowing my mind a bit.

It was exciting, and new, but at the same time, it also felt familiar. Like I was tapping into some part of myself that knew this was what I wanted to be doing, before I'd even had the chance to do it.

"There," I said, slowly getting up again once I got him all buttoned up. I took his hands off my shoulders, keeping one of them firmly placed in mine. "Now, let's go and play with some toys."

And as we walked down the corridor to the nursery, I knew that we had reached a massive turning point. Sure, our issues weren't magically resolved with this one thing, but I could tell we had just taken a massive step in the right direction.

"You weren't kidding when you said this place was always packed," Porter said over the hum of people talking and laughing. The music from the dance floor echoed through into the VIP section of Deffers.

"What can I say?" I said, settling back into the plush tan Chesterfield couch we were sitting on. I took in the busy scene in front of us, proud that the place that I once saw as a dream in my head was now a fully realized—and successful—reality. "Declan's article put us on the map, and since then, we've only grown and grown."

"Yeah, I can see that. Well, you should be very proud of yourself, Steel. Even though you're a silent partner, this place is a huge hit. Daylesford needed a Daddy bar like this."

"I couldn't agree with you more," I said, smiling. "Another drink?"

Porter looked down at his almost empty glass. "Sure, why not? Declan and Nick are still picking us up, right?"

I raised my hand in the air and waved it until I got Pierre's attention. "As far as I'm aware, yeah, that's the plan."

"Gentlemen." Pierre stood over us, his impeccable smile in place.

"Where?" Porter joked, snapping his head around in his maniacal fashion.

I shook my head at Pierre. "You'll have to forgive him, he's been making the same pathetic joke for years."

Porter gave me a friendly shove. "Hey, it's not pathetic. And since when does this place do personal service like this?"

He gave Pierre a good look up and down.

"Hey, I don't want us to be Daylesford's hottest Daddy bar just because we're better than The Laird. I want everyone here to experience amazing customer service, but especially in the VIP lounge. We wanted to do something that would take it to the next level."

"Well, I'm impressed." Porter picked up the drinks menu off the small table in front of us, his eyes scanning for...something. He looked up at Pierre again. "Have you got anything with a little...heat to it?"

"Uh..." Pierre shuffled on his feet as he considered Porter's question. "We don't have anything spicy, but the triple-distilled vodka we use in the appletini gives it a nice kick. Oh, and we only use local and organic apples in it too."

"Hmm, well that's too bad," Porter began, and I recognized that tone. That *I'm about to be an asshole and there's nothing you can do to stop me* tone. "Organic apples sound nice and all, Pierre, but last time I checked, Deffers was a bar, not a fruit shop."

I clenched my jaw. "Porter."

"What, Steel?" Porter's attempt at sounding innocent only irritated me even more. He flicked his eyes back over at Pierre. "I know of this great place that does these fabulous jalapeno margaritas. You might want to speak to your manager and let them know about that."

"Duly noted," Pierre said, trying to keep his voice steady.

"On second thought, I think we're good for drinks. Thanks, Pierre," I said, shooting him an apologetic smile.

A look of relief swept across his face as he turned on his heels and was out of there in a nanosecond.

"There was no need for that, Porter," I grumbled once Pierre was out of range.

"What?" His light green eyes widened as if he had no idea what I was talking about.

We both knew better than that.

"So, how are things with you and Nick going on the age play front?" he asked, settling back into the sofa and providing a very welcome change of subject.

"Good, actually." I bit my tongue and reminded myself who I was talking to before I said anything else. I'd have to tread lightly. "We're talking, which is a good thing."

Porter's face broke out into a friendly smile. "It is."

"And we made some...progress a few nights ago."

Both of his eyebrows shot up. He leaned forward. "Progress?"

"Yeah. We're both so new to this whole thing, you know, so

we're taking some time and seeing what works for us. Trying new things. Keeping what works, discarding whatever doesn't feel right."

Porter let the words sink in. "Well, that's good. I'm happy for you."

"Wait, that's it?" I asked, more than just a little bit surprised. I'd been expecting a Spanish Inquisition-style probe into the finer details of my sex life.

Porter shrugged. "What can I say? A man can change, can't he?"

"Yes, but you're no ordinary man, Porter. I saw you checking out Pierre before."

"Hey," Porter raised his finger in my face. "Looking is fine, anything else isn't." Then he said something I never thought I would live long enough to hear Porter Jones say. "I've found him, Steel. Declan is the one for me. No other man even interests me. Sure, I look sometimes, but I don't feel anything when I do."

"Whoa." It was the only word my brain could find.

"Tell me about it," Porter said with a soft chuckle. "How do you think it makes me feel?"

"How *does* it make you feel, Porter?"

His face went neutral for what felt like a very long time. Then he turned his head, his eyes sparkling like stars in the night sky as he said, "It feels like I've arrived home."

I clutched at my chest. "Oh my god, that's actually really beautiful."

"What can I say?" He fell back onto the couch. "I'm the luckiest Daddy on earth."

"I can think of at least three other Daddies who would be prepared to fight you for that title."

We both laughed.

"I'm glad to hear Declan is having such an amazing influence on you. I was worried there for a second."

Porter furrowed his brow at me. "Worried about what exactly?"

"That all your talk about me and Nick opening up our

relationship to a third person was, I don't know, you projecting something onto us that you wanted for yourself."

He grinned. "Steel, I am a lot of things, but you know that I don't beat around the bush. I'm direct—"

"Almost to a fault, some people might say."

"Stupid people might say that, yes," he said with a laugh. "But seriously, I was only suggesting it because I wanted to open your mind to the possibility. That's all. No projecting undertones, I swear. So, have you thought about it?"

"Only a little bit," I said, regretting I didn't have a drink in my hand for this conversation. "I just don't know if I could do it, Porter. Do I have it in me to share my boy with another Daddy?"

"Who says it has to be another Daddy?"

I cocked my head sideways. "What do you mean?"

"It could be another boy. A more experienced one. Kind of like a big brother for Nick. Someone who can guide him and teach him, lead him in any areas where he might lack experience. That sort of thing."

"Hmm." I shuffled on the couch. "I'd never even thought about that before."

The thought of another boy didn't trigger any alarm bells in me, so that was a good thing, I guessed.

"Besides, it could be hot. Having two boys play-fighting over who gets to ride Daddy's dick first."

"Oh, stop it, Porter," I said as a flash of heat travelled from my stomach to my cheeks.

Something about Porter's words inadvertently stirred something within me...and in my pants. I had to admit—to myself, because I would never divulge it to Porter—that the thought of Nick being with another boy turned me on.

"You know," Porter said, thankfully changing the subject yet again, "this will be the first year that no one from the quad squad is going to be entered in *Daylesford's Most Eligible Daddy* contest."

"I'm not complaining."

"Hey, me neither." Porter narrowed his eyes at me. "Has Nick mentioned anything to you about the contest?"

I shook my head. "No, why?"

"Well, it's just that Declan was asking me a whole bunch of questions about it the other day...right after he had hung out with Nick and Mikey."

"Maybe they talked about it and he was curious?" I suggested.

"Yeah, maybe." Porter didn't sound entirely convinced. "I think they're up to something, those boys of ours."

"They're just getting along well. I'm very happy about that."

A grin stretched Porter's lips. "So am I. But mark my words, Steel Crawford, our boys are planning something. Just you wait and see."

CHAPTER SIX

ADDISON

The cool air hit my face as I made my way down the street. I always loved this time of day—the thirty minutes or so before sunrise. The sky was still black, but the first signs of a new day were beginning to lighten it around the edges, like the night was trying to hold on for just that little bit longer.

For a photographer, there were two magic hours every day: sunrise and sunset. I was always an early riser. When I lived back in Sydney, I'd be at the beach just as the sun peeked over the horizon line, catching the waves with my mates. That morning stillness, the dawning of a new day and all the promise it held—that was my favorite magic hour.

Maybe I should get back into surfing? I smiled as I reminisced about how good it used to make me feel. Then again, I was a lot younger back in my surfing days. Nothing's better than being in your twenties feels.

And there it was again—my biggest issue.

I was getting older, and with each passing day, feeling worse and worse about it. Heck, I'd even let Kymmy talk me into that crazy so-called treatment with the snails. That was fucking gross... and desperate...and pathetic. Which pretty much summed up my life at the moment.

But I cast those thoughts away as I looked around the deserted street, enjoying a silence that I hardly ever got to experience in this normally bustling part of the city.

My backpack bounced around behind me, filled with my gear—both professional and personal. The shoot at Revolver had taken longer than expected. Despite starting just after eight, it was after three by the time we finished. It took until four to pack everything away. I was tired, but a good tired.

Revolver had become like a second home to me, especially after my marriage ended. Tyler and I had met literally one month before my student visa was going to end and I was due to go back home to Australia.

We fell in love in four short weeks and got married. Sure, we were met with some suspicion from immigration officials who incorrectly assumed our wedding was a ploy to keep me in the country, but we proved them wrong. At least, for seven years.

Then I did the worst thing a boy could do to his Daddy.

I turned thirty.

I had been getting more and more worried about it throughout my late twenties. Tyler's constant comments about wanting to stick his dick into any semi-decent-looking younger guy that we saw whenever we went out didn't help allay my insecurities. A wandering eye was one thing. I could handle that.

A wandering cock on the other hand...

Fucking Steve, the party planner he had hired to plan my surprise thirtieth birthday party, was about as awful as the sickly sweet chocolate *Thunder from Down Under* cake Steve had convinced him to get. The guy managed to steal my husband and fast track me down the path to diabetes all in the one night.

That was two years ago and I hadn't been with anyone since. Believe me, it wasn't for a lack of trying. I was on all the apps. I went out to bars with friends almost every weekend. I even put myself out there at Revolver. I did everything I could in the hopes of finding a Daddy that would want me. But it was all for nothing.

A thirty-two-year-old boy simply wasn't *a thing*, and like Regina George told Gretchen Wieners in *Mean Girls*, I should stop trying to make it happen.

Daddies wanted younger boys they could mold and guide over time. Boys with supple skin, tightly muscled bodies, no wrinkles on their faces, and thick heads of gray-less hair. Boys that were keen to serve, obey, and please their Daddies in all sorts of ways.

I still had that eagerness within me. Heck, age didn't dampen that fire at all. It raged just as hard now as it had when I took my first steps into boyhood in college. The desire to be controlled, dominated, and to surrender to just one man was so deep, and so strong, that I didn't think it would ever leave me.

But I wasn't in my early twenties anymore. My looks *were* changing, I couldn't deny that. My body was still muscular because I worked out at the gym for two hours, six days a week. But when I smiled, wrinkles formed around my eyes. They didn't completely disappear once I stopped smiling, either.

My forehead had a line running across it which was getting deeper, more pronounced. And tinges of gray were threatening my otherwise deep brown hair, appearing like unwanted extended family members showing up at Thanksgiving. I had come *this close* to buying my first bottle of *Just For Men* last week. Yep, it was getting that serious.

I was done.

Over.

A has-been.

My time had passed.

I was Daddy-less, and all the signs pointed to that being a long-term thing for me.

I heard some muffled footsteps behind me. I turned around but didn't see anyone there. I stopped at the intersection, but decided not to wait for the light to turn green. There weren't any cars on the road anyway at this time of morning, so I crossed to the other side.

I patted my front pants pocket and could still feel it in there and breathed a little easier. It was my safety. A little toy car that allowed me to connect with that part of me wherever I was, whenever I needed it. It was my version of American Express—I never left home without it.

I glanced over at the window displays in the storefronts I was walking past. The East Village was having its revitalization moment. All sorts of trendy stores were moving into the area, giving the place a hip, artsy feel.

I heard footsteps behind me again. Louder this time. I turned over my shoulder and saw two shadowy figures approaching me quickly, before one of them lunged at me.

"You fucking deviant." The words rang out as one of them yanked my shirt, pulling me in toward them, while the other one threw a hard right hook that landed square on my jaw.

My body stiffened, but I managed to pull myself away, trying to steady myself on my feet. They weren't done yet though. Another punch, this time pounding into my chest, pushing the air out of my lungs with such force it made my head spin.

They pushed me backward and I tripped over my own feet, falling to the ground. My thoughts turned to the gear inside my backpack. Fuck, I hoped it wouldn't break. I covered my head protectively, fear coursing through my veins as they started kicking my body like it was a football.

I heard another derogatory remark, then another. But then the words started to fade, my head filling with the unrelenting thumping of my heart. All I could see was the pavement before everything went black...

"Get the fuck off him."

The words stirred me back to life. I had no idea how long I had been out. All I knew was that the punching and kicking had stopped. I peered up and saw another figure, a large man, making light work of the two guys who were attacking me. A sweet, almost strawberry-like scent wafted through the air.

After he got them off me and threw a few punches their way, they scampered like the cowards they were. I heard their footsteps fading as they ran down the street.

"Are you okay?" The man dropped to his knees beside me. I flinched, covering my head protectively. "It's okay, I'm not going to hurt you."

I could hear him breathing sharply, but that was probably due to the fact that he had just saved my ass from two thugs.

I started to get up. I saw his outstretched hand but chose to ignore it. No, I had to do this on my own. I got to my feet, fuelled by adrenaline and a desperate desire to get the fuck off the streets and back to the safety of my apartment.

I was a little dizzy, but I figured I had enough time to get home before the pain really kicked in. The man, who despite his imposing size didn't look scary or threatening at all, bent over and handed me my backpack. It looked like he was trying to smile as he handed it to me, but I wasn't sure. I couldn't bear to look at his face. Even though he was a complete stranger, I hated him seeing me like this.

I felt so...reduced.

I looked down at my backpack, my hand fumbling around with it, feeling and listening for signs that anything was broken in there. It all felt, and sounded, alright. I silently prayed my gear had survived the fall without any major damage. At least that would be something.

"Hey."

His voice was friendly, and I knew I had no reason to fear him, but I couldn't look him in the face. Not now. Not when I was like this. I threw the backpack over my shoulder, wincing at the pain it unleashed on that side of my body.

"I can help you. We need to call the police. Please."

I shook my head, keeping my gaze firmly locked on my feet.

The guy was persistent though.

"My name is Nick," he said. "I own this bakery."

I turned and saw that we were standing in front of a bakery. His, as it turned out.

"Why don't you come inside? We can get you cleaned up... I have cookies."

Finally, I looked up. He was staring at me with wide brown eyes, his bottom lip sucked in between his teeth. He was so much younger than I had made him out to be in my head. He had a boyish face and long hair—just like me.

I must have looked like an absolute mess. Shame flooded my belly and rose up my body, like a searing, inescapable acid. I took a step back. I saw his face twisting, as if he wanted me to stay, to look after me and make sure I was alright, but I couldn't stay there anymore.

All I could whisper in a barely audible, hoarse voice was, "I like cookies too."

And with that, I turned around and took a few steps until I was feeling strong enough to break into a light jog.

"Hey, you dropped your..."

I barely heard what he yelled at me, but it wouldn't have made me stop anyway. I needed to get home. I could look after myself. What other choice did I have? No one else was going to do it for me.

CHAPTER SEVEN

NICK

My eyes widened as Mikey led me into their newly renovated kitchen. "Holy original line-up of Destiny's Child! Wow, Mikey, this looks amazing."

Mikey's bright blue eyes sparkled like glitter. "I know, right? Stirling and his team did an amazing job with it."

"It's huge."

"That's what he said."

I glanced over at my beaming best friend. It may have taken him a few years to find his inner-confidence, but now that he had, Mikey Harrison was one motherfucking sassy boy. And I was living for it.

"Stirling tore down two walls and basically extended the kitchen by about twelve feet in each direction," he explained as he pointed to where the old kitchen used to end.

"I guess that's one of the advantages of owning your own construction company," I said as I took in the massive island in the middle of the space, the exquisite black marble countertops and the huge oven, stovetop, and fancy inbuilt pizza oven by the window that looked out onto the back garden. "Now all you need to do is learn to cook."

I felt a gentle slap across my arm.

"Ha, ha. Very funny. Besides, having a massive island like this..."—he pointed to the island I was leaning against—"has nothing to do with cooking."

It took me a moment to figure out what he was saying, but when I did, I leaped off the island as if it were on fire.

"You mean—?"

"Yep, we christened it last week."

"Uh huh."

"And then over the weekend."

"Riiiight."

"And twice more last night, too."

"Okay, Mikey, I get it, I get it. The only way this island could get any more christened is if you hauled it over to the Vatican and had the pope give it a blessing."

Mikey burst out laughing. "C'mon, let's go into the lounge."

I followed Mikey and the sounds of his sweet laughter as we made our way out of the kitchen and plonked ourselves down onto the couch. He grabbed the remote and turned the television on, muting it.

"What are you doing?" I asked.

"*The Bold and the Beautiful* is about to come on."

I groaned. "You still watch that?"

"I do," Mikey said without the slightest hint of embarrassment. "And don't you act all high and mighty with me, mister. You used to watch it, too."

The show started and, as if I were passing an accident on the interstate, I couldn't stop my head from rotating to get a better look. Brooke's tear-stained face filled the screen. It was scary that I still remembered her name.

"By the looks of things, I must have stopped watching at least three facelifts ago."

"Shhh, things are getting really dramatic." Mikey waved a *shut up and don't interrupt me* arm my way.

I grabbed the remote and pressed a button, killing the image on the screen.

"Let me guess, she's still fighting Taylor for Ridge?"

"Well, yes, but this time it's different."

I sighed and gave my head an exaggerated shake. "Mikey, in the last twenty years, it's never been different. I don't know why those three don't just all hook up and live together."

Whoa, where did that come from? Of all the crazy stuff to come out of my mouth, I had never made a threesome joke before. For some weird reason, I felt my heart beating faster in my chest. I needed to change the topic. And fast.

"So, any more renovation plans?"

Mikey's face grew serious.

"No." He looked down at the ground.

"Mikey, what's wrong?"

He took a deep breath and I could see something building inside of my best friend.

"We were going to extend on the other side of the house as well, to match what we've done in the kitchen. Balance the design out, or something. The architect showed me the plans, but it was all just a bunch of lines and squiggles to me."

"Uh huh. Go on."

Mikey took his time. Something I guess he'd picked up from Stirling. "We wanted to add in a guest room and a...nursery."

"Oh, I see."

Mikey had told me about the fuckery they had gone through with the small-minded surrogate. I felt so bad for them both. As if trying to have a baby wasn't hard enough without having to deal with bigoted people.

"Is Stirling feeling better about it?"

I knew that it had hit him hard, possibly even more than it had Mikey, although I knew it had hurt him too.

Mikey gave a small nod. "Yeah, a little. We've decided to put a pause on that side of things. We just need some space to process everything before we keep going, you know?"

"That sounds like the right thing for you both." I reached out and gave his hand a squeeze. "Have you thought any more about what you, Declan, and I talked about last time we hung out together?"

Mikey's expression changed completely. "Wait, you guys were being serious about that?"

I sat up a little straighter. "Uh, yeah. Of course we were. It'll be the most epic-est thing ever."

"Wait, better than your world-famous, *shame it can't be nominated for a Grammy Award* flashmob performance?"

"Deffers better than even that," I said, smiling smugly. "That was just a warm-up act, kiddo."

A broad smile filled Mikey's face. "Well, let me think about it... Properly, okay? I honestly thought you guys were just joking around."

"Fair enough," I said. "And we have to loop Liam in, too. It will only work if all four of us do it. And you're right, we do all need to think about it. This is, like, majorly serious stuff."

"Okay, sounds good."

"Oh, and Mikey." I pointed my index finger toward him. "Do not breathe a word of this to Stirling, okay?"

I switched fingers, extending my pinky out. Mikey rolled his eyes but came in for a pinky swear.

Now that that was sorted, Mikey turned to me and asked, "So, how are things with you?"

It was a question he'd asked me a million times over the course of our friendship, but this time, it made a heavy feeling settle in the base of my belly.

"I'm okay, I guess."

"Which means that you're clearly not. Spill, Nick. What's up?"

I blew out a noisy breath. "A guy got beaten up outside the bakery a few mornings ago."

Mikey's eyes popped out of his head. "Oh my god, Nick. Did you get hurt? Are you okay? What happened?"

"Look at me," I said, throwing some campy bravado his way. "I'm a plus-size boy who knows how to throw a punch. I'm fine. But the guy they were beating up..."

My voice—and my thoughts—trailed off.

I hadn't been able to get that guy out of my head. The look of terror on his face did something to me. It made me want to protect him, look after him. Seeing him like that, so hurt and vulnerable, killed me.

There was something about him I recognized. I didn't actually know him, I knew that much. Maybe it was his eyes that were a darker shade of brown than mine, or his hair that was longer than mine, but there was something there, something that registered as familiarity, which was totally silly and illogical.

"Is this guy who was beaten up okay?"

"I don't know, Mikey. He ran off."

A look of a bewilderment swept across his face. "He did? Why?"

I shrugged. "I wish I knew. After I managed to get the two attackers off him, I tried to help him up, but he wouldn't take my hand. He didn't want to look at me. He barely said anything either."

I like cookies too.

The only words he had spoken to me echoed around in a never-ending loop in my head.

And then the small toy car that must have fallen out of his bag, or maybe his pocket, during the attack. It was a super tiny version of a normal-sized car. This one could fit easily into the palm of my hand. It was bright yellow and had dark black tinted windows. I had tried calling out after him as he ran away, so I could give it back to him, but he didn't stop. He didn't even look over his shoulder as he raced away.

None of it made any sense.

"Did you call the police?" Mikey's words interrupted my thoughts.

I nodded. "Yeah, I called Steel right away and he said I should do that. Even if nothing comes of it immediately, it's always good to have an official record of what happened."

Mikey tipped his head in agreement. "How...bizarre."

"I know, and I haven't been able to stop thinking about it since, Mikey. It's taken over my brain."

"Why do you think that is?"

I shook my head as I looked around the room. "There was just something about the guy. I felt this weird connection to him, which I know doesn't make any sense."

"You wanted to help him, Nick." Mikey's voice was soft. "You tried. And he wouldn't let you. Maybe it's a feeling of you wanting to do more, but not being able to?"

"Yeah, maybe," I said, squaring my shoulders and trying to put all thoughts of that guy, and what happened that morning, out of my head. At least for a little while.

"Okay, your mouth hasn't moved for the last sixty seconds, so as your Daddy, I believe I have an official responsibility to make sure that you are still alive, Nick Macklin." Steel's attempt at humor filled the inside of his brand-new, diamond white Jaguar XE as we drove down one of Daylesford's beautiful tree-lined boulevards.

I tore my eyes away from the blur of high-end shops I had been blankly staring at and looked at him. He was trying to hide it, but I could see the happiness bubbling away underneath his cool exterior. He was excited we were going to the social night for littles at Revolver. And I was too. When my mind wasn't consumed with thoughts of the guy outside my bakery.

"I'm fine," I said, trying my best to Swift-ize myself out of my mini-funk and shake it off, shake it off...

"No, you are not fine." Steel's voice was firm, but friendly. "And that's okay, baby. Are you thinking about the attack again?"

"Yeah," I replied glumly.

"Nick, we don't have to go to Revolver. The social night happens every month, we can go next time. If you want to talk about what you're feeling, or if you'd prefer—"

"No, I want to go." My voice was sharp. "This means a lot to me, Steel. I want to make some little friends. I think the clothes you bought have helped...a lot. But I'm still not entirely there yet. This is something that I really want to do. It'll be good for me...for us."

Steel kept his eyes on me for a little while longer. "Alright, but I'll be checking in on you all night, and if you change your mind at any stage, please tell me straight away."

"I will."

"You promise?"

"I swear...on Beyonce's life."

"Good. That means you're serious."

We both smiled and the energy in the car shifted.

"How are you liking the drive?" I asked.

I knew nothing about cars, but Steel owned at least a dozen of them. He was so excited by his latest purchase and would rattle off all sorts of design specs and use words that sounded like gibberish to me whenever he talked about them. My like or dislike of a car depended on its color and how big the cup holder in the center console was. Oh, and also the horn sound. I liked loud, but not mean-sounding honking.

"I love this car. It's so smooth. You know, you're welcome to drive it any time, baby."

"No, no." I gave a dismissive wave of my hand. "Like Barbara, Cher, heck even Tina Fey, I don't drive, darling. I get driven."

"I don't mind driving ya."

"Ooh." I snapped my fingers. "I love it when my Daddy gets a little sassy."

"What can I say?" he said. "I've learned from the best."

Steel's wide smile made my heart swell with joy. I was determined to have a good time tonight. We had packed my orange onesie—which had become my favorite—and I was excited about putting it on and playing with some other littles.

There was just one thing I wasn't sure about. "Steel?"

"Yes, baby?"

"Um, I don't know how to say this..."

He quickly glanced over at me before placing his hand in my lap. "Take your time, baby. I'm listening."

"Will the other littles at the club tonight, well, will they be...little? As in, small...? I'm a big boy, after all..."

Steel's face remained neutral. "Honestly? I don't know, Nick. I have a feeling that probably, yes, they will tend to be on the smaller side. But I'm not entirely certain."

"Right."

I felt his eyes lingering on me a second longer. "I hope I'm wrong though. There's nothing more beautiful than a big boy being a little."

I squeezed his hand tight and kept it close to me until we arrived at Revolver. I got changed in the private dressing area with Steel right by my side. He helped me get out of my jeans and T-shirt, and put the onesie on me as tenderly and with as much love as he always did. At the end, he buttoned me up and checked to make sure I was okay.

He pressed a kiss to my cheek. "Are you ready?"

I was. At least, I was as ready as I'd ever be.

"Let's do this." I placed my hand into his and we made our way to the open room that had been transformed into an adult baby wonderland.

There were at least thirty littles in the middle of the space, with their Daddies lined up against all four walls, like parents watching their kids playing sports on a Saturday morning.

Some littles were sitting quietly by themselves. They were reading giant picture books or stacking brightly colored blocks. Others were running around, playing catch, yelling out joyously as they got caught and it was their turn to chase their friends around.

Most littles were dressed in baby clothes, wearing either kid's pajamas or a onesie like I was, while others had on T-shirts with Superman, Batman or some other cartoon character emblazoned on the front. Some littles had diapers on, but not all.

"I see some people I know over there." Steel motioned with his head to the far left corner of the room. "I'll go over and say hello. If you need me, just raise your hand, okay, Nick? I'll come straight over."

I turned and met his gaze. "Thank you. I might just walk around a bit at first, before I settle down and play with someone."

"That sounds good. I'll have my eyes glued on you the whole time."

That thought filled my whole body with a delicious warmth. "Thank you, Daddy."

With a quick peck on the lips, I was off, exploring the little adventure land before me. This was the part I had been anxious about. I was worried that it would be a throwback to lunchtime at school, walking into the cafeteria and not being able to find anyone to sit with.

But it wasn't like that at all. As I moved around the room, every little that I made eye contact with smiled warmly at me. Some of them even waved and said a friendly *hello*.

Steel had been right about one thing. Most of the littles were small. A few, though, were broad-shouldered and muscly, but still on the lean side. As far as I could tell, no one was a plus-size boy like me. But no one seemed to notice or care. My breathing became slower as I continued walking, taking it all in.

Even just doing that, walking around and observing all the

littles at play, was shifting something within me. For so long, I had thought there was something wrong with me for wanting to explore being a little. I got that it wasn't entirely conventional, and that some people even had a problem with it, looking down their noses as if there was something abnormal about it.

But seeing so many guys here made me feel less alone. There was actually a community here of littles and their Daddies and it made it feel...normal.

I began looking around, trying to see who I might approach and ask to play with. I wanted a sign. Something that would make me know the boy I was playing with would be a good fit for me.

And then I heard the word. It rang out clearly above the din of giggles and excited chatter that filled the space. It also had a non-American twang to it, but there was no doubt in my mind that it was a sign from the pop diva goddesses themselves, all four of them—Shania, Mariah, Whitney, and Britney.

It was loud.

It oozed campiness.

It felt like fun...

"Yeppers."

The word came from my right, so I took a few steps in that direction.

And then I stopped—well, actually, I completely fucking froze on the spot as my eyes traveled the length of his long dark hair.

And then his brown eyes met mine. I swallowed what remaining saliva I had in my mouth.

His expression was impossible to read as he stood up.

He was moving in slow motion. I was too as I took a step closer toward him. He moved in closer to me as well.

The world around us faded away.

It was him.

I was standing face to face with the guy who had been attacked in front of my bakery.

CHAPTER EIGHT

ADDISON

I needed it.

I needed it so badly. To get away from everything that was going on in my life.

Thankfully, I had survived the attack without breaking anything, just a few bruises, mainly along my torso. My ribs were a little sore, so Kymmy suggested—and believe me, she can be *very* insistent—that I get them checked out. So I did. There was a little swelling but it went away after a few days.

I still didn't remember much about what had happened. The streets were pretty much empty at four in the morning, but there had been a few people milling about outside Revolver as I left. The sounds of footsteps still echoed in my mind and the anger in their voices as they called me all sorts of horrible names lingered at the edges of my memory.

I must have blacked out for a while, because I had no

recollection of the attack itself. I'd stumbled to the ground, and my only thoughts were to protect my head...and my bag.

And then it stopped. The kicking, the yelling, all of it. At first, I didn't know why. I was dazed, scared, and completely disorientated. But then...him.

The guy who had saved me.

Annoyingly, I couldn't remember much about him either.

He had long brown hair...I was pretty sure.

He said something to me...although I didn't know what exactly.

And he smelled amazing...like a field of strawberries. Funny, that was the one thing I remembered the best.

Although the physical pain had gone, the attack itself had scared the shit out of me. It dominated my thoughts. I had barely left my apartment since it happened, only going out during the day, and only to work or pick up essentials.

The night of the little social was the first time I had gone out at night since the attack.

But I needed to be here.

There were two places where I felt like I could truly be myself. One was behind the lens, and the other was when I was little. The social night for littles at Revolver had become my favorite night of the month. Here, it wasn't about looking for a Daddy—and being reminded how my age made that a nearly impossible task—no, nights like this were about one thing and one thing only for me.

Release.

Becoming a little, and playing with others, was like a security blanket to me. I'd started exploring the lifestyle in college, and despite being in it for over a decade, I was pretty mild by most standards. That didn't bother me. Nights like this showed me that there was no right or wrong way of being a little. It all came down to doing what felt right.

And this felt right. For me, that meant no diapers or binkies. My little age was probably about five or six. Sometimes I went a little older, very rarely a little younger. Some people might call that being a middle, but again, for me, I liked using the term little to describe it.

I liked to wear comfortable, loose-fitting clothing. Yellow was my favorite color, and I still had a soft spot for Big Bird. But my all time most-favoritest thing in the world ever was playing with my collection of toy cars and trucks.

It wasn't a particularly big collection, nor was it made up of super-expensive toys. In fact, it was a bit of a random hodge-podge of vehicles I had collected over the years. But that's kinda what I liked about it. They weren't all new, shiny, and expensive. Some were old, even a little worn, but they were mine. And they all had a place in the line up.

Standouts for me were the shiny red sports car that looked like an old school '80s Ferrari...or something, because yes, even though I liked toy cars, I knew nothing about the real-life ones. It used to be remote controlled, but over the years, I had lost the handset. Which meant that every time I pushed it, the wheels dragged slightly along the ground. The friction created a soft whirring sound that I explained away as actually being the car's engine.

I loved that car so much, but it shared the top place with the granddaddy of my collection, the classic and mighty Tonka truck. Yellow, of course. Even if the yellow had started fading and was interrupted by scratch marks, especially along the sides. But hey, it was a working truck. It was bound to get a little damaged.

Not many littles played with trucks at Revolver, so I was considered something of a novelty—for that, and my Australian accent too. But the regulars had gotten used to it by now. Besides, my accent and all of my Aussie-isms were starting to fade a bit. I'd been living in the States for over a decade now.

So, when a little I knew and liked, Josh, asked if he could join me and play with my collection, little-me couldn't help but exclaim an excited, "Yeppers."

Okay, so maybe a few Aussie-isms remained.

And that was the moment it happened. I had no way of knowing it at the time, but my life was about to change forever.

I felt it before I even saw him.

His presence radiated through the air and filtered in through my skin. And then that smell, that syrupy, strawberry-tinged scent that reminded me of summers spent at the beach, laughing and splashing in the waves and eating perfectly ripened mangoes, cantaloupes and...strawberries.

And then I saw him.

His eyes met mine.

He kept inching closer.

I got up...somehow. I had no idea how my brain or my body was functioning at this point.

I stepped in closer too.

I was scared. Not in a bad way, or because I thought he was going to hurt me. It was just that, even though we were both standing in a crowded room, surrounded by littles playing and having a great time, the moment felt so...huge.

His lips curled into a smile, and I instantly felt lighter. Like someone had patted me on the back reassuringly.

I gave a little wave, my own small gesture of goodwill.

And then it happened. There we were, standing face to face in front of each other. His sweet scent enveloped me, intrigued me, and made me curious to know more about him. I looked at his eyes. They were brown, like mine. But they had a naughty twinkle to them.

His hair was pulled back, but a few wavy strands had fallen down, loosely framing his face. He had thick, bushy eyebrows and glowing skin.

I looked down, taking his body in. My pulse quickened. It was the most splendid thing I had ever seen. He was big. Meaty. Solid. And the best bit? His beautiful body was covered in a snug orange onesie...and it had pictures of cars and trucks all over it!

I tried my best not to look like a chain of fireworks had just gone off in my chest. Because that was exactly what was happening inside of me. And that was why I was scared.

This wasn't normal. I didn't know anything about him. Who he was. If he was—

"Hi, I'm Nick."

Okay, so I knew his name. Oh, and that he owned a bakery. That part came back to me too.

I looked down at the floor, my cheeks flamed. For some reason, my words were trapped inside of me. I couldn't get anything out. At least, not anything intelligible. So I stayed quiet.

"I think I know you." His voice sounded as smooth as Britney's in any of her criminally underrated ballads.

I kept staring at the floor, holding my tongue. I'd thought about this mystery guy, the person who had saved me, every single day since it happened. I wanted to thank him for rescuing me. I had even been tempted to walk past the bakery during the day, in the hopes of getting another glimpse of him. But something always held me back.

The last thing I had been expecting when I came to Revolver was to run into him. Much less to see him dressed as a little. The silence was broken by Nick's words.

"Can I—can I play with you?"

I looked up. He shot me another friendly smile. I nodded, and we sat down in the middle of my collection with my assortment of cars and trucks scattered messily on the floor around us. I remembered I had agreed to play with Josh, but he must have scampered off somewhere as Nick and I had what must have looked like the most super weird greeting of all time with that whole thing that we just did.

"Ooh, I like this one." He picked up the bright red Ferrari. "It looks like something a badass Barbie would fuck Ken in."

A giggle bubbled out of my throat.

And then...*then*, the most incredible sound came out of his mouth as he ran the car along the ground. "Get outta my dreams, get into my car."

I couldn't believe it. He was singing. Softly, sure. But singing. It was like a gay choir of angels had lodged themselves in his throat.

It was beyond amazing. Nick was so confident, so carefree, so *I give zero fucks about anything and just do what I want.* Fuck. It lit me up on the inside simply being in his presence.

He kept on singing. "Get outta my dreams, get into my car."

I didn't know what came over me, but I couldn't hold back any longer. I had to burst free. I had to do it. The tightness in my throat evaporated like Lindsay Lohan's career as I joined him on the, *Beep beep, yeah* part.

"Hey, you know the song." His voice rang out excitedly, as if it were the best thing ever.

We both giggled, before his face tightened, turning pensive.

"So," he said softly as he reached out for the red Ferrari.

"I know that you like cars and trucks..."

He placed his hand over the car and continued to slide it across the floor, the gentle hum of the engine filling the silence between his words.

"I know that you're a great singer..."

He dragged the Ferrari around his front and to the side of his body.

"And I know that you like cookies..."

Our eyes met and, for the first time, I didn't flinch and look away. I met his gaze. Something inside me told me that it was okay to do that.

"But I don't even know your name."

My head dropped. Emotions tore through me, making me feel like I was about to topple over, even though I was sitting on the floor. A cold chill swept over me.

This was my fork-in-the-road moment. I knew it. I could feel it with every fiber of my being. Was I going to do it? Could I take the chance and just do something crazy...off the wall...completely...me?

"I'm in a trance," I started singing quietly. I felt so silly, so insanely self-conscious, but I pushed through it, determined to keep going. "And the world is spinning..."

"Spinning baby out of control," Nick joined in as I stopped, jaw-on-the-floor stunned.

"Oh my god, how do you know *that* song?"

It was the second track on Madonna's *Music* album. It wasn't a single or even a well-known song. But it was a fan favorite amongst true Madonnabes. Like me. And, apparently, Nick.

"Some people buy recipe books because they like to cook," Nick began. His voice was serious but there was an unmissable undertone of sass in there as well. "Others like to read about geography so that they can look at a map and know where certain countries—like Bulgaria, which is actually a real place, by the way—are."

He let go of the car and placed his hands into his lap.

"I am obsessed with pop culture, beginning in the '80s, because everyone knows that nothing significant happened before then. That's a scientific fact."

I let out a laugh—and about ten thousand hectopascals of built-up stress that I had bottled up within me.

"I can tell you everything about anything. The who did what to whom and where and why...and what they were wearing. All for moments like this."

"Moments like what?" The question flew out of me before I could even consider whether it was worth asking.

Nick tilted his head and smiled. "So that when a really nice...boy...sings me a random Madonna album cut—which, coincidentally was rumored to be about how she met her second husband, Guy Ritchie—I can sing along with him without missing a beat."

Who the fuck was this guy?

No, seriously.

Had he just fallen from the sky and landed in my lap? Once to save me and then to completely sweep me off my feet?

He was beautiful.

Funny.

He thought like me.

Kinda looked like me.

Was a little like me.

Was weirdly obsessed with pop culture like I was.

"I'm—I'm Addison."

"Hey, Addison," Nick said with a wide smile. "You already know my name. And this is my boyfriend Steel."

I spun my head around and my eyes landed on a stunningly gorgeous *GQ* cover model of a man.

"Hello, Addison," Steel said in an intoxicating deep voice as he sat down on the floor, joining us. "It's a pleasure to meet you."

CHAPTER NINE

STEEL

The first thing I noticed about the boy Nick was sitting with was that he looked as white as a ghost. A ghost who was about to faint. Or disappear. Or do whatever it was that surprised ghosts did. Which, come to think of it, were surprised ghosts even a thing? Weren't they the ones that usually did the surprising? My mind was uncharacteristically scrambled for some reason.

I cleared my throat, hoping it would also bring some clarity to my head as I looked over at the boy. "Are you alright, Addison?"

When I sat down to join them on the floor, that was when I noticed the second thing about him.

He was drop-dead stunning.

The only other time in my life that someone had been able to knock the wind out of me just by how physically striking they were, was the first time I saw Nick at my fortieth birthday party. The similarities between the two boys weren't lost on me either.

The same deep brown eyes. The same chocolate-colored

shoulder-length hair that fell wildly around his shoulders, framing his square face. The same heady combination of vulnerability, defensiveness, and playfulness that Nick had.

It was like I could tell that he had been hurt, that something had happened to him, and that his walls were up. He was guarding himself, but from what? Even though I had just met the guy, there was something about him that drew me in.

I'd had my eyes glued on Nick as he made his way around the space. I was worried for him, knowing how much he wanted to find a little to play with, but more importantly, an affirmation that he fit in. The longer he walked around, the more concerned I became.

But I shouldn't have been.

One of the best things about Revolver was how genuinely inclusive and friendly a place it was. It attracted people from all walks of life, each with their own stories, kinks, preferences, and appearances.

Nick didn't look like a conventional boy, but he had a place here, just like everybody else did. He was valued and he was seen. That warmed my heart and I hoped it would help him feel better about exploring his littlehood.

I saw him walking around, drawing smiles from littles wherever he went. I saw some hand waves and the mouthing of a few friendly *hellos*. I could tell he was tense, but he was pushing himself through it. I was silently willing him on as well, hoping that my love would remind him just how beautiful and amazing and special he was.

And then Nick saw Addison. I didn't have a direct line of sight, but I saw the reaction in Nick's body. It was visceral, like something within him was shifting. I wanted to see more of what was happening, so I excused myself from the conversation I was having and slowly moved closer.

I didn't want to intrude too early. This was Nick's moment, something he had to do on his own. But when I saw the way he was talking to Addison, my body moved of its own accord. I was drawn to the two boys, like a bee to a flower, inching ever closer.

I could see Nick's face lighting up, he was beaming. And Addison? Well, it was as if there were a halo around him. He was radiating an alluring energy—that intoxicating, breath-capturing mix of vulnerability, defensiveness, and playfulness.

Their presence, together and so close to one another, pulled me in. It felt so new and raw, yet had an undertone of completion that sent a spasm of electricity through my body.

For all of their similarities, there were a few differences that stood out too. Addison was older than Nick. Not by a lot, but by a few years. He was leaner too. Well-built and muscular, but without the softness and roundness that complemented Nick's massive muscles so beautifully.

His forearms were smattered with dark hairs, and when he smiled, the laugh lines settled on his face. There was just the slightest peak of gray hairs around his temple. He looked strong yet soft. Playful yet pensive. Young, but not that young. He was a subtle mix of contradictions and it suited him perfectly.

"Steel." Nick's voice interrupted my ruminations.

"Yes, baby," I said, my eyes darting between the still-scared-looking Addison and Nick, who was wearing an expression I wasn't entirely familiar with.

"We've been bonding over music."

My jaw slackened a little. "Let me guess, Britney?"

Addison's eyes widened as he turned to Nick. "You like Godney?"

Nick let out an excited squeal. "If by like you mean love so much that I own every piece of merchandise she ever put out—including the incredibly rare collector's edition of her *Greatest Hits* album that only came out in Japan—and I would literally donate my right ball to spend five minutes inhaling the same air as her, then yeah, I like her."

How he managed to get all those words out in one breath baffled me.

Addison clapped his hands together excitedly. Seeing Nick so happy, both of them so happy, filled my heart with an indescribable feeling. This was what I wanted so much for my boy. Someone on his wavelength, who he could share his love of music and pop culture—and all the other things that I knew nothing about—with.

Nick and I had an incredible connection in almost every way, but there were a few areas where I knew I was completely out of my depth, no matter how many pop diva puzzle sets we put together.

"Oh my god, have you heard the latest about her?" Addison's voice faded into a hushed whisper as Nick pulled in close and the two began giggling uncontrollably.

Addison's transformation was incredible. He went from looking like he was about to throw up when he first saw me to bouncing around on the floor with Nick as if he were having the time of his life.

The two boys moved in even closer, their knees touching. In his eagerness at recounting his story about the time a friend of a friend of a friend was at the same restaurant as Britney Spears'...body double—a story I had heard recounted at least two dozen times—Nick grabbed Addison's forearm. The sight of their touch instantly sent a pulse to my cock.

I settled back a little, watching the boys being themselves with each other. Their true selves. So open, so unaffected, so unconcerned with anything else in the world, completely engrossed in the conversation they were having. It was a beautiful thing to witness.

And it did something else to me. For a moment, it relieved me of the burden, the guilt, I had been feeling about not being a good enough Daddy for Nick. Try as hard as I could, there were still these few areas where we were different. I'd always assumed that meant we were incompatible, or that there was something wrong with me. But maybe, just maybe, different didn't have to mean bad?

"So, Addison," I said as their demeanors calmed and I correctly guessed that Nick had finished his story. "Why don't you tell...us...a little about yourself."

Addison's eyes found mine and a confident smile stretched across his face. "Sure. Well, I'm from Australia as you can probably hear."

I smiled. His accent was adorable. "Which part?"

"Sydney."

Nick looked at me before turning to Addison, gently resting his hand on his knee. I did my best not to let the sight of that thicken my cock but...too late.

"How long have you been in Daylesford for?" Nick asked, curious.

Addison looked up, as if he were counting the years in his mind. "I came here when I was eighteen. I'm now thirty-two, so that would be..."

Nick looked up as well, joining Addison in his mental calculations.

"Let's see now..." Nick started before trailing off.

My chest swelled as I chuckled at the two of them.

"Fourteen years," I offered. They both turned their heads to look at me.

"Thanks, Daddy."

My breath caught in my throat. Nick had never called me Daddy in front of anyone else before. Heck, it had taken a good year of *da-dudes* before he was comfortable using that word at home when it was just the two of us.

I narrowed my eyes at Nick, but there was nothing there. I was expecting to see him looking shocked, or embarrassed, or...something. Anything. Any slight sign of what he had blurted out. But no, his face looked fine. More than fine, actually. He looked happier and more carefree than I had seen him looking in a very long time.

And just like that, the thought of my boy being in a good place, and feeling so comfortable around this boy we had just met, hardened my dick like I was a teenager all over again.

We continued the small talk for a while longer, learning that Addison was a photographer by trade. That he was single and lived only a few blocks away from Nick's bakery. That he had a best friend called Kymmy who could drive him crazy like no one else, but who he couldn't imagine his life without. And that he came from a big family.

"Well, it's kinda huge actually," Addison explained. "My parents are still together, but this is the second marriage for both of them. So, they had children going in and then they had some more together, including me."

"Wait." Nick's lips tugged upward.

I could tell how much he was enjoying Addison's company. And now with this announcement, he was hanging off Addison's every word. Of all the things I knew Nick wanted in life—and it was one of the few things I couldn't give him—a big family was his greatest wish.

It probably had to do with the fact that he was an only child who had been raised by his grandparents. That's why hearing about Addison's large family was exciting him as much as it was.

"So, how many siblings do you have?"

Addison did that cute thing he did before when he was trying to calculate how many years he'd lived in Daylesford. He tilted his head and squinted his eyes. "All together I have seven brothers—"

"Holy shit." I thought I'd muttered it under my breath, but since Nick and Addison started laughing, I figured it must have come out louder than I had intended.

Addison continued. "And..."

"Wait, there's an *and*?" Nick asked, positively loving this.

Addison nodded. "Uh huh...and four sisters."

"Whoa," Nick and I said in unison and the three of us broke out into more laughter.

Something was happening here between the three of us. The conversation was flowing so easily, there was a feeling of familiarity despite having only just met, and my cock was going up and down more often than a go-go dancer working a pole.

Yes, something was definitely happening. I could feel it buzzing in the air between the three of us. I just had no idea what it was.

"Addison, I have a feeling you and Nick are going to be good friends," I said after a few hours of watching the boys playing, laughing, and talking.

The scene was beginning to wind down, with people starting to pack up their things and leave.

Addison's cheeks filled with a rosy red and he looked down awkwardly at the floor. "I'd—I'd like that."

Sensing he was uncomfortable, Nick stroked Addison's hairy forearm, gently running his fingers up and down. Each stroke soothed Addison until he was able to look up and give us both a warm smile.

This time, my cock didn't move, but my heart was practically bursting out of my chest. With pride. My boy was looking after someone, showering them with just the right amount of tenderness that they needed in that moment. It did something to me, seeing him act like that.

"Can Addison come over for a play date, Daddy? Please?"

I tapped my finger to my bottom lip as if the answer wasn't already a foregone conclusion. "Well, you've never had anyone come over for a play date before, Nick."

"Oh, Daddy, please!" Nick was squirming with anticipation.

And then Addison spoke. "Can we have a play date together? Please...Steel."

There was something in the softness of his voice that tugged a part of me that normally only Nick had access too. I looked over at my boy who was *this close* to jumping out of his skin, waiting for my response. His brown eyes were sparkling, warming me the way he always did.

"Of course Addison can come over for a play date, my sweet boy."

Nick let out an excited squeal of delight.

I turned to Addison. "We would love to have you over. What are you doing next Friday night?"

Nick bit down on his lower lip as he turned to look at Addison.

A smile broke out across Addison's face.

"I'm free," he said.

The exaggerated and overly dramatic sigh of relief that escaped Nick's mouth made us all laugh again...for about the eighty-seventh time that night.

"Great, well then, we're set," I said, getting to my feet.

I outstretched both of my arms as I stood up. Nick and Addison each grabbed one hand and they got up too. For a moment—a brief moment—the three of us were physically connected. Nick shot me a dirty smile, but it was gone so quickly I wondered whether it had really even happened. I brushed off the thunder clapping in my chest as being a result of getting up too fast... at my age, and all. That was what it had to be, surely.

We collected our things and made our way outside. I offered to give Addison a lift, but he said he preferred to catch an Uber. For the first time that night, there was a lull in the conversation between us. We had reached the goodbye part of the evening, and now we were wading into the always awkward *do we or don't we hug* territory.

Thankfully, Addison's car pulled up right at that very moment.

"See you next Friday," Nick said as he pulled Addison in for a hug, making the decision for them both.

"For sure." Addison smiled as he hugged Nick. As he pulled away, his face grew serious. "Thank you, Nick. For everything."

I pinched my lip, figuring I'd ask Nick what Addison meant by that later.

Addison looked over at me and a darkness filled his face.

"Uh, bye, Steel. It was nice meeting you." His words sounded so distant, and I wondered whether he meant them that way, or if he was just picking up on the uncomfortable, stilted vibe that had fallen over us since we'd left the club.

I squared my shoulders and sent him a warm smile. "It was nice meeting you too, Addison. I'm looking forward to next Friday."

"Great." He glanced over at his waiting car. "Well, I gotta go."

And with that, he jumped into the car. We watched as it drove off until it was completely out of view.

I threaded my arm around Nick's waist, pulling my boy in nice and close as we made our way through the almost empty parking lot in silence.

As soon as we stepped into the car, before I could turn the engine on, Nick blurted out, "That was the guy."

"What guy?" I turned to face him.

Nick's face was unreadable. One minute he looked like he was about to burst with excitement, the next, a sadness tore through him, making his mouth curl downward. "The one who got attacked outside of my bakery."

My eyes widened. "Are you sure?"

Nick nodded emphatically. "It's him. I recognized him."

"Did you ask him about it?"

Nick let out a heavy breath. "No. I was going to, but then you came over—"

"Oh, I'm sorry," I said, tapping my fingers nervously on the steering wheel. "Believe it or not, but I was actually trying *not* to interrupt you guys."

"Oh, no, it's okay, Steel. It was probably a good thing. I think that's why Addison said *thank you* at the end there. I don't think tonight was the right time to talk about it. In a way, I'm glad we didn't. I had the best time tonight."

"You did?"

Another dirty smile stretched his lips, and this time, it lingered for longer than the one I'd thought I saw before.

"I like Addison, Daddy. I think he might be my first little friend."

I placed my hand on Nick's lap and smiled. "That's good, baby. I'm so glad to hear it."

And I truly was.

CHAPTER TEN

NICK

Waiting for Friday night was like waiting for Jennifer Lopez to drop a new album: agonizing, but one thousand percent totally worth it.

"Nick, stop it."

I looked over at Steel. He was making sandwiches in the kitchen. His eyes were following me as I walked up and down the entire length of the kitchen. Repeatedly.

"The pacing?" I guessed correctly as he lifted his brows in acknowledgement.

"Sorry, sorry, sorry." I stopped moving, but the energy coursing through my body had to leave me somehow...so I started waving my hands about in front of me, as if I were dancing (badly) to a song only I could hear.

Noticing my heightened state, Steel put down the knife and came over to me.

"Hey." His fingers grazed my face and he stroked my chin. "Tell me what you're feeling, baby."

"Nervous. Scared. Excited. Thrilled. Worried. Aaaand...a little hungry."

Steel didn't look taken aback in the slightest. I guess he was used to my verbal torrents by now. God, he was the only man I had ever met who could handle me—the real, full, unfiltered me—while he somehow made it look like the easiest thing in the world.

He glanced over his shoulder. "I'm making sandwiches for you and Addison, but you can have one now if you'd like?"

I nodded and we walked over to where he had been standing. I pulled out a white bar stool and sat down on it, resting my elbows on the countertop, marvelling at the impressive spread Steel had been working on while I'd been having my mini panic attack.

I smiled because it took me back to the time when he had ordered every single pizza off the menu because he didn't know which one I would like. He knew I liked every sandwich known to humankind, so of course, he would go ahead and make pretty much every single type of sandwich possible. There was ham, beef, chicken, egg and lettuce, pulled pork, tuna...as well as the one I wanted right there and then.

"Can I choose?" I asked.

"Of course. Which one would you like, baby?"

I pointed over to the stack of peanut butter and jelly sandwiches.

"Surprise, surprise." Steel chuckled as he handed me the sandwich. "You know I spent hours googling unique sandwiches for your play date. The grilled chicken sandwich, for instance, has got celery, cranberries, and cashews in it. And I've been cooking the pork overnight so that it's tender and soft."

I shook my head in disbelief. I really had the best Daddy in the world. What kind of man does that, goes to all this trouble for their boy? And one who looked so fucking good doing it in his crisp white T-shirt that hugged his pecs so beautifully and faded jeans that were so tight, they should have been illegal.

"Thank you," I said in between chewy mouthfuls.

Steel let out a big smile as he watched me eating.

"Another one?" he asked as I finished.

Normally I would have said yes, but I knew Addison was arriving shortly, so I wanted to talk instead.

"I'm okay for now, thank you."

Steel handed me a napkin and I wiped my mouth. He looked down at his watch. "Addison will be here soon. How are you feeling about it?"

"Better now, thanks."

We had done everything possible to get ready for this play date. The nursery was all set up. Steel had the food situation under control. All I needed to do was to get out of my own head and...enjoy the experience.

"I just..." My voice trailed off.

"Just what, baby?"

I sucked in a deep breath. "I just hope I can, you know, be a little with him."

Steel's silver-gray brows pinched together. "You got on well last week at Revolver, didn't you?"

I nodded. "Yeah, but it's not really the same thing. Even though we were both there as littles, we weren't actually little together."

"Ah, I see." Steel considered my words for a moment. "Nick, if it works, it works. And if it doesn't..." Our eyes met as a flash of heat crossed my chest. "Then that's okay too."

"Really?" I asked softly. "You won't be disappointed in me?"

A look of complete confusion crossed Steel's face. "Why would I be disappointed with you, baby?"

I shuffled on the stool. "Well, because we went to Revolver so that I could get better at being a little—"

"Let me stop you right there," Steel said with the sexiest hint of his lawyer-ness coming through in his voice. "We did *not* go to Revolver because there's anything wrong with you. Or..." He glanced at his feet before looking back up at me. "Or anything wrong with me, for that matter."

What was he talking about? How could he even suggest that anything could be wrong with him? He was a walking, talking, living example of perfection.

He went on. "We went to Revolver in the hopes of making some new friends, others who enjoy being littles, so that we could possibly get to know them."

"Okay," I said slowly.

"We're both new to this, Nick. And we know that there are a number of different ways of incorporating age play into our lives. By meeting others and making some friends, it might help us to get some ideas. That's all. We're simply in an exploratory phase." .

Yep, that made sense.

"Thank you, Daddy," I said, lifting off the stool and walking over to give Steel a big hug. "I needed to hear that."

"Of course, baby. I'm here for you every step of the way. Remember that, and if you need me at any stage during your play date with Addison, I'm right here, okay?"

I nodded just as there was a knock on the door.

"I told the doorman to let Addison straight up," Steel said by way of explanation. "Are you ready, Nick?"

"I am deffers ready," I said, channeling my inner-Shakira spirit animal as we both headed over to the door.

My first play date was about to begin and I was so excited!

There was a knock on the nursery door, which was unnecessary since it had been left wide open. Addison and I both looked up from the car convoy we had created.

Steel's muscular frame filled the doorway. He smiled as he walked in, holding the tray of beautifully prepared sandwiches.

"I thought you boys might be hungry." He winked at me discreetly as he placed the tray on a side table, and then picked up the table and brought it over to where we were playing with Addison's toy collection.

"Thank you, Daddy," I said, picking out the infamous grilled chicken sandwich he'd told me about earlier.

"Thank you, Steel," Addison added as he went for the tuna and cheese sandwich.

Steel grinned. "My, what good manners you boys have. I'm very impressed."

Something about his words sent a thunderbolt straight to the tip of my cock. I always liked receiving praise from my Daddy, but given that I didn't always behave, I probably didn't receive praise as frequently as a boy, like, say, Mikey did.

But seeing Steel beaming happily at Addison and me felt all sorts of right. It settled any remaining remnants of nerves I might have had. Not that there were all that many of them left anyway.

From the moment Addison had walked into the apartment, I'd found myself relaxing. He had a warmth and a gentleness about him that seemed to have the effect of being able to chill me out, and get me out of my own head too. Maybe it was the Australian accent, maybe it was the baseball cap that he wore backward, or maybe it was the way he made everything feel so fun, light, and...well, normal.

He got changed in the guest bathroom, but like the other night at Revolver, he wore baggy clothing, not baby gear. I was in one of my car-and-truck-print onesies, the white one this time. I was so excited before he had come over, that I had put it on underneath my clothes, so I could peel them off when he arrived and be ready super quickly.

Steel walked us to the nursery. Seeing Addison's mouth gape

open as he stepped into the room was the sweetest thing ever. He couldn't believe how beautiful the space was. I squeezed Steel's hand extra hard as Addison took it all in, marveling at how big the room was, how many toys I had, and the pictures I had colored in and begun to stick up on the walls.

Steel left us on our own as he had sandwiches he wanted to finish making in the kitchen. Addison had brought his black backpack with him. I remembered it from the attack, handing it to him right before he ran away.

I was certain, in that moment, that I would never see him again, but here he was in front of me, opening the backpack and pulling out his collection of cars and trucks. A smile stretched his lips as he grabbed the red retro '8os sports car.

"You like that one, don't you." It was more an observation than a question. I could see he did.

He looked so joyous and free.

"I've got two favorites," he started to explain. "The red sports car, and then this."

He pulled out the yellow Tonka truck and handed it to me.

I giggled. "So manly."

He took his baseball cap off and whipped his hair around so that it hit him across the face.

"I can be manly," he said in the most campy, un-manly voice ever. We burst into hysterical laughter and didn't stop happily chatting away until Steel had walked back in with the sandwiches he'd prepared for us.

We ate in silence, except for the occasional compliment we gave Steel for the delicious sandwiches he had made.

"I guess I'll leave you boys to it," Steel said, and I picked up on an undercurrent of sadness in his voice.

I put my sandwich down.

"No. Stay, Daddy." I looked over at Addison. "I mean, if that's okay with you, that is?"

Addison finished chewing as a slight hue of red filled his cheeks. "I was just about to suggest the same thing, actually."

A look of sheer joy washed over Steel as he moved in a little closer to us, sitting down and crossing his bare feet.

"So, what are you boys doing here?" Steel said, motioning at the cars and trucks that were all lined up in one neat row.

"Just playing," I said, reaching for what was going to be either my third or fourth sandwich. They were just *too* damn good to resist.

"What's the game?" Steel asked.

"Just something I made up," Addison answered, waving his hand in the air. "It's silly, really."

Steel's face softened into a wide smile and I could see that it gave Addison the strength to tell him.

"Well, we basically get all the cars and trucks into an order. Then, we move them around the room. In line. They have to be in line, otherwise they get in trouble and get placed at the end of the queue."

Steel nodded reassuringly. "It sounds like fun. And it reminds me of a game Nick plays in the bathtub."

I grinned widely. "I like to take all of my bath toy animals from one side of the bath to the other."

Addison's eyes widened, becoming so huge they looked like they were about to fall out of his head. "No way. That's—that's incredible."

We lined the first few cars up, moving them forward one by one, and then moved the rest of the cars in line behind them.

"When I play by myself," Addison's voice was so low, Steel and I had to lean in just to hear him, "I like to pretend that the cars and trucks can talk to me. That they have personalities of their own. It's...dumb."

He waved his words away dismissively.

"No, it's not," I said, patting Addison on the shoulder. "It's really sweet. And yeah, they do all have personalities. I can totally see it."

Addison's voice remained soft as he peered up at me from underneath his dark lashes. "You can?"

"Deffers," I said with an air of my signature confidence. "Take this one."

I raised a faded blue old-timer Clyde. It was made of tin and its wheels wobbled precariously every time I had touched it so far.

"This is...Melvin."

"Melvin?" Steel and Addison said at the same time.

"Yeppers." I looked at Addison, his eyes twinkled with humor. "He was born in the 1950s, met the love of his life..." I snapped my fingers while searching for the perfect name. "Stanley. Until..."

Addison's eyes were glued to me. "Until what?"

"Until Stanley had to go away and fight in World War One."

Steel let out a low chortle, earning a sharp frown from Addison and me. "If Melvin was born in the 1950s, there's no way Stanley could have gone to fight—"

Steel must have felt the eye daggers that were being directed at him.

"Okay," he raised his palms into the air all truce-like. "Ignore my timeline corrections."

"I will," I said with a huff and a giggle as Addison and I fell into our own little word, giving each of the cars and trucks a name, a backstory—historical dates and correct timelines be damned.

Steel leaned back and just let us play, watching us be silly and get lost in a place that felt so magical, yet so real at the same time.

"How old are you, Addison?" Steel asked, timing his questioning to a lull in our crazy antics.

Addison frowned, his mouth opening and snapping shut a few times. "Would you mind calling me Marko, please?"

"Uh, sure. Do you mind if I ask why?" Steel prodded gently.

"Mark is my last name, but Aussies like to add an O to the end of any word that fits."

"Really?" I let out a giggle. "Like what?"

Addison cocked his head and looked upward, really

considering it. "Like afternoon. Aussies say arvo. Or, like, a service station. We'd call it a servo."

A smile stretched across Steel's face. "That's very cute."

I wasn't sure if he meant the words themselves, or how adorable Addison looked as he spoke to us.

"So, everyone back home called me Marko when I was growing up. Marko helps me get into my little headspace," Addison continued. "And stay there too. To answer your question, Steel, my age varies, but I'm not a baby or a toddler, or even a preschooler. I'm usually about five-ish. That's why I like to play with my trucks and cars so much."

My eyes landed on Steel and we smiled at each other. Then I turned to Addison and took his hand in mine.

"Thank you for telling us."

It was hard to tell what was going on with him, but he seemed to retreat. He looked like a shyness had overtaken him after telling us his little name. He was breathing heavily and kept his gaze firmly on the floor. Opening up like this was hard for him, and believe me, I knew what that felt like.

He gave my fingers a firm squeeze before saying, "I feel—I feel safe with you both. I don't know why."

"I'm glad," Steel said as he leaned in and cupped his hand over both of ours.

We were joined again, and my mind flashed back to Revolver last week and how Steel had helped Addison and me get up off the floor.

Something had tingled inside me when he did that, and it was making me feel all sorts of tingly goodness now that we were all holding hands again. I swallowed hard as my pulse kicked up a notch.

I hadn't been this confused since the time Miley Cyrus donned an oversized glove and twerked up on Robin Thicke at the VMAs.

Now I was the one breathing heavily. And staring down at the floor. Sweat started beading along my forehead the longer our hands remained clasped together.

I looked over at Steel. He looked fine.

I turned to Addison. He seemed fine too. A little shy, perhaps, but generally okay.

Great, so it was just me then.

What the heck was happening to me?

CHAPTER ELEVEN

STEEL

I shut the front door as Nick leaned against me, a loud sigh escaping from his mouth. I closed my arms around him, squeezing him firmly.

"Wow." His voice sounded airy. Like he had just woken up from the most wonderful dream.

I pressed a gentle kiss to his forehead, noticing it was slightly damp with sweat. "Are you hungry, baby? There are still quite a few sandwiches left over."

I could feel his chest heaving against my body as he giggled. "That's because you went so OTT with it, Daddy."

"OTT?"

We started making our way to the kitchen. "Addison said it tonight before you came in. It's Australian slang. It means *over the top.*"

I smiled. "Ah, I see."

Nick pulled out a seat as I opened the fridge and took out the platter of remaining sandwiches.

"What else did Addison say?"

Nick leaned forward on the countertop, his eyes glazed with a wistfulness I hadn't seen on him since Chris Evans accidentally leaked his dick pics online.

"Oh, well, did you know that *deffers* can also be said as *defo* in Australia?"

"No. I did not know that. Did you?"

Nick shook his head. "No way. Are you kidding me? Deffers is a Nick Macklin copyrighted, patented original, thank you very much."

I groaned. "Stop it, you're starting to sound like Porter now."

"But, you know those Aussies," Nick continued. "They like to add an O onto the end of everything they can."

His sweet giggle filled the kitchen with lightness. I unwrapped the tin foil and rearranged the sandwiches slightly to make them look more presentable.

"Daddy, you're fussing."

I guess I was. But as my fingers fumbled around the plate, clearing away crumbs from around the edges and moving the sandwiches closer to the center, the last thing on my mind was what I was actually doing. No. My head was flooded, filled to the brim, with thoughts of Nick...and Addison.

I honestly hadn't expected to spend most of the evening with them. But when they had invited me to stay after I brought the food in, somehow the thought of leaving them to play by themselves never crossed our minds. At least not for me, and I'm pretty sure not for them either, judging by how much fun we were having together.

As they played with Addison's cars and trucks, or when Nick offered for Addison to help him color in a picture he was working on, there was an air of things being...right.

Relaxed.

Easy.

I was happy watching them doing their thing, and judging by the occasional glances that both boys threw my way, they seemed to like my presence there too. I hoped it made them feel safe, protected.

I could see it in Nick too. There were no words in the English language to describe how beautiful he looked dressed in his white onesie, throwing his head back, laughing, his long brown hair waving around messily.

He was casual. Comfortable. Confident. All things that I wanted more than anything else in the world for my boy and things that, for some reason, Addison was able to bring out in him.

I could still feel the sensation that had torn through me as I cupped my hands over the boys' hands when Addison had opened up to us like that about his little name. I didn't know what that meant, but I knew what I would have to do about it.

After our bumpy start, Nick and I had well and truly learned the value of doing the one thing that most men don't like to do: talking.

I knew I had to be honest about what I was feeling. Even though I wasn't completely confident that I would be able to find the right words, I knew that I had to at least try. I also had more than an inkling that Nick was feeling whatever was happening between the three of us too. I hoped that by me stepping up—and opening up—it would encourage him to do the same.

Nick was already busily chewing away on a sandwich when I looked up at him. His eyes glowed with heat. "We need to talk, Nick. I'll take these sandwiches into the lounge room, okay?"

Nick nodded and silently followed me out of the kitchen. I placed the plate on the coffee table as we both slid down onto the white leather couch.

He licked his fingers clean. "What would you like to talk about?"

I felt my throat clench, but I pushed through it. "You. Me... Addison."

His lips tipped up at the corners. He outstretched his hands over the plate on the table and brushed the last of the crumbs off his fingers. "Go on, then."

"Well," I began, a little more nervously than I would have liked. "How was tonight for you? Did you have a good time?"

Nick fell back into the couch, beaming. "I had the most wonderful time in the world, Daddy."

His joy was infectious, and I felt my shoulders relaxing a bit. "That's good, baby. I'm glad to hear it. What did you enjoy the most?"

"All of it," he replied without missing a beat. "I loved playing with Addison, he's so much fun. I loved that you were there with us, watching us. It felt good having you in the room. And I loved..." His voice cracked slightly, so he sat up. "I loved how I felt...as a little."

I leaned in closer. "How *did* you feel?"

Nick chewed adorably on his bottom lip as he tapped his fingers against his leg.

"Safe..."

He started nodding his head softly.

"At ease..."

His torso started rocking.

"Free..."

He reached his hand out to mine and I saw his body trembling. I placed his fingers in my hand, holding them with a firm, steadying grip.

"I felt—" His brown eyes swerved up to meet mine. "I felt like I was...me. Not that I'm not always me, I don't mean like that. But I felt like I was a me that I had never been before, but a me that was always there within me."

My chest expanded hearing those words, as if someone was blowing up a balloon inside of me. Everything Nick had just said was everything that I had wanted for him so badly. And for some reason, the voice inside that normally would have responded with feelings of *Why am I not giving him those things?* wasn't there. Nick's happiness silenced that voice somehow.

"And how do you feel about Addison?" I asked as I studied his face for any subtle non-verbal cues.

Although I should have known better. Nick Macklin did many things well, but subtlety was not one of them.

His eyes brightened at the mention of Addison's name.

"I really like him, Steel. He's so much fun to play with. When we're playing with his toys, I just feel so calm. My mind melts and all I can think about is moving each car and truck, one by one, after each other from one place to the next. It sounds silly, but it's really cool."

"It doesn't sound silly," I said, moving in a bit closer, playing with a loose strand of hair that had fallen onto his shoulder.

"And I like his accent," Nick continued as I sat there watching him talk, mesmerized by him as I had been since the first time I laid eyes on him. "It's not super full-on and crazy, you know? I mean, I can still understand everything he says."

I chuckled. "Well, it is the same language."

"Yeah, but some people have really strong accents. He doesn't. His is really...nice."

"It is," I agreed.

"And..." Nick's voice went up about an octave. "The best thing is that, by hanging out with him, I'm bound to pick up more cool words and catchphrases that I can put my own sassy spin on."

We both laughed.

I waited until we settled down and a silence fell between us.

"And what do you think about his appearance?" I asked, keeping my voice as steady as I could. "Do you think he's attractive?"

I watched as a slideshow of emotions fell across Nick's face.

"Can I be honest with you?" he asked, and I detected an undertone of nervousness in his tone.

I stiffened slightly but smiled. "Of course, baby."

Nick looked down and paused before saying, "I think he's very attractive. Actually, no, wait, that's not entirely true."

He shuffled away from me, brought his legs up onto the couch and crossed them. After what felt like an eternity, he spoke again.

"I think he's one of the two most beautiful men I have ever seen."

"Oh?" I reached out my fingers and dragged them gently across his hairy calves. "One of two, huh?"

A smile curled itself around his lips. "Yeah. Wanna take a guess at who the other guy is?"

"I think I might have an idea."

"Chris Hemsworth," Nick said flatly, but the twinkle in his eyes revealed he was kidding, no matter how much he was trying to make it seem like he wasn't.

"That's the other guy, is it? Really? See, I'm more of a Chris Pine guy myself," I teased.

His cheeks started bubbling. He wasn't able to contain his laughter for long, and as the walls on the laughter dam broke and his loud, raucous sound filled the room, I leaned forward and kissed my boy hungrily.

He kissed me back with just as much force, cupping the sides of my face in his hands and pulling me even closer. Our tongues swirled, wetting our lips. My desire for Nick flowed through my entire body.

I pulled back, sitting myself down again. As much as I wanted to spend the rest of the night exploring the inside of Nick's mouth—well, actually, the inside of all of him—I knew our conversation was only half done.

Nick studied me for a moment, his eyes running across my face. "How did you find tonight?"

I cleared my throat. "I really enjoyed it. I love seeing you so happy. You have no idea how much that means to me."

"Aw, Steel." Nick took my hand in his.

"And I really enjoyed spending time with you both. Thank you for letting me stay with you. I wasn't expecting that, and it really meant a lot to me."

"Of course," Nick said, straightening up. "I want you there. Always."

"Really?" I asked. "I'm not in the way or, I don't know, cramping your style?"

Nick looked at me quizzically. "Uh, the only thing that would ever cramp my style is you saying the words *cramping your style* ever again."

My lips parted in mock surprise. "Okay, my bad. Won't happen again."

"Good." Nick shot me a searing look from across the couch. "And what about you, Daddy?"

I gulped. "What about me?"

"Do *you* find Addison attractive?"

This was it. The moment of truth had arrived. And of course I would be completely honest with him. The only reason I was slightly hesitant was because I wanted to be mindful of Nick's feelings.

"I do," I began slowly, carefully.

"Yeah?" Nick shot me a warm look. "What do you like about him?"

I coughed lightly. "Well, this is going to sound stupid, but...one of the first things I noticed about him when I saw him at Revolver was that he looks an awful lot like you. And that is, in some weird and twisted way, one of the things that makes him so appealing."

"Hey, there's nothing wrong with that." Nick moved closer. He ran his fingertips through the light hairs on my forearm. "I mean, I am pretty super fucking hot."

I laughed, but nodded my head in agreement. "That you are."

"So it makes sense that until cloning technology becomes sophisticated enough to create another me..."

I shook my head. "You really are something else."

"Well, duh."

"I don't know how I feel about this hypothetical future cloning technology though," I said, rubbing my fingers across my chin. "I don't think I want to share you with anyone else, even if it was a clone version of you."

Nick raised a bushy eyebrow. "I wouldn't mind sharing you."

"Really?"

"I mean, not with just anyone." Nick's fingers were making their way up past my elbow. "But if there was someone...special, then yeah, I'd be open to it."

I swallowed hard. "You would?"

Nick's fingers reached my shoulders. "Uh huh. I mean, if you think you could handle two boys, that is?"

"Well, I do have to wonder about that," I said, letting out a breath I had been holding in for way too long. "I seem to have my hands full with just one boy, sometimes."

Nick's fingers were now running across the front of my chest.

"There is nothing wrong with having your hands full, now is there?" he said as his hands dipped to the front of my pants, palming an erection I didn't know I had. I looked down, surprised at my own arousal.

I let out a low chuckle. "No, I suppose not."

"And," Nick said as he yanked at my zipper, "there's nothing wrong with having your mouth full either. Is there, Daddy?"

I was midway through another chuckle when Nick freed my cock, pulling my pants and underwear down my thighs. His warm fingers felt good wrapped around it, but the touch of his tongue against the underside of my swollen cock head felt even better.

"You know," he said, looking up, his fingers cupping my heavy balls. "I am killing this maturity thing. First, I'm using spreadsheets at the bakery, and now *this*. We're talking like...adults. I think you deserve a reward for that."

I barely managed a nod as I stretched my arms out on either side of my body and threw my head back, surrendering to the sensation. Nick licked my entire shaft from head to base, getting it nice and slick.

I moaned as his fingers ran along the flaming skin of my swollen cock. A heavy need was building within me, and I was chasing its release. He took me in his mouth, swallowing me slowly, teasingly, until I felt his nose pressing against my lower abdomen. Waves of pleasure rose within me.

I got lost in the warmth, the wetness of his inviting mouth, consumed by the love I had for my boy. His head bobbed up and down so beautifully. I brought my hands forward, tugging my fingers through his long hair.

And then I felt the jagged edges of my orgasm envelop me, tearing through my entire body, from my head to the tips of my toes. I gushed a heavy load into his mouth, and when I looked down, I saw Nick swallowing every last drop of it.

He smacked his lips, a satisfied expression lighting up his face.

"Come here, baby," I said.

I needed him close to me. I'd been worried about how our conversation would go. The reason talking had been hard for us was because being honest actually meant being something else: vulnerable. And that was hard as fuck.

But with Nick, I knew it was safe to open up, and he wouldn't judge me for anything I said. In the same way that I would never judge him for anything he told me.

As I cradled him in my arms, I closed my eyes. My post-orgasm high was fading, but I knew that our future had never looked brighter.

CHAPTER TWELVE

ADDISON

"I don't get feet." Kymmy tilted her head to the side, taking in the giant painting in front of us that took up the entire wall. A painting of a foot. In extreme close-up. Surrealist style.

"Maybe we're standing too close to it," I suggested as I grabbed her by the elbow and pulled her back a few steps with me.

"No, no, I get it. I can see that it's a foot," she said. "I just don't get why anyone would want to paint a foot in this weird kind of way."

"I take photos of faces," I countered.

"Yes, but see, that's real art, Addy. What you create is beautiful and soulful." Her lips pursed thinly as she waved her hand in front of us. "This is..."

I looked down at the brochure I was holding and began reading from it. "This is the artist's post-modern statement about the journey of pursuing self-love and acceptance. If the journey of a thousand miles begins with a single step, this is the part of the body that takes that step—"

"Oh, please stop, Addy." She groaned loudly. "I think I just threw up in my mouth a little. You know, of all the pretentious, bullshit artsy things you have taken me to over the years, this would have to be in the top...twenty worst ever."

I threaded my arms through hers. "Hey, you should be happy I didn't take you to see his previous work. It was a performance piece. All he did in it was open an envelope."

I felt Kym's body shudder against mine. "That sounds like a living nightmare. Alright, to make it up to me, please buy me a ridiculously expensive cocktail. Ooh, and I know just the place. Deffers."

My head swung around. "What did you just say?"

"I've never been, and it's meant to be this ah-mazing gay bar...with ridiculously expensive drinks," she said with a cheeky grin.

I shot her an incredulous sidelong glance. "What—what's the name of the bar?"

"Deffers. I don't know, I think it's a catchphrase of the owner or his boyfriend or something. I read about it a while ago in *The Daylesford Times*, so the details are a little fuzzy. I remember it was a cute story, though."

"Uh huh," I said, letting the dust settle in my mind.

Did Steel and Nick own a gay bar? Was that where the name came from?

It struck me in that moment how little I knew about both of them. And that wasn't even the biggest problem I faced when it came to the one fascinating boy and his equally wonderful silver fox Daddy I hadn't been able to get out of my mind.

"You alright, Addy?" I turned to see Kym's eyes scanning my face.

"Let me tell you all about it over a very expensive drink at Deffers."

Twenty minutes and one short Uber ride later, Kymmy and I were perched on a pair of high stools that had the most amazing back support ever, drinks in hand. She went for a long island iced tea, while I chose an espresso martini. I wanted to be alert for the conversation we were about to have, so I figured a caffeine-alcohol combo would help.

"Why do you keep looking around like that?" Kym asked, taking a noisy sip of her drink. "Are you looking to score tonight or something?"

I snapped my head back.

"No," I answered indignantly.

That was the last thing I wanted. The bar was pretty busy and I was trying to get a glimpse of Nick or Steel, on the off chance they were here, on the even off-er chance they owned the place at all.

I picked up a coffee bean from the top of my drink and rolled it between my fingers. "I'm not looking. In fact, I think I may have found someone."

Kym's eyes glimmered with excitement. "Ooh, do tell. Do tell."

"Well, actually," I began, feeling a sudden shyness sweep through me. "It's not a some*one*, it's a some*two*."

A confused frown dented her perfectly smooth forehead. "A *sometwo?*"

"Yeah, not one guy, but two," I explained, as if I hadn't just made up a totally weird-sounding word.

"Ooh." Kym was back on the same page as me.

"Yeah, and I think that they might own this place. That's why I was looking around, to see if they were here."

She took a sip. "Well, are they?"

I peered around the bar again. "No, I don't think so. Or at least, I can't see them."

"Perfect." Her hands tapped the top of the bar eagerly.

"How is that perfect?" I asked.

"It means you have all the time in the world to tell me every single last juicy detail. Go!"

I pressed my lips to the rim of the glass, wondering how I was going to frame this. Kym and I had the stereotypical *gay boy slash straight best female friend* friendship. We told each other everything, and I mean everything. She knew I was a little, and she was super supportive about it.

So, I told her the whole story. I started with what happened in front of the bakery—she already knew about the attack, but she didn't know that it was Nick who had saved me—and ended with me leaving Steel and Nick's apartment a few nights ago after the best play date of my life.

"Whoa. That's so...hot," she said when I was done.

"Which part?" I cackled.

"Uh, all of it. Nick sounds like he's an absolute riot..."

"And he's cute to boot," I said, and we both giggled at my spontaneous rhyming skills.

"And Steel..." Kym's tongue hung lazily out the corner of her mouth while she pretended to be wiping up drool off her chin. "Holy shitballs. He sounds like a fucking dream."

"He is. They both are. In fact, this whole thing feels like a dream, Kymmy. One that started from a nightmare, funnily enough, but has morphed into this incredible, beautiful, wonderful...thing."

Her eyes narrowed. "So, what's the problem?"

Damn. She knew me too well.

"I can think of at least two," I said glumly as I lifted my drink.

"I'm listening and will be judging you on the inside, as well as on the outside." Her tone was light as she threw a friendly smile at me.

"Number one, I know nothing about them. I mean, I didn't even know they owned this place."

I didn't say the other thing that I really wanted to know about them. I decided to keep that to myself, at least for the moment, but the question had been playing in my mind ever since that night at Revolver.

Were they open to...*more?*

So far, I hadn't seen any signs that they were. And the last thing I wanted to do was ruin what we had by letting my dick overrule my brain.

"Well, you don't actually know whether they do or don't own this bar, Addison. And besides, you've known them for less than a month. There's plenty of time for you to get to know them better...*annnnnd* for me to meet these two hunky spunks of love and tell them all of your embarrassing secrets."

"Don't you dare," I said, wagging my finger at her.

Her face softened. "So, what's the second thing, then?"

I let out a heavy breath. "Well, then there's the fact that they're new to the whole age play thing."

She scrunched her nose up at me. "So?"

"It's kinda hard to explain, but, they seem to blur the lines a bit."

"What do you mean?"

"Well, when I went over for my play date with Nick, Steel came into the nursery."

Kym's eyes widened. "They have a nursery?"

My chest warmed at the memory.

"They do, and you should see it, Kymmy. It's beautiful." I took another sip before continuing. "Anyway, Steel made these delicious sandwiches so he came in. And then Nick asked if he could stay."

"Is that a bad thing?"

I shook my head. "No. In fact, if Nick hadn't asked, then I would have."

"Okay, sorry, Addy, but I'm not getting it. What seems to be the problem here?"

I scratched the back of my neck. "Well, it just meant that for most of the night, Nick and I drifted in and out of being littles. Sometimes he and I would play together as littles, other times we would talk to Steel as adults. It was like, and this is hard to explain, but it was like I would keep going in and out of the little headspace the whole time."

"Did it feel bad or wrong?" Kym asked with an uncharacteristic delicateness in her tone.

I considered her question for a long time. "No. The weird thing was, it didn't. It should have, but—"

"Wait," Kym interrupted. "Who says it *should have*?"

Hmm, she had a good point. "I don't know, actually. I guess it's just that this is not how these things are meant to work."

"Again, says who?"

I flashed her an appreciative smile. This was exactly what I needed. She always gave it to me straight and helped me see things in a new and different light.

"I'm no expert at the whole age play thing," she began as a smirk filled her plush red lips, "but I am a boss at life..."

"I'll drink to that."

We both raised our drinks and gave a hearty clink.

"...And my number one life rule is this: fuck rules. Who made them? Why are we blindly following them? I remember when you told me you were a little, and I was blown away by your courage and strength."

"Really?" I asked with a high-pitched squeak.

"Really." She gave my arm a quick rub. "It takes balls to be who you are in this world. You're strong, Addison. Stronger than you probably realize. So if it feels good, or right, or like something that you want to do, then fuck the rules, and fuck what anyone else thinks, and follow your heart."

"Thanks, Kymmy. I'll—I'll try to do that."

"But not before you buy me another drink." She tipped her head at her near-empty glass.

I smiled as Kym's words settled over me. She was right. Screw rules and expectations. Screw what people thought was normal or how things should be.

There were already enough people in the world with issues—including those who had a problem with the whole age play thing in the first place. I didn't want to be one of those people who limited himself just to fit into others' preconceived ideas and expectations. I wanted to be the kinda guy who did what he wanted and followed his heart.

Because if I did, I knew exactly where it would lead me.

A high-pitched bell jangled loudly as I opened the door to Nick's bakery the next morning. He was standing behind the glass counter but ran out and hugged me like his life depended on it as soon as he saw me come in.

"Oh my gosh, Addison! It's so great to see you."

His excitement was contagious, buzzing through my veins as I sniffed in his sweet strawberry scent.

"It's good to see you too, Nick."

We pulled apart and stood there looking at each other. It could have been ten seconds or it could have been ten years, but suddenly, time passing by stopped being a thing that I paid any attention to. I was lost in his eyes. Those rich, warm brown eyes of his.

My gaze turned down. The usual pinkness of his lips was hidden behind a thin layer of what looked like it could have been either flour or icing sugar.

"Have you been baking?" I asked, tapping my own lips to indicate what I was referring to.

He smiled a little sheepishly.

"Eating," he responded. "I don't really bake. But I don't mind sampling the goods."

I grinned. "There's nothing wrong with that."

Our eyes lingered on each other again, before Nick motioned over to the glass counter.

"Do you feel like anything? The chocolate croissants are to die for. So are the doughnuts, and the apple crumble is pretty good too, oh and I really like the peach cake."

"So, basically everything?"

Nick let out a giggle. "Yeah. You can't go wrong."

If only that applied to real life and not just pastries.

"I'm okay for now, but thanks," I said with a smile. "Actually, I was hoping you and I might be able to talk. Privately?"

I looked over at the other guy who was standing behind the counter. Nick lifted his brows, catching my drift.

"Hey, Remy, I'm going out for a bit. You okay to hold down the fort?"

The young guy shot Nick a toothy smile. "Sure thing, boss. Fort is being held."

"I could do with a coffee," I said once we were outside. "I noticed a coffee truck parked at the end of the block."

Nick grumbled. "Urgh, sure."

"What's the matter?" I asked.

"Well, it's the only place around here that does coffee, but the coffee is terrible."

"Uh, I hate to break it to you, Nick, but that goes for most of America. The coffee in this country is bad across the board."

"Are you serious?" He sounded surprised.

"I am. Aussie coffee is, like, a million times better. That and Tim Tams are what I miss most about home."

"What are Tim Tams?"

I explained what the slice of heaven wrapped up in a chocolate biscuit was to Nick as we waited for my coffee. Once I got it and took a sip, I had to admit he was right.

"Okay, even as far as shitty American coffee goes, this is shockingly bad."

Nick laughed. "Told you. There's a park across the street. Let's go there."

We walked over and sat down at an empty bench. I took another sip of the godawful drink, my need for caffeine overriding the logic of my taste buds.

"So what did you want to talk about?" Nick asked after a few moments of silence had passed between us.

I looked at him, his eyes warm, his face friendly. "I know we haven't really talked about it, but I wanted to thank you for saving me when I was getting beaten up."

He looked taken aback. "Oh, you don't have to thank me for that. I'm just glad that I showed up when I did and was able to get those cowards off you."

Another silence, shorter this time.

"By the way," Nick said. "I called Steel straight after and asked for his advice about what to do."

"And what did he say?"

"He said I should file a police report. Just so that they have it on record. So I did. If you ever want to do anything about it—"

"I don't." My words were firm and, thankfully, Nick didn't press any further.

Another silence, this one hung around for a while.

"I have something for you." Nick reached into his pocket and pulled out...my yellow car!

"Here you go."

He passed it to me and I felt so happy I thought I would cry. "It must have fallen out during the attack," he said. "I did try calling out after you, but maybe you didn't hear me?"

I played with the car between my fingers like I had done countless times before. It felt so good to be able to hold it again, and having it in my hand helped me fight against the shame that threatened to fill my insides.

"No, I heard you," I finally managed to say. "I was just so scared and embarrassed and felt so...awful."

"Hey." I felt Nick's hand land on my shoulder. "It's okay, Addison. You have every right to feel however you feel about what happened."

"Why—why did you keep it? The car, I mean."

Nick leaned back against the bench and a part of me wished he hadn't. I liked having his hand on my shoulder. I quickly pushed that inappropriate thought away.

"I guess because it reminded me of what happened and a part of me wanted to keep remembering it. That's weird, isn't it?"

"Yeah, you should have just said you liked the car, or something."

We both laughed and I felt relief washing some of the shame away.

"I couldn't stop thinking about you after it happened."

"Really?"

Nick nodded. "Yeah, just ask Steel. He'll tell you. I talked about it every day."

"Why?"

Nick's eyes met mine. "Honestly? I don't really know. I just felt...something toward you, Addison."

The words hung in the air between us.

"I'm glad we got to meet again," I said, breaking the silence.

Nick flashed me a wide smile that warmed my insides. "Me too. And I'm glad you stopped by today."

"So am I."

We both got up and started walking back in the direction of the bakery. I threw the rest of my unfinished coffee into a garbage bin.

"You know," I said, "you really should start selling coffee at the bakery, Nick. Anything would be better than that coffee."

CHAPTER THIRTEEN

NICK

"Ohmygod, ohmygod, ohmygod."

Steel looked up from his desk as I burst into his home office with the fierceness of a drag queen entering the workroom on *RuPaul's Drag Race* for the first time.

He lifted his thick, black-rimmed Anderson Cooper-esque glasses and smiled at me. "Well, someone's excited."

My ass found its usual spot at the edge of his desk. And yes, my ass had a *usual desk spot*. After more than a few excited run-ins into his office, where I would sweep all of the papers and whatever else was on his desk off with my forearm in an overly dramatic fashion before plonking myself onto his desk to share whatever major news I had, Steel had the good sense to clear the left-hand corner of his desk for occasions that required such grand entrances.

Such as this one.

He leaned back in his chair, taking in all of the dazzling radiance I had going on. My hair was pulled up loosely in a bun, just the way he liked it. I was sporting a fluorescent pink midriff-baring tank top and skin-tight black leggings with my favorite pair of Mickey Mouse knee-high socks. For me, pretty much standard around-the-house fare, but I knew Steel loved it. I mean, the guy was practically drooling as his eyes traveled over my body. I couldn't blame him one bit. He was a red-blooded gay male, after all.

"You'll never guess who I ran into today."

"Oprah?" he guessed with zero hesitation.

I rolled my eyes. "That's your default answer every time I ask you that question."

His lips curled into a devious smile. "Oh, you think you've got me figured out, do you?"

I cocked my head. "Uh huh, I do actually. You're totally predictable. Take another guess."

"Kim Kardashian," we both said at the same time.

"Ha, see, I knew it. She's your second default. You always say Oprah first, then Kim Kardashian second."

"You got me. You know me too well, baby."

I flashed him a look of cocky acknowledgement but decided to get back to my big announcement. It was too majorly major to put off any longer.

"So, are you ready for it?" I asked, the anticipation in my voice building.

He gave a nod, his light blue eyes still gleaming teasingly.

"Addison."

Steel rocked up in his chair until he was sitting way too upright. "Addison? How? Where? Why?"

I giggled. I liked seeing the cool, calm, and collected Steel Crawford in moments like this where he was so unguarded, spontaneous.

"He stopped by the bakery this morning."

Steel lifted a brow. "This morning? And you've managed to go all day without calling or texting me about it? I'm very impressed."

"You should be. I believe it's called self-control."

Steel patted his hands on his thighs, and I accepted his invitation, sitting myself gingerly on his lap. I was getting better at it, and it was happening less and less often, but there was still a part of me that worried about placing too much weight onto him. Despite his constant reassurances, his firm insistence on it, and the fact that Steel's massive thighs felt like they were made of, well, steel, some things just took a while to get used to, I guess.

He rubbed my lower back as I sat down. "Are you comfortable, baby?"

I readjusted myself until I was.

"Yes, thank you," I said softly. I didn't think he'd ever really know how much little questions like that made me feel so protected.

"Now, tell me all about it."

So I did.

I told him about how amazing it felt when I saw Addison walking through the front door of the bakery. How I couldn't help but run up to him and give him a huge hug. I mentioned that Addison wanted to talk, so we got a terrible coffee from that awful coffee truck down the block before we went to the park. I told him how I gave Addison back the little yellow car that must have fallen out of his pocket or backpack during the attack.

The whole time, Steel sat there, listening to my every word and rubbing my back lightly. I clasped my hands together in my lap when I was finished.

"So, there you have it. Pretty much a blow-by-blow, minute-by-minute retelling of my time with Addison today."

Steel kept looking at me but he didn't say anything. The silence wasn't awkward though. We both just needed a moment to process it all. It gave me a moment to reflect, too.

I had been buzzing with anticipation all day after Addison had walked me back to the bakery. Part of it was the joy I felt at seeing him, and another part of it was the thought of telling Steel about it. I didn't know why that made me feel so happy, but it did.

"Well, it sounds like you had a nice time with him," Steel observed.

"Yeah, I did. And it was nice seeing him as an adult too. Most of the time we're together, it's as littles, you know?"

A frown formed across Steel's forehead.

"What is it?" I asked.

"I've been thinking about that," Steel began. "I'm wondering if we are actually doing the whole age play thing correctly."

It was my turn to frown. "How do you mean?"

"Well, I was online before, checking out some age play websites, and a couple of comments stood out for me."

"Uh huh."

"I guess I'm just worried that my presence with you boys—as much as I love it, don't get me wrong there—distracts the two of you. Maybe in some ways it prevents you both from really getting deep in your littlespace."

Steel looked serious. I looped my arm around his neck.

"I love having you with us. If anything, I've never felt more comfortable. Having you there helps me be a little."

Steel half-smiled, but I could tell his thoughts were somewhere else.

"And what about Addison?" he asked softly. "He's more experienced at this than we are, baby. Maybe his expectations don't necessarily align with what we're doing here."

I *hmpfed* loudly.

"Has he said anything to you about it, Nick?"

I shook my head. "No, he's never mentioned anything. See, there's really no problem here, Steel."

He still didn't look convinced. "Just because he hasn't said anything doesn't mean there's nothing going on with him. I think you and I both remember the time when we weren't so great at talking. It might be hard for him to feel like he can talk to us. Just look at how much it took for him to tell us about his preference for being called Marko."

"That's true," I said. I had never thought about it that way before, that Addison might have found it hard to talk to us because there were two of us and only one of him.

Or that we weren't doing the age play thing right.

Because it felt so right to me. I loved having Steel in the room with us, watching as we played together, and sometimes joining in on the conversation too. I couldn't imagine him not being there. Just like I couldn't imagine the scene without Addison. I needed both of them right there with me.

"Well, maybe we can talk about it with him next time?" I suggested.

"Next time?" A smile lightened Steel's face. "You'd like that, baby?"

I practically bounced out of his lap. "Are you kidding me? Of course, I would."

"Great." Steel was beaming. "I'll get in touch with him to arrange something."

"Something *soon*," I said, rubbing my hand across Steel's wide chest.

He chuckled and I could feel his torso vibrate under my fingers. I liked being so close to him that I could feel every movement of his body against mine.

"So, what did you do today?" I asked looking around the stacks of paper piled on his desk.

"Mainly just work," he said. "Then a little bit of online research."

I felt something stir under my ass, so me being me, I wiggled deeper into his lap, pressing into the growing firmness of his cock.

"And then I masturbated," Steel said, looking all sorts of sheepish-cute. Like he always did when he told me he'd jerked off. He knew I had no problem with it—hell, I thought it was super hot. But he seemed to always get so cutely shy about it for some reason.

"Why do you always get a little funny about telling me you've masturbated?" I asked, keeping my voice tender.

"I don't know," he said, looking away for a moment. "I guess I'm just a little old school about that. It feels weird talking about it."

"Well, get new school about it, please," I said, playfully. "So tell me, what were you thinking about when you were jacking off?"

"You."

Heat filled my chest. That was another question Steel always answered predictably every time.

"...With Addison." Steel gulped so loudly I could have heard it from the moon.

"Oh, well, there's no need to feel bad about that," I said reassuringly, brushing my fingers down his arms. "Actually, I think that's kinda hot."

"You do?"

"Uh huh."

Steel's body practically melted underneath me. Well, except for his cock. That was as hard as granite.

I ran my fingers along his square jawline. "What were you imagining?"

Another loud gulp. "He was—he was fucking you."

"Mmm...nice. And what were you doing?"

"I was watching." I felt his cock twitch beneath me.

"Well," I said as my fingers made their way into his thick silver mane, gently dragging across his scalp. "Why don't you tell me the rest of what you were thinking about while you're fucking me?"

CHAPTER FOURTEEN

ADDISON

I studied my face in the elevator mirror as it zoomed me up to the top-floor penthouse. I ran my index fingers underneath my eyes, hoping to stretch away the wrinkles that were getting deeper and deeper every day. At least in the relatively dim lighting I was standing under, the gray hairs that were starting to appear on the sides of my head weren't so visible.

I stepped back and took a deep breath. I'd been a bundle of nervous energy ever since Steel had called two days ago, inviting me for another play date with Nick. I kept replaying that conversation with him over in my mind. It was on the short-ish side, friendly but formal-friendly, and it had an undertone of something else. But I couldn't quite put my finger on what, exactly.

I wanted Steel to like me the way Nick liked me.

With Nick, it felt so natural. Like we'd known each other forever, but had been apart for a few years and were reconnecting again. There was an easy flow between us. He made me feel warm and welcome, and I hoped I was helping him get more comfortable exploring his little side.

But with Steel, it was different. I mean, I liked him, and I kinda-sorta thought he liked me too, but it didn't feel quite so effortless.

And I thought I knew why.

I took another look in the mirror and grimaced. Even bad lighting couldn't completely shield the truth. I wasn't a boy like Nick was. I was a thirty-two-year-old something-in-between. And Steel, like pretty much every other Daddy I had encountered, wasn't interested in thirty-two-year-old *somethings*. I couldn't really blame him for that.

I pushed my shoulders back and put on a smile as the elevator made a low pinging sound. Before the doors had even fully opened, Nick lunged at me and flew into my arms. Steel followed a few steps behind with an exasperated look of defeat on his face.

"You're here," Nick exclaimed as I smiled.

I looked over at Steel who mouthed the words, "I'm sorry."

I breathed in Nick's sweet, fruity smell and allowed myself to enjoy the warmth of his hug.

"Someone couldn't wait to see you," Steel said as Nick finally peeled himself off me. I looked at Steel. We did that awkward *half-sideways, half-forward step, arms outstretched but not wanting to smack into each other* thing, before hugging quickly.

Nick didn't seem to notice anything. "Right, so the nursery is all set up. Steel has ordered a whole bunch of Chinese food and I have a new set of building blocks I am *dying* to show you."

I smiled, unable to remain unaffected by Nick's enthusiasm.

"Well, let me get changed and we can get started."

I saw Nick flick a glance at Steel, before he turned to me and said, "Sounds good, Marko."

"Uh, okay."

Less than five minutes later, I had gotten changed into my go-to loose-fitting clothes and was sitting beside Nick in the nursery. We were playing with his colorful new blocks. Or rather, I was carefully stacking them, and Nick would gleefully smack them down every once in a while and make me start all over again. It sounded annoying and if it were anyone else doing it, then maybe it would have been. But with Nick, I was having the time of my life.

"Hey." Steel's voice rang out sharply as he entered the nursery with a tray full of Chinese food. "What are you doing, Nick?"

Nick didn't look taken aback or surprised in the slightest. "We're just playing, Daddy."

"Yeah, well, I just saw you knocking down Addis—Marko's pile he was building there. Play nicely."

Even Steel's finger wagging once he had set the tray down on the table didn't seem to bother Nick. It was the first time I was seeing a hint of his bratty side, and I kinda liked it. Steel had his hands full with this one.

"You boys hungry?"

We both let out a loud *yeah* as we walked over to the table. Steel must have bought every single item on the menu because there were at least twenty containers of food. He was laying them out across the table, opening the lids as Nick and I sat down.

"He tends to go OTT," Nick said as he took in my face.

I giggled as Steel handed me a bright blue plate.

"I know what that means, and...yes, I do like to go OTT."

I giggled again, louder this time. He said the word right, but it still sounded funny to me with his American accent.

After we'd filled our plates and begun eating, Steel looked at me and asked, "Do you mind if we have a conversation? We'd like to ask you a few questions."

"Sure," I replied. I finished chewing and looked at them.

Nick was being quiet, which wasn't like him at all. And Steel was looking more serious than I had ever seen him.

"Look, as you know, Nick and I are both new to the whole age play thing. And I guess—I guess we just want to make sure that we're doing it right. With you," he quickly added.

My chest tightened a little. "What do you mean exactly? What's *doing it right* look like?"

"Well, that's exactly it. We don't really know. I mean, as much as I love watching you boys and spending time with you, am I cramp—" Steel stopped himself and looked over at Nick, who let out a loud groan. "Am I ruining things by being in the room with you? Do I need to back off and let you boys be littles?"

Nick chimed in. "And I'm confused about the whole Marko thing. I called you that out near the elevator when you arrived. I did it because I was so excited to see you, but I think that was the wrong time, right?"

The firmness gripping my chest loosened, and I let out a relieved breath. I couldn't believe these two. They were so thoughtful, so considerate. That they had picked up on these things meant that they not only had self-awareness, but that they cared...about me.

I smiled as I mentally prepared my answer. I knew exactly what I was going to say, and it was going to be short, sweet, and to the point. They were both staring at me intently. I pushed the plate away and leaned my forearms on the table.

"Fuck rules," I said, summoning my own inner-fierceness.

Steel's eyes widened so much I thought they'd pop out of his head, while Nick let out a loud laugh. After giving them both a moment to recover from my somewhat forceful response, I continued.

"Look, just because I have more experience with this, it doesn't change the fact that every age play situation is different. The three of us are not the same as my ex-husband and I were."

Steel nodded along as I was talking.

"That makes sense," he said.

"And yes, maybe you shouldn't have called me Marko by the elevator, and yes, maybe we should be clearer on littlespace boundaries around Steel, but again, fuck rules. Fuck shoulds. And fuck shouldn'ts."

"Amen to that." Nick outstretched his hand and we high-fived, the smack echoing loudly around the nursery.

I looked over at Steel who was still deep in thought.

"I want you boys, actually all of us, to be comfortable with this situation." He turned his gaze to me. "Nick and I had a tumultuous start to our relationship—"

"That's putting it mildly," Nick chimed in.

"It is," Steel agreed. "But we don't have all night to fill Addison in on it all right now."

We all laughed and it lightened the atmosphere between us.

"And here's what we learned. We have to communicate. I know it's a tired, old, and overused cliché, but it really is true."

"I agree with you, Steel," I said. "Especially with age play stuff. Talking is key."

"It is," Steel replied. He smiled warmly at me and his face softened for the first time. "So, I would like to propose that the three of us make an effort to talk to each other about whatever we are feeling. Whether it's good or bad, easy to talk about or really difficult, it doesn't matter. We have to push through all of that and just...talk."

"Deal," Nick said, clapping his hands together. "I'm in."

"So am I," I added as my heart swelled with happiness.

"Great. So, we're all in."

"Yay!" Nick grabbed me by the hand. "Now, can we keep playing... Marko?"

I was about to get up when Steel interjected.

"Nick." His voice was firm. "You haven't asked if Marko has finished with his food yet."

And there it was. Nick looked down and his cheeks flamed a bright red. He was back to being a boy. In fact, a good boy who wanted to please his Daddy.

"I'm sorry," he said, turning to face me. "Have you finished your meal, Marko?"

I wiped the corners of my mouth with the napkin. "I have, Nick. And I would love to play with you."

I was expecting shouts of joy, but I was met with silence. Nick was looking over at Steel. He was waiting...waiting for his Daddy to give him permission. Wow, he could actually be super obedient when he wanted to.

"Alright, boys, you go play. I actually have a work call that I couldn't get out of, so I will leave you to it." Steel gathered up all of the plates and containers, placed them on the tray, and walked over to the door.

"Play nice, boys. And Nick," his voice lowered, "please behave."

"Oh, I will, Daddy. I'll be a very good boy."

And with that, Steel left and I turned my attention to Nick. My heart was beating fast. I had been looking forward to this play date from the moment Steel had invited me over.

Nick grabbed my hand.

"I am so excited." He sounded as thrilled as I was feeling.

I squeezed his hand back. "Me too. I could barely sleep last night."

"OhmyGod. I couldn't either. We are going to have so much fun, Marko." He looked around the nursery. "What would you like to do first?"

CHAPTER FIFTEEN

STEEL

I felt like I was walking on air as I left the nursery to make a quick business call. The play date was going way better than I could have hoped for. The three of us had an honest and upfront conversation and cleared a few things up I had been worried about, and most importantly of all, we'd made a promise to talk.

I had a really good feeling about...this, even if I still wasn't entirely sure what *this* was exactly. Or what it was going to be. Or what I wanted it to be. As much as I was on board with the *fuck rules* sentiment, it did mean that things were a little more up in the air than I would have liked them to be. But hey, that's life. You can't always control every last aspect of it, as much as you'd like to.

I was only on the phone for a few minutes with Mason Gray, my business partner and the co-owner of Deffers. Even though I was a silent partner at the bar, Mason needed my advice in planning the upcoming *Daylesford's Most Eligible Daddy* contest. There were a lot of logistics involved that I knew about, since I'd been involved with the event over the years—as well as being a three-time winner of the title.

I answered all of Mason's questions as thoroughly—and quickly—as I could, tapping my fingers impatiently against the side of my body, eager to get back to my boys.

Wait, I meant, my boy and his...friend?

Play date?

Object of my masturbatory fantasy that one time? Okay, maybe twice.

Hmm, I wasn't exactly sure what Addison was to me. Or us. Or even what I wanted him to be.

I said goodbye to Mason and stepped back to the nursery, pausing for a moment to collect my thoughts before going in. Being in a *fuck rules* limbo meant I had to be clear within myself on how I wanted to handle things. I was still a Daddy, and it was important for me to project an image of strength and look like I had the faintest clue of what I was doing, even if that wasn't necessarily the case.

From the moment I stepped into the room, I knew that something was wrong. Addison was packing up his toys, forcefully shoving them into his backpack, while Nick was kneeling behind him looking all sorts of upset.

"What's going on?" I asked, approaching them both.

"Steel, you're here." Nick's voice was thick with panic. He leaped to his feet and strode over to me.

Out of the corner of my eye, I could see Addison slowing down his packing.

Nick leaned against me, his cheek grazing mine as he whispered, "We were playing, having fun, when..."

"When, what?" I said it quietly into Nick's ear, not looking at Addison directly, but keeping him in my periphery.

"Addison got an...erection."

"Oh."

"Yeah, and he feels really bad about it." Nick pulled away and I could see his panic was giving way to sadness. His big brown eyes were on the verge of tears.

I slid my hand up and down his forearm. "Let me handle this, baby."

I walked over to Addison and sat down. "Hey."

Addison didn't look up at me, but he did stop packing. "Hey."

"How are you feeling, Addison?"

"Nick told you what happened?" There was so much shame in his voice, in his slumped shoulders, in the dejected look on his face. It tugged at my heart.

"He did," I said carefully. This was a tricky situation and I needed to proceed carefully. "You still haven't answered my question, Addison. I'd like to know what's going on inside of you."

A few moments of silence followed. Addison's face wasn't giving too much away, but I could see he was struggling with something. I decided to give him a gentle nudge.

"Remember our deal?" I kept my voice as calm as I could. "We said we would talk about anything. No matter how difficult it was. That's really important to me, to Nick...and I think to you as well, right?"

He gave an instant nod in response to that. He looked up at me, his dark brown eyes as teary as Nick's had been just a moment ago.

"I got turned on playing with Nick...as a little. That's never happened before. I feel so embarrassed." He said the last word so quietly I was barely able to hear it.

At that point, Nick walked over and sat down next to the two of us.

"Are you okay, Addison?"

I could see Nick reaching his arm toward Addison, but then he pulled it away abruptly. That was probably smart. I knew he wanted to console Addison, but given what we were dealing with, touch probably wasn't the right way to do it.

Addison shook his head. "No."

He tipped his head up, his eyes roaming between Nick and me.

He looked lost, hurt, and it did something to me. Now I was the one fighting the urge to reach out and give him a hug. Or a pat on the back. Shoulder. Arm. Something, anything to help make him feel better. Somehow, I had to find the right words within me.

"Thank you, Addison," I said.

His thick eyebrows bunched together in confusion. "For—for what?"

"For talking. It's one thing to make a promise to communicate, but when you're faced with a tricky situation, it's so easy to retreat or run away from that promise. I know it feels like that would be easier, to pack up your things and get outta here, right?"

He gave a sheepish nod and placed the car and backpack he was holding on the floor.

"But you haven't done that, Addison. You're still here, and you're talking. That takes real strength."

"It does," Nick added softly. "I'm really proud of you, Addison."

"You are?"

Addison and Nick exchanged a look, one filled with friendship. I could see there was something happening between them, the chemistry they had was off the charts. But underneath that, there was something else too: the possibility of a genuine connection.

They were similar in so many ways. Even when they were different, it was like they were still complementary. Two parts of a whole that fit so well together. Seeing them exchange that look lit up a light bulb in my head.

My mind raced back to the advice Porter had given me about my situation with Nick and his suggestion of bringing in a co-Daddy. But that didn't feel right to me. Truth be told, I was probably too possessive to be able to share my beautiful boy with anyone else, even if it was only temporarily. Besides, I wanted to be all the Daddy he needed. I'd do whatever it took to be that for him...on my own.

But then Porter had mentioned the idea of another *boy*. He'd used the expression *an older brother*, which was perfect. That's exactly what Addison was, or at least could be, for Nick. Someone to take his hand and guide Nick as he explored his littlehood. I could see how Nick looked at Addison, and I felt it returned in equal measure by Addison.

I was filled with such happiness I wanted to jump out of my seat and run around the room. But then I was struck by another thought. A dark one. One that stopped any ill-fated ideas about jumping for joy dead in their tracks.

What about...me?

It was one thing to want Nick to have the experience of an older brother, but where did that leave me? Was Addison even looking for a Daddy? Would he be interested in someone like me? Could I even be a Daddy to both of them when I was having trouble being a good Daddy to just one boy?

"Steel." Nick's voice lifted me out of my thought bubble.

"Yes, baby?"

"You seemed to have drifted off. We've both been looking at you for the last two minutes." Their eyes were fixed on me.

"Right," I said, clapping my hands on my knees. "I think the three of us need to have a talk...as adults."

Both boys nodded at me. "It's getting late, and I know you have to wake up early, Nick. How about dinner tomorrow night?"

"But that's ages away," Nick whined...wait, no, that wasn't Nick—that was Addison—putting on a totally accurate American accent that seriously made him sound just like Nick. The three of us looked at each other and laughed, sharing our first in-joke. The heavy mood in the room lifted.

"You sounded just like me," Nick laughed as he grabbed Addison's hand. "Let me help you finish packing, okay?"

The boys cleaned up and when they were done, Nick, Addison, and I walked to the front door.

"So, tomorrow then?" he asked, nervously adjusting the backpack on his shoulder.

I shot him a warm smile. "How does seven sound?"

"Perfect."

Our eyes met briefly. He stepped in closer and gave me a quick, light hug, our bodies barely touching. Nick, on the other hand, gave him a Hudson-style bear hug, lifting Addison up off the ground and swinging him around as if he were light as a feather. Their bodies pressed together so closely made me need to adjust the way I was standing.

"I'll see you tomorrow," Addison said as he left.

We said our goodbyes, watching him walk into the elevator and waiting until the doors closed and he was gone before shutting the front door.

Nick leaned in toward me. "I saw the way you looked at me when I hugged Addison, Daddy."

I folded my arms around his neck. "Oh, did you now?"

He brought his face closer to mine, smiling seductively. "Uh huh. And if it's okay with you, maybe next time, we could put on more of a show for you?"

"You'll have to talk to Addison first," I said, swearing that would be the last logical thing to come out of my mouth that evening. The mere thought of Nick and Addison together made my skin heat and my cock stand at attention.

"Of course I will," Nick said, pressing his fingertips to my lips. His sweet scent filled my nostrils. "But you know what they say: erections don't lie."

I let out a chuckle. "I've never heard that expression before. Who says that?"

"I could answer that question..." his hands drifted down the front of my shirt.

"Or I could find something else to do with my mouth..."

I quirked an eyebrow. "Such as?"

"Follow me." So I did, walking an inch behind Nick as he led me into the kitchen. "Pants off." His words were strict, but the smile on his face let me know he was just being playful. And that was fine with me.

I followed his instructions. I was about to take my shirt off when he raised his hand. "Uh, you might want to keep that on."

"Why?" I asked slowly.

He had that cheeky look in his eyes that I knew only too well.

"Because I want you on here." He tapped his hand along the white marble countertop.

"Huh."

"You're so beautiful, you little ripper. Sorry, you missed that one. Addison said it when you were on your call. It's another Australian expression. One that I'm stealing."

"Uh, Nick, I'm standing pantless in the kitchen here. Focus, baby."

"Right. I want you on here. On your back. Legs in the air, waving 'em around like you just don't care."

I smiled and obliged. I could feel the coldness of the countertop against my back as I lay down. Nick's suggestion of keeping my shirt on was a very good one. He helped me shuffle down so that my ass was positioned right at the edge of the countertop.

"I am going to go to town on your ass," he said, before diving down and hungrily lapping at my hole.

The incredible sensation tore through me as I stared at the ceiling. I'd never known anybody who enjoyed rimming me this much—and was so damn good at it.

Nick spread my cheeks apart and dove in even deeper. All I could hear was his licks smacking against my skin. All I could feel was wave after wave of sheer, unadulterated pleasure, rising within every part of my body.

I grabbed my cock and began to jerk myself off. Slowly. I was so turned on I knew it wouldn't take long for me to blow, and I had every intention of letting Nick's tongue work its magic over me for as long as humanly possible.

Suddenly, Nick stopped what he was doing. I peered down at him.

"Everything alright, baby?" I asked.

Nick never stopped mid-rimming. A hurricane could have swept through Daylesford and he still would have kept his lips locked on my ass.

Something wicked danced in his eyes.

"You know what would make this even better?" he asked.

"What?"

"If Addison was here with me, joining in on this feast."

I threw my head back heavily against the marble. God, just the thought of having two willing boys eating me out released a surge of adrenaline inside of me.

"Imagine how good it would feel, Daddy. Two tongues. Two mouths. Two sets of hands."

I grabbed my dick again, formed a tight fist, and began stroking furiously. I was so close, Nick's words had brought me to the edge. I felt his tongue slurping noisily at my hole. The sensation. The warmth. The idea of him and Addison...

"Fuck," I yelled loudly as a heavy moan tore from my chest. My whole body rocked. I came hard, rope after rope of creamy cum covering my shirt.

Nick waited until my body had stopped shuddering, before lowering my legs gently. He offered me his hands, helping me to sit up at the edge of the countertop.

I was feeling faint and a little dizzy...in the best way possible.

"You really think you could...share me? I asked, still breathless from the aftermath of my intense orgasm.

Nick gazed up at me, his eyes burning with desire.

"With Addison," he breathed. "Only with Addison."

CHAPTER SIXTEEN

NICK

"So, I took your suggestion and rimmed Steel on the kitchen countertop last night."

Mikey snorted and a thick stream of caramel milkshake poured out of his mouth and flew across the table. Mikey looked around the crowded lunchtime diner, trying to regain his composure.

"Ew, Mikey. Don't be gross." I handed him some napkins and he began to hurriedly clean up the mess.

"I'm sorry," he said, clearing his throat and wiping the table down furiously. "You just caught me a little off guard there." He looked around and gave a firm nod, all traces of caramel milkshake had been cleaned up. "And I'm sorry, when did I ever give you *that* idea?"

"When you showed me your kitchen," I reminded him. "The countertop in your new kitchen that you and Stirling had been christening like crazy."

"Oh, yeah." Mikey pulled the milkshake in toward him, a soft smile curling his lips. "That's still happening. But I was just telling you what we were doing, not recommending you do it yourself."

I shrugged. "But I did...and it was the best thing ever."

We both giggled as our burgers arrived. Betty's really was the best diner in town, and I needed to fuel up because tonight was the night Addison was coming over. And I had a feeling dinner wasn't the only thing that was going to be on the menu.

"You seem happy," Mikey observed, taking his first bite.

I had told him all about the previous night's play date with Addison earlier that morning in a torrent of text messages. Self-control was overrated, I couldn't wait until lunchtime to spill my heart to my best friend.

I grinned. "I am. I can't wait for tonight, Mikey. It feels like something is shifting."

Mikey swallowed. "Shifting?"

"Yeah," I said as I grabbed a handful of fries. "Things are great with Steel and me. I love him like I never thought it was possible to love someone. He's like the George Clooney to my Amal."

A soft groan fell from Mikey's mouth.

"The Tom to my Giselle."

More groaning, louder this time.

"The Harry to my Megan."

"Careful, there." Mikey lifted a brow. "That reference could age very badly."

I waved my hand in the air. "Anyway, what I'm saying is that I've found my true love."

Mikey reached over and grabbed my hand. "And I couldn't be more thrilled for you, Nick. You deserve it more than anyone."

"And now with Addison," I began. "I can't explain it, but it's like he fits in with us...somehow."

Mikey kept eating his burger, but his big blue eyes remained focused on me. "Is it the little thing?"

"That's part of it," I said, putting way too many fries in my mouth. I chewed for a moment as I thought about what it was I was trying to say. "He definitely relaxes me, and being with him, I find that I'm able to get into my little headspace easily. Whatever blocks I have disappear whenever he's around."

Mikey smiled warmly. "That's really good."

"Yes, it is. But it's not just that. There's something when we're together—the three of us, I mean—that feels really good. Is that...wrong?"

"Why would it be wrong?" Mikey asked, gripping the straw to his milkshake between his teeth.

"I don't know..." I looked around the lunchtime crowd at the diner, my eyes not able to settle on anything for too long. Kinda like my mind at the moment. Mikey noisily slurping his milkshake turned my attention back to him.

"I like him, Mikey. Addison does something to me."

"Does Steel like him too?"

I nodded emphatically. "Uh, yeah. Very much."

That, I was certain of. He was jerking off thinking about me and him being together, *hello!*

"And what about Addison? How does he feel about things?"

"That, I don't know. But, he's coming over for dinner tonight, so I guess I'll find out."

"Well, that's good." Mikey flashed me a toothy smile. "I have a positive feeling about this, Nick. You and Steel are totally couplegoals. I think you'll figure this thing out with Addison."

"Thanks," I said as I let out a breath. "You've cheered me up."

Mikey beamed. "I'm glad. And I've been doing some thinking—and talking—with Stirling too."

I narrowed my eyes. "About the surprise?"

Mikey tipped his head. "But before you freak out, don't worry. I didn't say anything. Unlike you, I have the ability to actually be subtle."

Hmpf. He had a point there.

"And?" I asked expectantly.

"I'm in."

"You got the sign you needed from Stirling?"

"Yeah, I'm pretty sure."

My heart felt like it was overflowing with joy. "Yay, Mikey. This is going to be the most brilliant surprise ever."

Mikey's blue eyes gleamed wildly. "I know, it will be. I can't wait. And I spoke to Liam last night too."

"Ooh, and what did he say?"

"He's totally in too."

My eyes widened. "Really? That's awesome."

"You sound surprised," Mikey observed, reading me like a...book, or whatever it was people read these days.

"I guess I am, a bit. Don't get me wrong, I like Liam, but I'm not super close with him, simply because he and Hudson are away so often. I wasn't entirely sure which way he'd go."

"Well, funnily enough, I think it might be Declan who's the holdout."

I bit down on my lower lip. "Why's that?"

"You know, their whole contract thing. They only renew it every six months."

"Oh, right. Well...let's see if that happens. If it's meant to be, it will be."

"Exactly," Mikey said with an elated tone ringing in his voice. "That goes for this monster surprise we're planning...and it goes for you, Steel, and Addison too."

"Some more wine?" Steel glanced over at Addison, who replied by cupping his hand over his near-empty wine glass.

"No, I'm good. Thank you."

Steel turned to me. "Can I get you anything, baby?"

"I'm all good," I replied with a smile. "But I do want to know more about Addison's photography."

The whole evening was going swimmingly. From the moment

Addison arrived—looking mighty fine in his customary all-black outfit, this time it was a relaxed-fit button-up shirt and pants, with his long hair loose and flowing—all the way to the amazing conversation we'd been having over dinner.

Steel, being Steel, had hired one of Daylesford's top chefs to prepare the meal for us. While he was busily working away in the kitchen, preparing what I was sure would be a scrumptious dessert, the three of us were sitting in the formal dining room. It wasn't a place we used a lot, although my ass had copped a pounding, or five, on the giant oak table we were having dinner on.

I turned my attention back to Addison and onto a *non-sex on the dining table* topic.

"There's really not that much to tell," Addison began modestly. "I got a scholarship to Daylesford University—"

"What did you study?" Steel asked. He was zeroed in on Addison as much as I was.

"Fine visual arts," Addison replied.

"What happened after you graduated?" I asked.

"I actually had some early success." Addison finished off the last of his wine before continuing. "I don't know if you guys remember back in the day when *The Daylesford Times* used to run an annual photography competition?"

We both shook our heads, although Steel chimed in with, "Vaguely."

"I entered the year I graduated. And I won."

"Oh wow, that's amazing," I said, but my glee wasn't matched by the melancholy look that swept across Addison's face.

"It—it was." His voice had changed. Deepened. But he kept talking. "I won some money and the opportunity to show my work as part of a collective exhibition in New York. It was meant to be my big break."

Steel and I glanced at each other, both sensing this story didn't have a happy ending.

Steel flashed Addison an encouraging look. "What happened?"

"Nothing. Nothing happened. That's the point. Despite showing some early promise, my big break never materialized. Before I knew it, I was no longer the hot next thing. I became yesterday's news. Forgotten about like..." His voice trailed off.

"Tara Reid?" I suggested.

"Nick, that's terrible," Addison said, his cheeks burning up. "I was going to say more like Mischa Barton."

We both burst into a fit of giggles while Steel looked at us like we were speaking another language.

"Or Heidi Montag," I said.

"Nick Carter," Addison added.

"Aaron Carter."

We only stopped throwing names out because we were too busy laughing. Steel still had no idea what we were talking about, but he started laughing anyway, probably at the sight of us being so silly and ridiculous.

After we'd settled down, Steel asked Addison, "But you still shoot now, don't you?"

"I do," Addison said, his face still beaming from all the laughing. "I mainly freelance, and then I shoot my own passion stuff on the side."

"What's your passion stuff?" I asked curiously.

Addison looked down for a moment, before looking back up at me. "Faces."

"Faces?" Steel and I said in unison.

Addison cocked his head to the side and let out a slight chuckle. "Yeah, I like erotic photography. I don't focus on the bodies, but on people's faces while they're..."

"Fucking each other's brains out?" I offered, trying to be helpful.

Both Steel and Addison laughed. "I would have gone with *doing it*, but yeah, one and the same, I guess."

"Are you showing your work anywhere?" Steel asked.

"Oh, no," Addison said, brushing away the question as if it were silly. "It's just something I do for me. It's not good enough to show publicly."

"Well, I'd like to see your work sometime." Steel's voice was low and it stirred something in my belly...and a little lower down too.

"Me, too, I'd like to see it as well," I added, before changing the subject completely. "How did you know you were a little?"

Steel was used to my abrupt changes in direction, and Addison handled it deftly too, barely blinking an eye.

"It was probably around the time I came to Daylesford to study," Addison began. "The city's so progressive. I knew I was gay, but I also felt like there was something else. Something more about my sexuality that being gay just didn't cover. One night, through a friend's friend, I got invited to Revolver and it happened to be little night. One look and I was hooked. I found that extra something that had been missing."

"That's amazing," Steel said, lifting his wine to his lips. "Was it something that you jumped right into?"

Addison shook his head.

"No. It actually took me a long time to get fully comfortable with it." His eyes met mine as he said it, and I felt relief and heat flushing through me.

"Why do you think that is?" I asked.

"I guess because I'm...different. I'm not into diapers, or binkies, or any of that typical baby-age stuff. I don't have anything against any of it. I tried it, but it wasn't the right fit for me."

"Fair enough," Steel said.

"So, it took me some time to find my groove, so to speak. And then when I met my husband—ex-husband I should say—he was really good at encouraging me to be me."

"What happened? With your ex, I mean?"

"Nick," Steel looked at me. "That's a very personal question."

"I don't mind," Addison answered. "Besides, we have a deal, remember?"

He smiled so sweetly I thought I would melt.

"But only if you're comfortable," Steel said. "We don't want you to feel pressured into talking about anything that you don't want to."

Addison blushed again. "Thanks, I appreciate that. But it's okay. My husband dumped me for a younger boy."

"I'm sorry, what?" I leaned in closer. "I must have misheard you, because it sounded like you said he dumped you for someone else."

Addison looked at me and shot me a tight, pained nod. "Nope, you heard right. He cheated on me with the party planner for my thirtieth birthday, ironically."

My blood heated. "What a fucking idiot."

"Nick." Steel's voice was even louder than mine.

"It's okay," Addison said as a smile broke over his lips. "He is a fucking idiot."

We laughed, and the mood lightened instantly.

"I'm sorry, I didn't mean to be offensive or rude, it's just that I don't get how anyone could leave you. I think you're amazing, Addison," I said, calming myself down a bit.

"Thanks," he replied, stretching his hand out across the table. "I think you're pretty amazing too, Nick."

I looked over at Steel as I placed my fingers in Addison's warm hand.

He squirmed a little in his seat, but I caught his reaction. I could see it in his eyes. Keenness. Wonder. Arousal. He wanted to see me with Addison, and I wanted it too. Badly. The Aussie did something to my insides that made me want to be near him.

"Well, now seems to be as good a time as any to talk about...us," Steel said.

"Us?" Addison looked slightly perplexed.

"Yeah, us." Steel waved his hand between the three of us.

"Oh." Addison pulled his hand away from mine and looked down.

I turned to Steel and motioned for him to keep going.

"Unless you don't want to, Addison."

Steel was giving him an out and while I appreciated the kindness behind the gesture, I sure as fuck hoped Addison wouldn't take it. He had to be feeling this too, right?

When he looked up again, his eyes had turned even darker. "I—I don't want to fuck things up. I'm really enjoying my play dates with Nick, and I like hanging out with you both."

"We like it too, Addison. So much," I said.

"But..."

Shit.

What?

Why had he just said *but*?

Buts were never good—unless we were talking about my fine ass, that is. Or slurping on Steel's delicious hole.

And then Addison said the words that made me practically fall off my chair. "I've got feelings. For both of you."

Steel and I looked at each other again, my skin filling with a million tiny pinpricks of desire.

"Feelings are okay, Addison."

How was Steel able to keep his voice so steady like that? It was taking everything I had in me not to jump out of my own skin...and straight onto Addison's mouth.

"They are?" Addison's voice was on the cusp of cracking, but I heard the hopeful undertone it carried.

Steel nodded as he reached over for my hand. "We have feelings for you too, Addison."

It was as if a stormy cloud had lifted off his face. Addison smiled wider than I thought he possibly could.

"I don't suppose you'd want to skip dessert?" Steel asked, looking at the both of us.

"Normally I'd say, *Steel are you out of your flipping mind?*" I began as I heard them both chuckling at my over the top-ness. "But I can think of something I want for dessert more than food."

"Oh yeah?" The look in Addison's eyes was pure, unadulterated lust.

"Yeah," I shot back with a cheeky grin. "I think Daddy would like to see us put on a show for him."

"Well, in that case..."

The three of us stood up and I grabbed Addison and Steel by the hand, marching them to our bedroom. With the door firmly shut behind us, I led Addison to the massive California king bed. Steel sat down at the edge, while Addison and I stood, facing each other.

I stared into his deep brown eyes, joined only by the slightest touch of our fingertips, still interlaced with one another. I could see a whole world of something going on in his mind.

"How are you feeling?" I asked.

It looked like his breath caught in his throat. His fingers slipped out of mine and his lips quivered. Finally, he spoke.

"Scared."

"Why are you scared, Addison?"

"I—I haven't been with anyone since..."

"Your fucking idiot ex-husband?" I suggested with a smile.

Addison's jaw loosened. "Yeah."

I looked over at Steel. He stood up and approached us.

"Addison, you don't have to do anything you don't want to do. There is absolutely no pressure. I need you to know that. We can go back out to the dining room and have some dessert if you'd like."

Addison's dark eyes met Steel's gaze. He was assessing the situation, thinking it through. It was like I could see the cogs in his brain rotating, weighing up the options.

Dessert or me, dessert or me.

Then his head turned and his eyes roamed up and down, taking me in. All of me. And the scales of desire tipped in one very clear direction.

Fuck dessert. Addison chose *me*.

He grabbed the back of my neck and pulled me into him. Our lips locked. The touch felt warm and sent a pleasant tingle down my spine. My eyes met Steel's briefly. The look he shot me was so fucking hot I thought I would combust. He liked this, seeing me and Addison kissing. I liked it too.

And my cock, it was achingly hard and desperate to free itself from the pesky pants and underwear it was contained in. But first, back to this kiss.

Addison's initial confidence at initiating the kiss were wavering a little. It was up to me to step things up a bit. I led him over to the bed, right into the middle. Out of the corner of my eye, I saw Steel perch himself down at the end, leaning back, taking in the scene that was playing out before him.

I wondered momentarily if this was how he'd imagined it when he was fantasizing about us. I hoped it was everything he'd thought it would be...and more. I didn't know why I needed him to be so into it, but I did. Even though I was the one kissing Addison, it felt like Steel and I were doing it together.

We were on our knees, facing each other, when our lips collided again. This time, the gentleness was gone, replaced with a need. A hunger. A hunger freeing itself from the constraints of inhibition. Whatever was holding Addison back was loosening. I could feel it in the way his tongue lapped at my lips, before opening my mouth and flicking around madly, exploring every corner.

I kissed back just as hungrily, my hands running through his hair before tearing at his shirt. Damn those annoying buttons. He smiled, pulling away.

"Let me help you with that," he offered, but I wasn't about to let his lips get away from me that easily.

"I was just going to tear it off, but then I thought it might be a favorite shirt or something," I kiss-spoke, our lips smacking against each other.

"Tear it off."

I couldn't resist his offer. I grabbed at his shirt, stuffed fabric into each hand, balled my fists, and then in one abrupt movement, ripped the shirt off him. The sound tore through the room as buttons flew everywhere.

But it had the desired effect. Addison's ripped abs and slightly hairy chest were now exactly where I wanted them to be—under my hands. I ran my palms over his skin, the ridges of his stomach, the hairs that covered his chest. He took what was left of his shirt off while I got rid of mine too.

Our eyes locked, then he looked down. At me. At my body. I inhaled sharply, suddenly realizing this was the first time he was seeing me shirtless. Panic filled my throat, before I pushed it away.

Fuck, I'd been with Steel for so long now that I'd forgotten this feeling. The first time someone saw my body. It was the only time I still felt the slightest inkling of self-consciousness.

It's one thing to see me with clothes on. I mean, I could wear Walmart and make it look like something off the Paris runway. But without material, it was just me. My protruding belly. My muscular arms. My soft, squishy pecs. What if he didn't like it? What if it didn't turn him on? Worse, what if it grossed him out? Or what if—

"Fuck," he exclaimed as his fingers landed on the skin of my stomach. He ran them side to side.

It was almost a little ticklish.

"What?" I whispered back, my heart in my throat.

"Nick, you are—you are the most beautiful boy I have ever seen."

I let out a sigh as his words washed over me, removing that last niggle of self-doubt that remained, even after all these years. I knew I didn't need his—or anyone's—approval, at least not ninety-nine percent of the time. But the one percent of the time that I did, I was sure glad to get it.

"I mean, no offence, Steel," Addison added hastily, casting a glance to the corner of the bed where he lay. "I mean, you're hot too, in that whole *if Anderson Cooper had a hotter younger brother* kinda way."

I heard a low chuckle and a *thanks* coming from Steel.

I cleared my throat.

"Back to me, please," I teased. "Or do I need to take these off?"

I didn't wait for Addison to answer. I flipped onto my back and freed my legs from my pants. He took me in as he lay down beside me. His hands seemed glued to my body like magnets to a fridge. He couldn't keep them off me, running them up and down, stopping when they found something he liked.

He really seemed to like my big belly.

And then I felt his finger tugging at the waistband of my briefs. I lifted my hips, silently inviting him to take them off. He looked at me and smirked as he slid them off. Then his eyes widened as he glanced back at me.

Yeppers, he seemed to *really* like my dick.

"You know, this is a little unfair." I ran my hand down my chest seductively. "Here I am lying naked in front of you, and you're still wearing pants. Steel, do you think that's fair?"

"No, grossly unfair," Steel said a little breathlessly.

And with that, Addison stepped off the bed and stripped off his remaining clothes. He looked at Steel as he unbuckled his pants and peeled them off his legs.

I could see the tentpole that had formed in Steel's pants, his light blue eyes were filled with desire as this gorgeous slab of Aussie hunkdom got nakeder and nakeder.

Once the pants were off, he made light work of his white briefs. He bent over to draw them down his legs and when he straightened back up, I was face to face with his rock-hard cock.

"Ooh," I said, keeping my voice low. "You really should be careful, Addison. You could take a boy's eye out with that thing."

"Is that so?" Addison replied, crawling back onto the bed. And those were the last words we spoke for a long time as our mouths reacquainted themselves with each other again. It had been too long—way too long—since I'd had his tongue inside of me.

"How are you feeling now?" I asked, pulling away even though I didn't want to. But my need to check in with him and make sure he was alright seemed to override my desire to never have his tongue leave my mouth.

"I'm good. I feel good." He gave a firm nod and looked back over at Steel. When he turned back to face me though, something was on his mind. "Oh shit, I just realized. I don't have any condoms. Do you?"

"Uh, no," I said, straightening up a little, my cock starting to deflate. "We don't use them anymore."

We both turned to Steel with what I could only imagine were desperate pleas in our eyes.

Steel shook his head, as if he were waking himself up from a dream. A few seconds later, his brain came back online too.

"I'll get condoms for next time. But now, I mean, there's no reason why you two boys can't...blow each other?"

"He has a point," I said, stroking the side of Addison's face.

He smiled back at me. "I deffers agree."

"Well, what are you waiting for?" I said as I placed my hands on his shoulders and not so subtly directed his mouth toward my re-awakened cock.

Addison stuck his tongue out as he traced it slowly down my neck and across my chest, making sure both of my swollen nipples were tended to, and then began to slurp his way down my belly until he reached my cock.

I gripped the sheets and closed my eyes as he delicately flicked the tip of my cock with his tongue. I could feel him squeeze the head, and then he noisily slurped up what I assumed was probably a pool of my precum.

His hand gripped the base of my cock as he took me in his mouth, sliding up and down slowly. The warmth and wetness and suction he was creating felt beyond divine, like my cock was riding a never-ending rollercoaster of pleasure.

I opened my eyes and looked at Steel. At some point, he had stripped naked too. There he was, in the corner of the bed, stroking himself. My Daddy was enjoying the show we were putting on for him almost as much as I was enjoying what Addison's skilled mouth was making me feel.

Addison's mouth left my dick as his fist slid up and down my saliva-slicked cock. His grip was firm, insistent. He was jerking himself off, too.

"Oh fuck," I threw my head back, feeling my balls tightening. I was at the top of the rollercoaster and there was only one way it would go from there.

I howled loudly as I came, spilling cum messily all over myself, the sheets, Addison's forearm. My body bucked and shuddered even after the last drops of release had left me. The aftereffects tingled throughout my body.

Addison moved so that he was lying behind me, his strong arms covering me. I could feel his pounding heartbeat against my back, his warm breath across my neck and ears, his own sticky release between us.

I looked at Steel. He had come as well, the evidence sprayed all across his chest. We smiled warmly at each other.

This was the best feeling in the world. Steel in front of me, Addison right behind me. But the best part wasn't what had just happened. It was something Steel had said earlier, when he mentioned that he'd get condoms.

Two words that echoed in my head as my eyelids grew heavy and a feeling of contentment settled in my chest.

Next time.

CHAPTER SEVENTEEN

ADDISON

A week after being with Nick and my mind was still frazzled as fuck.

I stepped out of the Uber, slung the black backpack across my shoulder, and looked up the length of the massive apartment building to the very top. Yep, that's where it had happened. Nick and I having sex while Steel watched—the single hottest sexual experience of my life.

Also, the single most confusing sexual experience of my life. Well, apart from that one time Natalie Portman—no, not *that* Natalie Portman, this Natalie was one I went to primary school with who just so happened to have the same name as the Academy Award-winning actress—tried to get me to kiss her in sixth grade. I did, out of politeness, of course. But it left me feeling weirded out for way longer than it should have.

The *having sex with Nick* part didn't weird me out. Not at all. In fact, it had set off a chain reaction in me that made me want him even more than I'd wanted him before. How was that even possible?

Nick Macklin truly was something else. A one-in-a-million boy, for sure. And his lure drew me like a fisherman hauling in the catch of the day.

It was the *Steel watching me have sex with Nick* part that concerned me. It wasn't the fact that he had watched us that bothered me. That was totally fucking hot. Knowing we had an audience, an aroused audience who was jerking off his massive meat because of us didn't bother me in the least.

No. It was my mind racing away with me, wondering why Steel didn't want to join us. And then it was my mind doing that thing it always did when it answered a hypothetical question with a hypothetical answer, which I proceeded to believe. And the hypothetical answer that I had come up with as the reason for Steel not joining in was that it was because of...me. Specifically, the fact that he didn't find me attractive. Which, of course, made me feel like absolute shit.

I took a deep breath in and felt the cool night air sweep across my face. I needed some more time before going in. That elevator was the fastest elevator ever invented, making it a less than ideal place for a last-minute panic attack before a play date, or sex date, or *whatever the hell this was* date. It also had a mirror, and they were my sworn enemies at the moment.

I felt my camera pressing into my back through my bag and smiled momentarily. Well, whatever kind of date this turned out to be, I'd come prepared. Even though it still didn't change the fact that Steel didn't like me.

I could feel it in the lightness of his touch whenever we hugged, or in the way his eyes never stayed on me for a second longer than they had to. He'd dart his attention to me infrequently, and when he did and I happened to look back at him, he looked away immediately. As if even holding my gaze was too much for him.

That hurt a little... Okay, a lot. I mean, sure, I wasn't some sprightly twenty-year-old jock, but I wasn't a complete monstrosity either.

I worked out, watched what I ate—heck, I hadn't eaten a carb or even a carb-adjacent food since the Obama presidency—and any spare money I had at the end of the month I spent on the highest of high-end beauty products. So, yeah, I might have suffered from the terrible condition of being a thirty-two-year-old gay male, but I was a pretty damn decent thirty-two-year-old, thank you very much.

At least that was what I kept telling myself as I walked into the imposing building, shot up the elevator, and stood waiting after I had knocked on their front door. I was blowing out another massive breath when the door was opened by a walking Greek statue.

Sorry, my mistake, it was just Steel. But with the way the light from inside illuminated his muscled frame and lit up his thick head of silver hair, he looked...transcendent. I snorted slightly as I forgot to finish exhaling.

"Hey, Steel," I managed to croak.

He looked at me questioningly. "Hey, Addison. Are you okay?"

"Fine," I said, stepping past him as he motioned for me to come inside. "Just. Mouth. Dry. A little."

Great, now my brain had decided to leave for a vacation too. *Come back soon,* I pleaded. *I'll be needing you.*

"In that case, let me get you something to drink." He looked at my backpack. "Can I take that off you?"

"Oh, thank you."

I'd always heard that some people found manners sexy, but I'd never got it. Until that very moment. I mean, what's so sexy about a guy saying *please* or *thank you*...or offering to take your backpack from you? Uh, it makes you feel special, that's what.

Our fingers gently grazed each other as I handed him the backpack. My face flamed as I looked around the kitchen. Steel carefully placed my backpack by the wall and out of the way before turning back to me.

"What can I get you? We've got alcohol, soda, coffee, tea, water."

"Water will be great, thanks," I said as I carefully pulled out a stool and sat down on it. "Where's Nick?"

Steel smiled as he handed me a glass of water.

"He's getting ready." He leaned in closer and covered his mouth, as if he were whispering. "That's code for: be prepared to wait a while."

The water and his humor relaxed me.

"Well, you can't rush perfection," I said, and for the first time, the walls of awkwardness and distance between Steel and I lowered a little.

Sure, he hadn't hugged me when I arrived, and the vacuum of not having Nick around was huge, but somehow, slowly, we were navigating our way through this. Baby steps for sure, but steps, nonetheless.

"Did someone say *perfection?*" Nick asked as he stepped into the kitchen. "Because I thought my ears were burning."

I turned around and almost fell off my stool. Nick looked beyond amazing in a midriff-baring black tank top and super-short Daisy Duke shorts. His furry belly was on full display, and so was that delicious ass of his, hanging out the back of his shorts invitingly.

He leaped over to me and wrapped me up in the warmest, tightest hug.

"It's so good to see you, Addison."

He ran his fingers through my hair softly.

"It's good to see you too, Nick."

I closed my eyes and breathed him in. Our bodies were pressed firmly together. I never wanted the moment to end. As my eyes opened, I noticed Steel looking at us. There was an expression on his face that I couldn't read. Whatever it was flickered away as Nick and I pulled apart.

"So, I wasn't sure what kind of play date this would be," I said as

Nick pulled up a stool next to me and moved in closer. Our knees were gently bobbing against each other. I liked the touch. Even if it was small and incidental, I really liked it.

I got up, sliding my fingers over his knee and up his leg to gently move it out of the way as I walked over to my backpack.

"So, I've brought little clothes..."

Nick leaned in over the white marble countertop. "Uh-huh."

"And I also brought my camera, because I thought it might be nice if we took some photos tonight. But we don't have to, it was just a silly idea."

Steel stepped in a little closer too. "I think that's a wonderful idea, Addison."

"And then I also brought something else." I reached my hand into my backpack, fumbling around until I found it. "Now, before I pull it out, you can totally veto this idea and I won't be mad. I promise."

Nick clapped his hands together excitedly. "Ooh, show us, show us!"

I felt my heart clanging against my chest. "Alright, here it is."

I pulled out the box and held it up so they both could see. Nick's eyes widened as he let out a high-pitched squeal, while Steel's mouth fell to the floor.

I slid the box across the countertop to Nick.

"Where did you get this?" he asked, his eyes as wide as footballs. "It's a limited edition. Kind of like your new car, Steel."

I saw Steel rolling his eyes, but then a good-natured smile fell across his face. "Well, maybe it's not the exact same thing. My new car probably cost a little more."

"Maybe," I said jokingly, sitting down beside Nick again. "But this is guaranteed hours of fun."

Nick was staring at the box. "How... Where...?"

I smiled. "I got it for my thirtieth birthday, actually. From my ex."

Steel's eyes landed on me, and this time, he didn't flinch or turn away. Instead, there was a look of pain and compassion behind his eyes. He pressed his lips into a smile, as if encouraging me to go on.

"After I caught him cheating and we broke up, I put this away in the back corner of my closet. I knew I'd want to open it one day, but I wanted to wait for the right time."

Steel's tight smile melted, replaced by a wider, genuinely warm one. He cleared his throat and glanced at Nick. It might have been brief, but again, even his small looks my way were baby steps in the right direction.

Nick swung around to look at me. I met his gaze and my heart skipped a beat, he was still so excited.

"Can I open it?" His voice had all of the reverence of an archaeologist uncovering an ancient tomb and opening up a crypt for the first time in millennia.

"If that's what you boys would like to do, how about we move into the lounge room? You can use the table in there," Steel suggested.

As we stood up and followed Steel out of the kitchen, Nick grabbed my hand. He raised it to his lips, planting a soft kiss on the back of my index and middle finger.

"What's that for?" I asked.

Nick looked at me with eyes the color of the most delicious, decadent chocolate in the world.

"For waiting," he replied. "I hope we've been worth waiting for."

My skin felt like it was on fire.

"You have," I said as Steel peered back over his shoulder at us. "You've been worth waiting for... Both of you."

"Deffers?" Nick asked seriously.

"Deffers," I replied firmly.

Nick's lips pulled upward into an irresistible grin, while Steel's face tightened sharply, as if he were in pain.

I let out a sad sigh. If only Steel felt the same way about me.

CHAPTER EIGHTEEN

STEEL

As my eyes settled on Addison, the familiar warring inside of me flared up again. It was an unfamiliar feeling for me, scary. It made me feel unsure of myself, and that was a feeling I absolutely hated.

And then he said that word. The word that I'd been hoping for and dreading, but for entirely different reasons.

Both.

He liked both of us.

I snapped my head around faster than I ever had as the boys followed me into the living room. I looked down at the box I was carrying, grateful for the temporary distraction from the more serious matters pressing on my mind.

Britney Spears looked back at me, smiling as always, frozen in an innocent late-'90s time warp. The limited edition of her *Piece of Me* jigsaw puzzle jangled in the box. I had hoped my days of pop diva puzzling were over. And for a while, they had been. We had completed every single pop puzzle in existence, even plumbing the depths of boy bands such as the Backstreet Boys, NSYNC, and Seventy-Eight Degrees, or whatever they were called. But apparently, there was still one jigsaw puzzle we hadn't done.

I smiled as I recalled the endless hours Nick and I had spent sitting around whatever puzzle we were working on at the time, chatting away, laughing. It was funny how such a simple act, like hanging out and putting jigsaw pieces together, could really bring two people closer.

Or three people, in this case.

I pushed through the cold dread that was gripping my chest as we sat down. I handed the box to Addison, who opened it and tipped all the pieces onto the coffee table. I positioned myself on the couch, giving myself a good view of the two boys.

My cock twitched at the memory of the last time I had watched them playing together. Although that time there had been far fewer clothes involved. Seeing Nick and Addison together—whether they were launching into a jigsaw puzzle, or onto each other's bodies—did something to me. It was more than just a sexual response, it felt like I was tapping into needs and desires I didn't know I had.

In all my years, the idea of having a threesome had never entered my mind, except for whenever Porter would regale us with his sexploits that involved three, four, and sometimes more men.

It was never an idea that I entertained for myself, mainly because it had never come up with anyone I had been with before. I certainly had nothing against it. Hell, the thought of Nick and Addison even touching knees catapulted me straight into Boner Land.

But what was happening here between the three of us was different. It was more than just a purely physical attraction.

Could I name it?

No.

Could I try to explain it?

No.

But could I feel it?

Fuck yeah, with everything I had in me.

It was real.

It was happening.

And it was scaring the life out of me.

"Hey, Addison." My words came out as a croak. Both boys looked up from the puzzle pieces scattered over the coffee table. I swallowed hard. "You mentioned you brought your camera over?"

He nodded. "Yeah, it's in my backpack."

"Do you mind if I take it out and have a look at it?"

"No worries. Go for it."

I grinned at his hint of Australianism as I went back into the kitchen and pulled the camera out of his backpack.

"It's light," I said as I gently cupped it in my hand, returning to the room. "And small, too."

"It's an Olympus OM-1," Addison said without looking up, intently focused on the more important task at hand: finding whatever puzzle piece he was looking for. "It's not the best camera in the world, but it was when it came out back in the early '70s."

"That's around your time, isn't it, Steel?" Nick joked naughtily. He and Addison broke out into a cacophony of mischievous giggling.

"Hey, watch it, mister." I wagged my finger in his direction, resisting the smile that threatened to fray the edges of my lips.

Once they'd both settled down and resumed the very serious task of putting together the Britney puzzle, Addison continued.

"It's got a cloth focal-plane shutter with speeds from 1-1/1000 sec plus B, two-CdS cell metering system, fixed pentaprism with interchangeable viewing screens, single-stroke wind lever, mirror lock-up, and motor/winder compatibility."

I liked hearing him rattle off the camera specs the way I'd share the details about the latest car I had my eye on with Nick. Ah, and now I understood the vacant look that Nick wore whenever I would do that, feeling like a similarly blank expression had landed on my own face. I knew nothing about cameras, but Addison's passion for his work was crystal clear.

"Do you mind if I take a few photos of you guys?" I asked.

Without saying a word, Nick practically leaped over to the other side of the table.

"This is my best side," he explained to Addison, who was just as startled as I was by the sudden movement.

"I think both sides of your face are your best side," Addison said.

Nick's face softened as he gave Addison a long, tender look.

Click.

That was the first photo I took, knowing it would be a good one. The boys had an undeniable chemistry, and I wanted to capture some of it. They kept putting the pieces together as I sat back and snapped away every time one of them laughed, or looked adorable, or stuck their tongue out the corner of their mouth...so basically, I was pretty much taking photos damn near nonstop all evening.

Midnight rolled around way faster than any of us wanted it to. But after ignoring Nick's first three yawns, I decided it was time. We had to call it a night.

"What should we do with the puzzle, Daddy?" Worry filled Nick's eyes as he looked down at the progress they had made.

"I can move it into the nursery. That way, you two can work on it next time."

Two sets of eyes lit up at those words.

Next time.

My lips curled up, happy in the knowledge that they were both enjoying our time together as much as I was. I handed the camera back to Addison.

"I hope I got some good ones there," I said a little sheepishly.

He was a professional photographer, I was sure my amateur snaps would be terrible compared to what he could do.

He smiled warmly. "I'm sure they'll be ah-mazing."

"Of course they will be," Nick added, hooking his arm around Addison's neck. "I mean, how can you go wrong when you're photographing this generation's boy version of Linda Evangelista and Claudia Schiffer?"

"Wait." Addison turned to Nick. "Which one am I?"

"Claudia," Nick replied without missing a beat. "It's the cheekbones."

We all laughed, and the mood stayed light until we reached the front door. Acting on what looked like pure animal instinct, Nick pulled Addison into him by his belt buckle. Their lips swirled around in a messy, enticing display of tongue flicking and lapping. My cock thickened as the sounds of lips smacking and moans escaping mouths filled the air between us.

Addison ran his hands down Nick's back, landing on his meaty ass. I could see him pressing Nick's flesh hungrily. As if he wanted more. What could I say? Nick had that effect on men.

When they finally pulled apart, all I could manage was a bewildered whisper. "That's hot."

Both boys flipped their heads to look at me, then back at each other, before they erupted in laughter.

Not exactly the reaction I had been expecting.

"Uh, what's—what's so funny?" I stammered.

My question only set them off even more.

"He doesn't know," Nick managed to gulp out.

"That's what makes it cuter," Addison added, wiping the tears from his eyes.

I bit down. "Does someone want to fill me in here?"

"No, I think we'll leave you hanging for a bit longer, Paris Hilton."

I shook my head, and for what felt like the millionth time that evening, tried to suppress a smile. But I couldn't with these two. Even though ninety-nine percent of their pop culture references went straight over my head, I wouldn't have changed them for the world.

They were both so perfect individually, but when they came together, god, they were out-of-this world spectacular. They weren't like the puzzle they had been putting together earlier, incomplete pieces needing to be connected. No, they were both fully formed, fully realized on their own.

Addison stepped in toward me. And with the half-step he took, it hit me that he and I had never kissed. Somehow, we'd managed to avoid it, or at least, I had. That familiar feeling of being torn in two was rising within me again.

Deciding the last thing I wanted to do was to draw any attention to it, I pulled Addison in for a hug, my lips dragging lightly across his cheek. There, that was a kiss. Nick saw it too, so there'd be no awkward questions the second Addison left, with Nick wanting to know why I hadn't kissed him.

Because, technically, I had. In the lips-touching-skin sense, which was what a kiss essentially was, right? My lawyer's mind was way overthinking this.

I ran my hand across the back of Addison's head. His hair felt as soft as Nick's, but it smelled different. Less sweet, more earthy. It was appealing in an understated way.

We pulled apart and I glanced at Nick. He cocked his head to the side, lifting both bushy brows up. But he wasn't thinking about the awkward hug-slash-barely-there kiss Addison and I had exchanged. His mind was already racing ahead to the future.

"When can we see you again, Addison? Can we come to your place next time? I want to see where you live." His voice was alive with excitement.

For a moment, Addison looked taken aback. I couldn't blame him. As good as he was at taking all of Nick in, it took some time to really get used to him.

But before I could interject to try and save him, Addison answered, "How does Friday sound?"

Nick responded with an enthusiastic nod before turning to me, his brown eyes all wide.

"Can we, Daddy? I think we're free that night."

"Of course," I said, stepping in, my hand finding the small of Nick's back. "That sounds wonderful."

Friday was still a few days away. That gave me just enough time to round up my friends and get some advice about how to handle the situation.

We watched as Addison left. Thankfully, he didn't seem to pick up on my weirdness around him. Or at least, I hoped he didn't. The last thing I wanted for Addison to think was that it had anything to do with him, when it was actually about me.

All about me.

"Now this," Porter said, lifting his glass into the air, "is one motherfucking seriously good drink."

I looked over at Stirling. He rolled his eyes playfully, before my gaze shifted to our recently returned friend, Hudson. His face was tanned and he looked about five years younger. Van life, and being head-over-heels in love with Liam, was a good look on him.

He threw Porter a diplomatic, yet *I still know you're up to something* look as he returned to examine the drink in front of him on the table.

The feeling of having my three closest friends—brothers, really—back together as we sat in a corner booth in the VIP section of Deffers warmed my heart more than even Porter's jalapeno margarita could. Well, almost. That was one seriously spicy drink.

I had relented to Porter's incessant pleas to add it to the drinks menu, and as much as I hated to admit it—and never would to him—we had a hit on our hands. It had even made one of those online listicles, roaring into the top five must-try drinks in Daylesford. Who knew that was even a thing?

"Just be careful," I warned Hudson as he brought the salt-frosted glass to his lips. "It's hot."

Gingerly, he took a sip before his eyes rolled back in his head.

We all stared at him, unsure if his reaction was a sign he liked the drink, or if he was about to have a heart attack.

"Damn, that's wicked good," he rumbled, and we let out a collective sigh of relief. "I've missed you guys."

"We've missed you, too," Stirling said. "And you're back for a while, right?"

"Six weeks," Hudson replied.

"Ooh," Porter's voice shifted an octave. "That means you'll be here for *Daylesford's Most Eligible Daddy* contest."

Hudson ignored Porter's reaction and turned to face Stirling and me.

"My tenants have moved out, and I'd like to do a few repairs around the place before we lease it out again. Besides, it'll be nice to sleep in a full-size bed and shower in a full-size shower again. Being six foot six and living in a van can be...challenging."

"I bet," Stirling said.

The four of us continued catching up.

First, Hudson filled us in on all of the good work Liam had been doing. He really was using his platform to expand people's awareness of important issues like climate change, but he was doing it in a way that made it accessible and easy to understand.

I had to admit that before Hudson met Liam, it hadn't been a topic that I paid much attention to. But after following Liam on social media, and reading through his posts and messages, I now saw climate change as one of the most pressing issues of our time. And he'd gotten me to make small changes too. Every light at home had been changed to LED, and all the taps in the penthouse, in my office, and at Deffers had been fitted with special washers to reduce water waste. Not huge things on their own, but hey, if everyone did it, it would quickly add up and make a big difference.

The conversation moved on and Stirling talked about how he and Mikey were feeling after having had their hopes dashed in the baby-making department. I was glad to hear that they were both in a much better place with it now. In fact, it sounded as if they were almost ready to restart the whole process again.

Porter filled us in on how great he and Declan were doing. I was so happy for him. Not just because he'd finally settled down and found someone, but that he was able to live a true and authentic life. Declan's article had really moved the needle and people were open to the idea of a Dom mayor in a way I don't think any of us had ever expected.

I had explored kink and BDSM in my twenties, and as much as I enjoyed certain aspects of it, I didn't have that deep, primal, innate desire for it like Porter did.

For me, it was all about age play. Although, as I was seeing with the boys, I was even doing that somewhat...strangely. A part of me still couldn't believe that Nick and Addison were getting everything they wanted with me in the room with them.

It definitely wasn't the traditional age play scene. Heck, the last time Addison had come over, when he and Nick worked on the puzzle together, they hadn't even changed into their little clothes. Surely they couldn't be happy with that, could they?

"And what about you, Mr. Crawford?" Hudson's deep voice stirred me out of my thoughts and back into reality, as did the three sets of eyes glued on me. "Have you and Nick progressed on the age play front?"

I took a sip of the ridiculously tangy drink, letting it burn the back of my throat. I told them all about it. About how Nick and I were both so new to it, and the night at Revolver when we met Addison.

I talked about how the three of us had started hanging out. And as I looked at the three men around the table, I could feel their love and support pouring out of them and into me. All they wanted for me was to find happiness.

So with a deep breath and another gulp of the spicy margarita, I opened up my heart and soul to my brothers. I told them everything.

How Nick and Addison had sex while I watched.

How incredible the attraction and connection between the three of us felt.

How I enjoyed spending time with them, even if we were blurring the traditional boundaries of age play every time we hung out.

And how I felt like my soul was being ripped apart.

"Whoa, what—what do you mean by that?" Stirling asked, his voice laced with uneasiness.

I blew out a breath, trying to summon the word gods to smile down on me. "I have no problem with Nick and Addison being...together."

I squirmed in my seat, until I felt Porter's hand land gently over mine. "Take your time, Steel."

I cleared my throat. "But when it comes to me and Addison, I don't know, you guys, it just feels wrong for some reason."

"Wrong, how?" Hudson prodded in his customary delicate way. God, how I'd missed him being here for conversations like this.

I searched for the right words.

"It's as if there's something wrong with me for wanting it," I finally said.

"But, you don't feel that way about when Nick is with Addison, do you?" Stirling asked.

I shook my head.

"No, not at all. If Nick was with another Daddy, then I know I would have an issue with that. But with Addison..." I drifted off into a warm memory reel at the mention of his name.

The guys let the silence linger.

Finally, Porter rested his elbows on the table and cleared his throat to get our attention. "Let me tell you all a thing or two about how men operate."

"Oh, please do," Stirling shot back with uncharacteristic sassiness. "Just because we're all men here, don't let that stop you."

Hudson and I snickered. Porter ignored all of us and steamrolled ahead. "We are visual creatures. Men need to look, it's an outlet for us. I need to, even though when I do, I'm left with nothing. I don't even know why I do it half the time. But if you told me I couldn't look, then the switch in my brain that activates whenever I get told I can't do something would get triggered."

We all pondered his words for a moment. He did make some sense. I mean, I loved the sight of Nick and Addison together. It was the most beautiful thing I'd ever seen in my life, and I'd seen the northern lights over Lake Michigan.

"It might not make a lot of sense," Porter continued, "but there's really nothing wrong with looking, and in your case, there's nothing wrong with touching either, Steel."

His words torpedoed into me, unlocking a hidden box next to my heart that I'd kept closed for far too long.

"Do you guys agree with that?" I asked, looking over at Stirling and Hudson for some additional validation.

Hudson gave a firm nod. "Absolutely. I think that far too often, we let our internalized feelings of shame—especially when it comes to love and sex—take over. Based on what you said, Steel, you, Nick, and Addison are communicating openly and honestly about this. You're not hurting anyone here—"

"Well, that's not entirely true. You are hurting someone," Stirling interjected.

I furrowed my brows, unsure what he was talking about. He lifted a finger and pointed it straight at me.

"You. You're the only one who's suffering here."

He was right.

They all were.

All my fears, doubts, and insecurities, they were only hurting me.

"Another round?" Porter asked as he raised his hand to get the server's attention without waiting for a response.

"Maybe beer this time?" Hudson said. "My throat needs some

time to recover."

"There's a joke in there," Porter laughed. "But I have matured, so it won't be coming from me."

Hudson shot Stirling and I a look of utter disbelief.

"Okay, I know I've been away for a few months, but what have you guys done with my friend? This man might look like Porter Jones, but there is no way my friend would ever say something like that."

Our laughter was interrupted by the server coming over and Porter placing an order for a round of beers. As soon as he left, Porter leaned over the table and launched into his *the boys are up to something* conspiracy that I'd heard plenty of times before.

I tuned out, my thoughts returning to our previous conversation. I was struck by how blinded I had been to what was right in front of me.

Me.

The problem wasn't with Nick or Addison, it was with me. Pure and simple.

For whatever reason, I felt a misplaced sense of guilt for having the feelings and attraction that I had for Addison. If I wanted to change that, first, I had to own it.

And second, I had to do something about it.

My feelings for Addison didn't diminish my love and adoration of Nick in the slightest. And my love for Nick gave me room, permission almost, to create a space for Addison in my heart too. All of a sudden, I went from feeling conflicted and torn up to having a wave of realization sweep through me. The mere thought of it ignited my insides.

It was true.

Possible.

Probable.

Heck, even likely.

Suddenly, I had an idea how this was going to end.

I could be a Daddy to the two most beautiful boys in the world.

CHAPTER NINETEEN

NICK

"This is so much fun," Mikey squealed, practically falling off the couch with elation. "I can't even remember the last time the four of us were together like this."

I looked at my over-excited best friend who was sitting next to me on the couch. Then I flicked my eyes over to Liam and Declan who were sitting on the opposite couch.

"You know, this is kind of where it all started for us."

Declan scrunched up his eyebrows. "What do you mean?"

"Well..." I glanced around Porter's sunken living room. "This is where Steel had his fortieth birthday. Mikey and I were hired as naked butlers and Mikey practically came in his briefs the second he laid eyes on Stirling."

The guys laughed, including Mikey. "Hey, can you blame me? I have the hottest Daddy in the world."

The laughter stopped.

"Uh, read the room, Mikey," Declan teased. "In the interest of investigative integrity, I cannot let that statement stand as fact."

"Ooh, look at you Mr. Big Shot Reporter," I said with a giggle.

As I looked at the three boys, my heart was overfilled with joy. We had each found our own perfect Daddy, the one that was just right for us. And we were each, in our own way, creating happy, healthy lives for ourselves. Whether that meant having children like Mikey and Stirling, travelling the country like Liam and Hudson, or writing up BDSM contracts like Declan and Porter, we were all living out our version of a happily ever after.

Mine, though, wasn't fully finished yet. I couldn't help but let my imagination wander, exploring how it might end.

"Hey, I really liked your article about Daylesford's new recycling center," Liam said, looking over at Declan. "You did a really good job."

Declan blushed slightly. "Thanks."

I smiled as the background talk continued around me. It was good having the boy gang gathered together. Mikey and I might have been best friends since forever, but Declan and Liam were very welcome additions to our posse.

It was nice, rare even, to find a group of like-minded people who you could be your true, authentic self with. There was no judgement with these guys, no need to apologize for who we were or hide any part of ourselves. It was...freeing. Even for a super-confident (and sexy, and funny, and all-round superstar) boy like me. It was nice knowing these guys had my back, just like I had theirs.

"So," Mikey said, using his *I'm going to try and sound like a proper adult now* voice. "Liam and Declan have filled us in on what they've been doing, and I've told you guys what's going on with me. So, that just leaves..."

Three sets of eyes landed on me. On all of me, and the only fair and right thing to do was to allow them some time to soak it up and take it all in. My choice of outfit had definitely been inspired by someone, a certain *sexy Australian photographer* someone. A different look for me for sure, but hey, I still pulled it off.

Gone was the camp color and traces of glitter that were my fashion staples. Instead, I had gone for a sharp all-black look. A super-tight black shirt that clung to my every curve, every muscle, every pore of skin like it's life depended on it, and a pair of MC Hammer-style balloon pants I had picked up from a thrift shop a few weeks back. Yes, it was a risky choice, covering one of my top ten all-time best features—my ass—but hey, sometimes you gotta take risks in life.

"Yeah, how are things with you and Steel going?" Liam asked, settling on the sofa. "I've heard there's been some...progress, since last time I was in town."

I cocked my head to the side. "Oh yeah, there's definitely been progress."

I channeled my inner-Porter and filled the boys in on everything. I wasn't ashamed of anything, so I wasn't going to hide any part of it. The truth of the matter was that I, no, wait, *Steel and I* were falling for Addison.

Hard.

Completely.

Totally and utterly.

Mikey beamed. "That's so great, I am so happy for you... For all three of you."

"So am I," Declan said. He looked like he was about to say something else, but stopped himself. After a moment, he pushed ahead. "What—what about the age play thing? How are you feeling about that?"

The nervousness I heard in his voice made sense. I had shared with them all how difficult it was for me to break through into being a little, I guess it was time to give them an update about that as well.

"That's going well." At least, I kinda-sorta thought it was. Or rather, hoped it was. "I think we've found something that works for us. It's a bit of a hybrid thing, but, yeah, it's going okay."

Mikey narrowed his eyes. "You don't sound convinced, Nick Macklin."

I wasn't.

I scratched the back of my neck. "I guess there's just a lot going on, you know? When Steel and I went to Revolver that night, we were hoping to find a friend. Someone I could be a little with and who might help me navigate through things. I certainly wasn't expecting to find..."

"A third?" Declan suggested.

"A big brother?" Liam chimed in.

"Love," Mikey said, and with that one word, he broke shit down to the heart of the matter.

Love.

Was that what was happening here? Was I falling in love with Addison? Was Steel? And what was Addison feeling? I sighed. I hadn't had this many unanswered questions since I'd re-binged *Lost* for the third time and still couldn't figure out what the hell was going on.

Liam peered up at me through his long lashes. "How does Steel feel?"

"He feels the same way I do. He really likes Addison, and he loves it when we spend time together."

"I couldn't do it," Declan announced. "Don't get me wrong, I think all love is great. Whether it's between two people or twenty people. I just think I'm too jealous. I couldn't share Porter with anyone else."

"Fair enough," I said. "I mean, you've managed to tame one wild-ass man. You gotta have some good D, there."

We all laughed.

"Don't get me wrong, he looks at other guys," Declan said.

"And that doesn't bother you?" Mikey asked.

Declan shook his head. "No, not at all. Some men are just wired like that. He can look all he wants. It's just something that he needs to do, like how a dog needs to scratch itself."

More group laughter followed.

"Oh, and you're right, Nick," Declan said, casting his gaze in my direction. "I do have some good D. And he loves all nine inches of it."

Another round of giggling ensued.

"I think the important thing," Mikey started, "is that you guys follow your hearts. I mean, look at each of us. We're all different and we have completely different relationships with our Daddies. Whether it's obedience, or BDSM, or any other way we want our relationships to be, we're each following our hearts. And how good does that feel, right?"

Mikey's—AKA Mini-Oprah's—question had the audience, I mean, Liam and Declan—nodding their agreement.

I knew Mikey was right. You could never go wrong when you followed the voice deep inside. It was just that Steel had his own inner voice and Addison did, too. Were all of our inner voices saying the same thing?

Thankfully, Liam decided to change the topic. "So, *Daylesford's Most Eligible Daddy* contest is coming up in six weeks. And we are still in, right? We're going ahead with this crazy, hairbrained scheme?"

We all nodded, before Mikey turned and shot me a worried look. "Wait, Nick, what are you going to do?"

I frowned. "Huh? What do you mean, Mikey?"

"Well," he said, choosing his words carefully. "Usually, these things only happen between two people. You technically have three."

Shit. He was right. I hadn't even thought about it.

Declan smiled. "Nick, don't worry about it. Remember, just follow your heart."

So much easier said than done.

Fuck rules.

Follow your heart.

All totally cute and stealable catchphrases which I could see myself printing onto some of my homemade T-shirts. But all of a sudden, real life hit me like a ton of bricks.

I had no idea how any of this was going to end.

CHAPTER TWENTY

ADDISON

"Are you sure this is safe, Addy?"

Kym stood behind me in my tiny bathroom, scissors in hand and looking just as nervous as I was feeling. This time though, the crazy beauty treatment idea was on me.

"Of course it's safe," I said, lifting my hair off the back of my neck, pulling it up into a high ponytail. "It's medical grade, Kymmy. It's fine. Now, you'll probably need about four to six inches."

Our eyes met in the mirror before she broke out into a saucy grin. "I need a whole lot more than that, believe me."

If my stomach wasn't in knots, I probably would have laughed at her joke. Kym took my silence as a sign that she should get down to business.

Her face tilted down as she cut the tape to the required length.

"Done," she said, proudly waving it for me to see in the mirror.

"Great."

I ran my fingers along the back of my neck, double-checking to make sure no wayward strands of hair remained. My mind floated back to the feeling of Nick's fingertips grazing my skin there. God, I loved how he made me feel.

If only I could get Steel to feel the same way about me that I felt about Nick. Well, maybe this would go some way toward that. At the very least, it couldn't hurt. I hoped.

"So, what do I do now?" Kym asked.

"Place the tape on one side of my neck," I said, mentally replaying the YouTube tutorial I had watched a hundred times earlier that day.

"Okay, done."

I felt the tape stick to my skin on the left side of my neck.

"Now, pinch the center of my neck slightly, gather the excess skin toward the middle, and pull it under the tape. Then, press the tape down and over the excess skin, so that it stays in place, and stretch it over to the other side."

The look of concentration on Kym's face was priceless. I'd owe her big time for this, or I could just call it even for her crazy beauty treatment idea. Yeah, I'd go with that.

"Alright, Addison Mark, you are all done." She stepped back from me like an artist stepping away from their just-completed masterpiece.

I let my hair out, watching it as it fell around my face. I shook my head gently. Then I leaned closer to the mirror, studying my neck. Kymmy came in for a closer look too.

"Does it look any different?" I asked, patting the skin peeking out from the top of my shirt.

Kym scrunched her nose. "How is it meant to look different?"

"The tape is meant to pull the neck skin back, so I should look younger and less...saggy."

"Addy." I felt her hand land softly on my shoulder. "You don't have saggy neck skin. You look great—"

"For my age?" I interrupted, sounding snarkier than I'd meant to.

"For *any* age." The kindness in her voice snapped me out of my brief detour into jerk-ville.

"I'm sorry," I said. "I just—"

Kym raised a finger into the air that caught my eye in the mirror. "I don't mean to interrupt, Addy, but can we please have this conversation somewhere that isn't your bathroom?"

I smiled. "Sure."

We stepped out of my miniscule bathroom into my miniscule combined   living-slash-dining-slash-pretty-much-the-only-room-that-wasn't-a-bedroom room in my apartment. We huddled up on the loveseat in the corner by the large window overlooking a beautiful brick wall.

"So, tell me everything. Why has my otherwise normal and mostly sane best friend just made me cover his neck in tape?"

I tried to find something witty or funny to answer that question with, but instead—annoyingly—a big-ass lump formed in my throat.

"I just, I mean, I feel so...old."

And then I said it, the words that broke it down to the very core. It was my biggest fear. The thing that I was ashamed of and tried so desperately to escape from but couldn't.

"I'm too old to be a boy."

Kym ran her fingers down my arm.

"Addison." Her voice was uncharacteristically soft. "You're thirty-two. That's not old."

"It is for me. No Daddy wants someone my age."

"Addison." Her voice had a firmer edge to it this time. "That's not true. But if it was, then it only proves my point."

"Which is?"

"That men are stupid," she said flatly. "Do you know that I had a guy come up to me at a bar last week and ask me if I was Margaret Cho? I mean, how stupid was he? I was so mad and offended."

My eyes were wide with shock. "I don't blame you."

"Yeah," Kym continued, picking at a piece of fluff on her top. "I mean, Margaret Cho is like a million years old. But am I going to let some dumb fucker bring me down? No. Next time anyone says something like that though, I'll just pretend they mistook me for Lucy Liu instead."

I smirked. "You know, Margaret Cho and Lucy Liu are actually the same age."

"Really?" Kym squeaked in disbelief. "That's so...weird."

I shrugged. "Facts is facts, y'all."

Kymmy let out her signature cackle. "God, I love your random pop culture knowledge...and your terrible attempts at talking like an American. You always sound like such a hillbilly."

"Oh really?" I asked, feigning seriousness. "I was going for Walmart-shopping trailer trash."

The mood in the room lightened a bit.

"Hey, what are these?" Kym asked as she leaned over and picked up a pile of photos off the small coffee table.

"Steel took some photos of Nick and me when we were hanging out. They're nice, right?"

Kimmy carefully flicked through the photos, one at a time.

"Yeah, wow. They really are, Addy." I noticed a wistfulness in her tone.

"Why do you sound like that?"

She placed the photos back onto the table and looked at me.

"Because, Addy, that's what love looks like." She motioned with her head toward the photos. "You guys just look so...happy together."

I smiled. "We are."

At least, Nick and I were.

Her face turned solemn.

"You don't need to change anything about yourself to find love, Addison. And even if you wanted to, what good would it do? The second the tape thing wears off, or the Botox, or whatever other crazy beauty treatment you try, at some point, you're going to be left with you. And the you underneath all of that stuff is so amazing, so beautiful, so fucking worthy of being loved. You just have to believe that."

Her words hit me hard.

I knew she was right. I could feel the truth in what she was saying. But how could I do it? How could I make myself believe that I was worthy of being loved when all my life, the world had told me that boys like me had an expiration date?

Or worse, when Daddies like Steel lost interest in me once I passed a certain milestone birthday?

I wanted things to work out with Nick and Steel. I was falling for them, for both of them. But I had to be smart about this, too. For my own sanity, I had to use my head as much as my heart. There was a difference between what was real and what I wanted or hoped was real. As much as I wanted to be with them both, there was a good chance that would never happen.

A tightness formed in my belly as it dawned on me that I had no idea how any of this was going to end.

CHAPTER TWENTY-ONE

NICK

"Come on, come on, come on." I was hurrying Steel, tugging at his arm to get him to follow me up the stairs to Addison's apartment.

"Baby, I'm coming. Relax."

Yeah right, as if I was going to be able to do that. It had felt like ages since we'd seen Addison, and I was bursting with anticipation. Our busy work schedules meant we'd had to postpone this visit twice. I didn't care if the entire world blew up and only Steel and Addison could fix it, this date was going to happen.

We reached his front door. I felt Steel's warm breath behind me. I stretched my arm out to knock on the door just as Steel wrapped my fingers in his.

"Before we go in," he rumbled from behind me, which coincidentally was exactly where I liked him to be, "I just want to check in with you. How are you feeling?"

"I'm good, I'm good, I'm good."

I felt his low chuckle vibrate through his chest. He spun me around so that I was facing him and cupped my face.

"I love you. We're going to have a good time tonight."

"I love you, too."

Our lips met in a gentle kiss. I closed my eyes, silently acknowledging the wonderfulness of my Daddy. Other men would have tried to calm me down, or force me to be quieter, stiller, less...me. But not him. Never Steel.

Sure, he'd always check in with me to see how I was feeling, and in those moments, I grounded myself a little. But he was doing it out of concern for me. Never to control me and deffers never trying to change me. Because....good luck if he so much as even tried.

I turned back to face the door and was just about to knock, when I looked over my shoulder.

"And how are you feeling?"

There was a pause, one that went for longer than expected. I felt Steel's strong hand running across my lower back as he leaned in and said, "I'm good, baby. Now knock on that door before you explode with excitement."

I giggled as I gave the door a gentle knock. Addison opened it a moment later and holy fuck, did he look ah-mazing. Dressed in all black as usual, his hair cascading loosely around his shoulders, he was one of the most gorgeous creatures I had ever laid my eyes on, and yet, he looked almost a little nervous.

"Hey," he said.

"Hey, yourself."

I stepped in and our mouths met. Mine was slightly open and without hesitation, Addison slid his tongue inside. I cooed softly. He felt so good, like he belonged there.

I pulled away after a few blissful moments and moved so that Steel could have a chance to say hello. I wanted to see them kiss. It struck me that I'd never really noticed them kissing before, at least not in the way that Addison and I did.

Steel moved in and instead of kissing Addison on the lips, he dipped his head in and around him, kind of mimicking some weird birdlike movement you see in a nature documentary, before finally giving Addison a peck on the cheek. Okay, that was weird. Addison looked uncomfortable until his eyes met mine and he smiled.

"Come on in," he said.

Steel closed the door behind us as we stepped into the cozy apartment. The memory of *the kiss that wasn't* lingered in my mind, but I didn't want to focus on that right now. I'd bring it up with Steel later.

"It's not much," Addison said as he pointed to a loveseat for Steel and me to sit on. "But it's home for me."

"I like it," I said as I took it in.

Yes, the place was small. But it was cute, and best of all, it had signs of Addison everywhere.

"I made a margarita pitcher," Addison said. "Let me go grab it."

"I'll give you a hand."

Addison looked like he wanted to rebuff Steel's offer, but Steel was on his feet before Addison could say anything.

It gave me a chance to stand up and look at the photos on the wall more closely. Every single photo was a close-up of a face. People of all different ages, looks, shapes, and sizes, but all looking so beautiful. I smiled, liking the fact that Addison had a way of bringing out the best in others.

"Here we are," Addison said as he placed the pitcher on the small round coffee table.

Steel placed the glasses down and sat next to me. Our hands clasped together tightly. Addison poured the drinks and handed them to us.

"No jalapenos in this one?" Steel asked with a smile, but was quickly met with two confused faces. "It's a long story, I'll tell you boys about it some other time."

I took a sip of my drink and settled into the evening. As always, it was brilliant. The conversation flowed smoothly, the pitchers kept coming, and the three of us were getting along so well. It was everything I'd hoped it would be.

When the three of us were together, all my worries and doubts disappeared. At least for a while. Things felt so right, so natural. I could tell that this was meant to be. That the three of us were meant to be together.

Somehow.

Steel stood up and walked over to the wall, taking in all of the amazing photos that lined it. Addison got up and joined him.

"This was from my first exhibition. The one in New York."

"It's good." A smile stretched Steel's lips as his eyes scanned the images. "I can see why you won."

Addison shuffled from one foot to the other. He looked so adorable whenever he was caught off guard. I took a moment and just watched them. Sure, maybe their kiss by the front door had been a little awkward, but they liked each other. That I could tell. But I also couldn't shake the sense that I was picking up on something else, perhaps a slight hesitancy. I just couldn't tell which one of them it was coming from.

"Have you got anything more recent you could show us?" Steel asked as he sat back down on the loveseat next to me.

Addison dropped his head down. "I do, actually."

Steel leaned over the table and reached for his hand. Addison looked up, let out a breath, and met his fingers. The touch between them sent an instant jolt of electricity to my dick. I may have normally been an above the marquee A-lister, but right now, I wanted front row seats at the Steel and Addison show.

"Would you be comfortable showing us?"

Addison gave a firm nod and slipped his hand out of Steel's. He walked over to his bedroom and he emerged a few moments later, holding a black leather-bound photo album. He handed it to Steel.

"Here you go."

Steel moved his legs toward the middle of the loveseat and carefully placed the album on his lap. I shuffled over, and he waited to make sure I was in position before he opened it. When he did, my heart clenched in my chest. The images were so beautiful. All black and white. Only faces. All men.

"Is this your passion project?" I asked.

"Yeah," he answered with an airy smile. "It is."

Steel turned the page carefully and I looked back down again. The men in the photos were making love, that part was pretty apparent. But the zoomed in, super close-ups on their faces gave the images a sense of honesty and intimacy that I hadn't ever seen before.

Steel thumbed through the rest of the album in complete silence, only taking his eyes off the images to make sure I was ready for him to turn the page. When we were finished, he closed it and placed it carefully on the coffee table.

"You're being awfully quiet, Steel," Addison observed. He was chewing on his lower lip. He looked nervous. I guess showing someone your passion project was really putting yourself out there.

I could see Steel's jaw clenched tight. He looked at me, before turning to Addison. "Why aren't you showing this somewhere?"

Addison looked surprised. He let out an exasperated half-sigh. "They're just some silly photos I take at Revolver. It's not like they're anything good or—"

"Hey." Steel's voice was deep, and it reverberated loudly off the walls." There's nothing silly about these photos, Addison. They're amazing. You're insanely talented."

Addison blushed. "Well, so are you, then."

He reached around behind his seat and pulled out a small pile of photos, handing them to Steel.

I peered over and could see the photos Steel had taken of Addison and me.

"Ooh, these are good," I said.

"They are," Steel added, but he kept his eyes on Addison. "But yours are good because you're a talented artist. Mine are good because I got lucky and was photographing the two most beautiful boys in the world."

I looked over at Addison. He looked like Steel's words had stunned him. I stood up and walked over to him.

"Steel's right," I said as Addison stood up to face me. His face was just inches away from me. "We are the two most beautiful boys in the world."

Addison smiled and I ran the back of my fingers across his soft cheek.

"Especially when you smile," I added.

I looked over at Steel and could see the look of lust in his eyes.

"Especially," I said, leaning in and gliding my tongue across his jaw until I nibbled on his earlobe, "when you're fucking me."

I could have been all demure and said something lovely about kissing or hugging, but screw that, I wanted to get right down to the main event.

This time we had come prepared, and judging by the hardness I was palming in the front of his pants, Addison was just as ready.

We made our way to his bedroom, in a blur of hands and lips and groans, and somehow managed not to kill ourselves. I took a quick look around the room. It was small, a little messy, but it smelled like Addison. That's what made it perfect.

"Over there." I directed my Daddy to a chair in the corner of the room while I pinned Addison down on his bed. I liked being on top once in a while, not that I ever actually topped. But the position made for a nice view.

Addison's body was tanned, hard, and had just the right amount of fur. Steel handed me a condom, while Addison reached his arm under the bed, and fumbled around for a little while until he produced the prize he was chasing: lube.

His eyes shot up to meet mine. "I cannot wait to fuck you, Nick."

"Then don't wait," I breathed, lifting an eyebrow and inviting him—no, *daring* him—to take control.

CHAPTER TWENTY-TWO

ADDISON

There were lots of things I could control in my life. What I ate—and just as importantly, what I didn't—how often I dragged myself to the gym, the insane and questionable beauty treatments I was willing to torture myself with. But having Nick Macklin on top of me, with that glint of mischievousness in his eyes, saying those fucking words to me. That had me losing any last shred of self-control I had been trying to hold onto.

"Oh, you fucking got it."

I gripped his wrists and with my well-earned core strength, flipped myself up...over...and around him until I was the one on top of him, my fingers pinning down the most stunning boy in the world to my queen-size bed.

He gazed up at me with eyes filled with surprise—and lust. He wrapped his legs around my ass.

"Fuck me, Addison."

He handed me the condom. I ripped it with my teeth and slid it over my fully erect dick. I couldn't remember the last time I had been so hard. I grabbed the bottle of lube and slicked my cock, using what remained on my fingers to press against his hole.

The change in Nick's expression as my slicked fingers gently explored his ass was breathtaking. He went from cheeky to vulnerable quicker than the shutter speed on my camera. I slowed my fingers down, spreading the lube out not just against his hole, but around it too.

The outside street light shone through my bedroom window and illuminated his face with a gentle blue hue. With my eyes firmly fixed on his glowing face, I entered him.

One finger.

He breathed out so heavily I felt I was swimming in a pool filled with strawberry milkshake. His sweet scent settling over me reminded me that there was so much more to Nick that I wanted to know. Every time my mind settled and thought, *Right, now I've got you figured out*, he'd say or do something—or even just exhale in a way—that made me realize there was so much more to discover.

"How does this feel?" I said as I gently probed his inside wall with my index finger.

"So good, Addison. So good. I want more."

A heat hit my chest. It felt good being wanted. I hadn't realized how much I had missed that feeling. Or maybe I did, but I'd just gotten used to ignoring it.

I pulled out and lubed up my index finger on my other hand. With each finger nice and wet, I placed them to the left and right of his hole.

He looked down at me and smiled. He trusted me, I could see it all over his face.

"Relax. Breathe," I said as I gently stretched his hole, pressing the tip of each index finger into his flesh and spreading them wider.

"Oh, man."

Nick's head fell back onto the mattress, making it bob like we were out on a boat. The rocking felt good, and I went with it, pushing both fingers deep into him at once. He blew out noisily as his warmth encased my fingers.

"You're doing well, Nick."

"I've had a few years of practice."

We both glanced at each other before turning our heads to Steel. He had moved my clothes onto the floor and was stroking himself in the corner.

"Like what you see?" I asked, my heart pounding at my own audaciousness.

I saw a nod and heard him grunt before I felt Nick's hands on the back of my hand, pulling me into him. I kept fingering him while our mouths mashed together. His sweetness was now all around me—gripping my fingers, filling my nostrils, in my mouth.

I pushed back and took a deep breath. Slowly sliding my fingers out of him, I stroked my cock, making sure it was still properly lubed. It was. And it was time to give Nick what he wanted.

I spread my knees out a little wider on the bed, lining the head of my cock up against Nick. Slowly, the tip entered, meeting the barest of resistance. With his legs wrapped around my ass, and his fingers pulling my hair, I gently pushed forward, inching my way deeper and deeper until finally...I was all the way inside him.

The sensation that followed was indescribable. I closed my eyes as I felt his ass clamp down around my cock. His legs wrapped tighter as he kept clenching and releasing, clenching and releasing.

Mmm, now this was the kind of bossy bottom I liked.

"How does that feel?" Nick asked, not that he needed to.

My eyes were rolling around in the back of my head, and I probably looked like a zombie that had come back to life. But he didn't seem to care. He was fucking my cock with his ass...and loving it more with every single squeeze.

I couldn't find any words to speak, so he stopped. I took that as my cue to start actually fucking him since, yeah, that was what was supposed to happen next. I had no idea where my brain had gone, but it was clearly no longer functioning. Thankfully, instinct took over as I began to thrust in and out of him, my cock feeling like it was on fire.

Our bodies slammed against the bed, and the boat we were on? Yeah, now it was in a fucking wavepool. My trusty old queen bed started squeaking with every forceful thrust. God, I hadn't heard that sound in forever. I enjoyed hearing it, like it somehow made what we were doing even hotter.

If that was even possible.

I rocked into him, harder, stronger, putting all of my body weight into each thrust. My balls tightened and I let out an almighty scream. I was yelling out words for sure, but what they were, I didn't even know.

I released what felt like a lifetime of pent-up energy inside Nick.

CHAPTER TWENTY-THREE

STEEL

Addison's head flew back as he cried out, "Oh, holy fucking shit. This feels so good. Oh my fucking God, I'm gonna lose it. I'm coming, I'm coming," in what seemed like one incredibly long and uninterrupted breath. His torso twisted, and the ripples of his orgasm shuddered through his entire body.

I kept my grip firmly around my cock, determined not to come. Not yet, anyway. I'd been enjoying the show too much and I didn't want it to end.

As Addison's body began to settle down, Nick tenderly stroked his hair. Addison leaned in for a kiss, before throwing a glance at me.

"I think it may be time for your turn."

My eyes widened. "You mean...?"

"Yeppers," Addison replied with a cheeky twinkle in his eye. "It's my turn to watch the two of you."

Nick flipped over onto his hands and knees. Addison shuffled up so he was sitting against the headboard with Nick's face right in front of him, while Nick's beautiful, meaty ass was right in front of me.

He gave it a little wiggle as he looked over his shoulder. "I should be all nice and warmed up for you...Daddy."

A shiver tore through me as I reached for the lube and greased my dick up with it. Nick was right, he was warmed up. I could feel it as I slid my cock into him. It felt good, and more than just a little bit filthy, to think that mine was the second cock inside of my boy tonight.

I entered him fully and as I looked up, I could see Nick and Addison kissing, unable to keep their mouths off each other. My cock jolted as I started sliding in and out of my beautiful boy's stretched-out hole. The sight of the two of them fucking was burned into my memory—and held a permanent place in my spank bank too—but right now, watching them kissing so hungrily, passionately, as if their lives depended on it, turned me on like nothing else ever had.

Addison suddenly pulled away and reached into the top drawer of his nightstand.

"Do you mind if I take some photos?" he asked, pulling out his camera. "Just faces. Private collection. No one will ever see them."

"Baby?" I stopped thrusting and Nick turned to look at me over his shoulder. "How do you feel about this?"

Nick threw a lust-filled look at the both of us. "Let's do it. I trust Addison."

"I do, too." I flashed him a warm smile. "Now, which side is my best side?"

"The side of you that's fucking me. Now, get back to it."

Nick wiggled his ass. God, I loved my bossy bottom.

"Let me figure out the details," Addison said as he lined himself up at the top of the bed. "As much as you can, just completely ignore the fact that I'm here."

I was so lost in the moment that I didn't even notice Addison or the camera that was pointed at us. I dragged my fingers along Nick's scalp and pulled on his hair. I loved the way it made his back arch. It changed the angle of his ass and it felt like heaven on a stick.

After a few more pumps in and out, I felt that guttural sensation behind my balls. That deep heavy feeling that could only mean one thing. The normally long march to release would be crazy short as the sight of Nick's back arching and rocking in time with mine sent me over the edge.

I came hard. Just as I did, I felt Nick's balls slapping against me. He was jerking himself while still kissing Addison. After a few strokes, I felt his ass clamping down against my still-hard cock, and then he released. I felt it all, down to the very last drop, as he came just as hard as I did.

I pulled out of Nick as Addison put the camera away. We lay together as close as we could be, three sets of legs entangled. The air was filled with the aroma of sweat, cum, and strawberries, of course. Nick lay in the middle, between us, but I could feel his and Addison's bodies heaving, gently stirring the bed with a slight motion that made me feel like I was floating.

Because I was.

And as I lay there, listening to the sounds of the two boys breathing, I closed my eyes and let out a smile. I never wanted the night to end.

CHAPTER TWENTY-FOUR

ADDISON

"That was…" Nick began as the three of us headed toward the door after we had showered—separately, because that was how freaking small my bathroom was.

"Incredible," Steel said.

"Magical," I whispered.

"Ev-er-y-thing." Nick's wrap-up took the cake.

I gave his hand a tight squeeze, feeling like I was still half asleep and not wanting to wake up and end the beautiful dream I was having.

"I don't want you guys to go."

Holy shit. That woke me up. Why had I just said that? I shuffled away from Nick as I opened the front door for them.

"I don't want to leave, either." Nick's eyes pleaded with Steel.

"Maybe next time," Steel said, placing his hands on both of our shoulders, "Addison can come over to our place and stay the night?"

His eyes flicked over to me.

"I'd like that," I said quietly.

I felt Nick's fingers hook under my chin, lifting my gaze to meet his.

"I'd like that too. So much."

His words echoed in the dark hallway as they stepped outside. We embraced each other, all three of us at once. The heat still coming off their bodies felt good against mine.

"We'll call you tomorrow," Steel said as Nick threaded their fingers together, and I watched as they walked away.

I closed the door, leaning against it as I closed my eyes. When I opened them again, it was as if I was seeing everything through a new lens, pun unintended. My apartment, which I had always loved and felt good in, despite being the size of a sardine tin, suddenly felt cold and alien.

The photos that I'd clung to as a reminder of my former glory looked like something that belonged in a time capsule, not something I should be hanging on my walls. Why was I displaying something I associated with defeat so prominently in my own house?

My past and present were colliding with the future, or one of the many possible futures that lay before me.

I sat down on the couch, picking up the photos Steel had taken of Nick and me.

Again, it was the two of us. Nick and me. Always just us.

Never him.

Never me and him.

We even took turns fucking Nick. It wasn't something we did together. It was always kept separate, distanced. He hadn't made even the slightest move or gesture to indicate that he wanted me...that he wanted to fuck me.

I knew the future I wanted, but as I looked around my dimly lit apartment, I figured I'd just have to settle with the future that was destined for me. One where, at the end of the evening, I'd be left by myself.

The pain clenched my heart as I walked back into the bedroom, the smell of sex assaulting my senses. The crumpled bed sheets, the air still thick with all of our smells. I threw myself onto the bed and grabbed my camera, glancing through the photos I had taken of Nick and Steel.

God, Nick really did have one of the most expressive faces I had ever shot. I could see so much in his eyes—the thrill, the excitement, the rush—and Steel's handsome face behind him was such a steadying force.

How I wanted that. All of it. But it wasn't going to happen. They already had their thing and I had...I looked around my tiny bedroom, I had this.

I placed the camera onto my nightstand and lay down. My mind was racing but it couldn't settle on any one thought. A feeling of sadness swept over me. I tossed and turned, willing my brain to switch off and let me fall asleep.

Finally, after what seemed like hours, I closed my eyes and drifted off into a light, lonely sleep.

CHAPTER TWENTY-FIVE

NICK

When we'd left Addison's apartment a week ago, there were two things I wanted to change.

First, I wanted to get clarity on the whole hybrid thing we were doing. In the beginning, I had enjoyed it, and it had worked. Addison made me feel so comfortable that regressing into my little headspace had gotten easier and easier for me. But lately, it had started to hinder rather than help me become a little.

I think that came down to me being confused. It was a good stepping stone, but now I was ready to move on to something more concrete and better defined. I was one hundred percent sure I was ready to take the next step, and I got the sense that Addison felt the same way too.

So I did that mature thing that adults do, I got Steel to take Addison and me out to Montrachet, Daylesford's finest French restaurant. Sitting in the beautifully appointed private dining room, with the three of us bathed in the glow of candlelight and enjoying the most delicious lightly grilled scallops I had ever tasted, I told Steel and Addison my plan.

We needed better boundaries between the different headspaces Addison and I occupied. I was ready to move further, deeper, and more fully into my littlehood than ever before.

I double-checked with Addison who had been nodding at me as I spoke, and he backed me up. He was feeling the same way, just like I'd suspected. He needed clearer boundaries, too.

So I proposed two words. They weren't safewords, they were more like mood words. I made a mental note to remind myself to ask Steel to check in with Porter to see whether that was a copyrighted term, but basically it worked like this.

We all needed to know which space we were in. Whether we were little or adults. It wasn't about whether Steel was in the room or not, it was about how we interacted together wherever the three of us were together.

I suggested we use two simple words to communicate what space we would like to be in: little and big. That gave us all a chance to talk about it and agree on where we were in that moment.

It also meant that after some time in one space, we could use those words to indicate we wanted to change to the other space. It was kinda what Addison and I were doing anyway, flipping from little space to adult space, but because we weren't talking about it, it wasn't clear when it was happening. That was the confusing part and what was keeping me from being able to regress farther into my littlehood.

By the time we had finished dessert that night, the three of us had agreed to the system.

And over the week after that conversation at Montrachet, we had put it to the test. It was working beautifully, like I knew that it would. Because when the three of us were together, there was magic in the air.

Addison had arrived at our place less than twenty minutes ago, but after taking one look at him, we both said the word at the same time.

"Little."

He was dealing with a difficult client who was making his life a living hell. He had come over every night this week, in need of some little time at first, before we made the switch to big time.

"Knock knock," Steel said as he pushed the ajar door open with his foot.

"It's so funny when he says that," I giggled, giving Addison a friendly push.

We were sitting on the floor with his truck and car collection spread out in front of us. He was wearing his usual baggy clothes and I was snugly wrapped up in my favorite orange onesie.

Both of us had damp cloths in our hands, because once a week the vehicles needed to be cleaned. His rules, not mine, but I was more than happy to go along with them.

"I know," Addison replied with a smile. "The door is always open, anyways."

"Good manners are always important," Steel said as he placed a tray down on the table. "I know we are having dinner a bit later, but I thought you boys might be hungry now. I've cut up some fruit pieces, and there's carrots and some hummus dip here as well."

I rolled my eyes. "That sounds so...healthy."

"That's right," Steel said, straightening up. "I want my boys to be healthy."

That wasn't a slip of the tongue. I looked over at Addison who had been gently wiping down the side of the red Ferrari. He paused, his movement suspended as he took in Steel's words.

My boys.

Yeppers. It was clear that what was happening between the three of us was more than just friendship and play dates—it was relationship-level stuff.

We were falling for each other. And just like we'd set clear boundaries around our little and big spaces, this thing between us also needed a boundary. So tonight, over dinner, Steel was going to ask if Addison would like to become our boyfriend.

I had a pretty good feeling he would say yes. I mean, we'd been spending all our spare time together, and we loved every minute of it. It didn't matter if we were little or big, every time we hung out, things were so fun and free and easy.

But it was more than just that. We had a genuine connection. It was the beginning of a feeling I had only ever experienced once before in my life...with Steel.

Love.

I was falling in love with Addison.

And so was Steel.

And tonight, if Addison was feeling the same way, we would have a chance to turn those feelings into a relationship for the three of us.

"Will you stay and watch us play, Daddy?" I asked, giving Steel my double combo of cuteness: puppy-dog eyes and droopy lips.

He inhaled sharply in response. "As much as I would love to stay and watch you boys, I'm getting dinner ready, so I won't be able to. I'll call out once it's ready."

If it were just some regular dinner, I would have been a brat about it and started protesting. But it was more than just a meal. It was special. I knew Steel wanted to get everything just right. So I simply said, "Okay, then."

Addison looked over at Steel. "Thanks for bringing us the food and looking after...us."

I could tell by the twinkle in Steel's eyes how happy Addison's words made him. They filled me with joy too. I was starting to get excited, thinking about how awesome we were going to be as a throuple.

Steel had been urging me to slow down and not get too ahead of myself, but as if that was going to happen. My mind was already racing away with thoughts of Addison moving in with us, holidays we could go on, and the one thing—the only thing, really—that I desperately wanted to see and that I hadn't had the chance to yet: Steel and Addison making love.

For some reason, that hadn't happened yet. Addison and me? Oh yeah, and it was spectacular. Steel and me? Holy hell, we were having some of our most amazing sex ever in front of Addison. But the two of them, or the three of us for that matter? Not yet. But hey, the anticipation was almost as good as I knew the release would be.

But I put all of those adult thoughts out of my mind as Steel left the room and Addison and I continued playing as littles.

"All done," Addison said with a satisfied smile as he carefully inspected his now thoroughly clean collection.

"Can we play with them now, Marko?" I asked hopefully.

Addison rested his hand on my knee. "Sure. Same as always?"

I nodded enthusiastically. "Yeppers."

We both smiled as the word I had stolen from him and replaced as my official catchphrase filled the room.

"Alright, well, you can lead today, Nick."

So I did. The first thing to do was to pick out the order the cars and trucks would be lined up in. Once I had done that, I set out the path they would be going on. "We'll take them from where we are, around the table with the food on it, and then into the corner of the nursery by the window," I explained to Addison.

"Sounds like a plan."

And with that, we were off, as my little headspace took over.

For so long, I had thought that being a little was about the clothes, the environment, or the accessories, such as diapers and binkies. For some, those things played a really important part, and that was great.

But for me, I'd had all of those things and yet, I wasn't able to get there. Yet with Addison, I could. With him, regressing into my little space felt...safe. It was like closing my eyes and walking backward slowly with him watching me every step of the way. He would never let me bump into something or fall over, and just his presence gave me all the reassurance that I needed.

"Are you having fun, Marko?" I asked as he finished getting the Tonka truck into place.

"I am." He looked at me and his face lit up in a bright smile. "And what about you?"

"I am too," I said, biting down on my lip.

"Nick?" His voice was gentle, yet laced with concern. "Do you want to switch to big?"

I shook my head.

"No," I said, my eyes locked on the carpeted floor. "I want to say this as a little."

He placed his hand over mine and the warmth radiated through my entire body.

I finally looked up and into his dark brown eyes.

"I like being like this with you. It feels like, like..."

"It's okay, Nick, take your time." His fingers stroked my hand as the hugeness of my emotions washed over me.

"It feels like you're my older brother."

I meant every single one of those words, but hearing them out loud felt like I was having an out-of-body experience.

"Well, it feels like you're my younger brother."

"Really?" I asked, my voice shaky. "But you already have so many brothers."

"None like this." His fingers ran up my forearm lightly. "And no younger brothers. I'm the youngest in my family."

"You are?"

How did I not know that? I guess we still had a lot of stuff we needed to learn about each other.

"Let's keep playing," I said.

"Sure," Addison replied. "Help me move this truck over here, little bro."

And with those words, I drifted back into my littlespace and happily joined Addison in our truck and car moving game.

I didn't know how much time had passed, but when I next looked up at the door, Steel's muscular frame was leaning against it.

"Dinner's ready," he announced, his eyes flicking between Addison and me. "How about you boys finish up, get changed, and we can have dinner in big mode?"

"Sounds good, Daddy," I said as Addison and I started to tidy the toys up and put them away. A few minutes later, we had both changed and joined Steel at the dinner table.

"Mmm, this smells delicious, Steel," Addison commented as he sat down.

"Is this Mikey's mom's recipe?" I asked as I looked down at my plate of spaghetti bolognese.

Steel inclined his head.

"Yeah, Stirling gave me the recipe, with Mikey's and his mom's permission, of course. It's not going to be as good as if she had made it, but I hope it's...okay?"

The slightest flutter of nervousness danced across Steel's face. I didn't know why he was so worried about the conversation we were going to have. I was sure Addison would be all in.

"I'm sure it will be fine," Addison said as he took his first bite.

"Well?" Steel asked, glancing between the two of us.

I took a bite.

"This is very good, Steel," I said with way too much pasta in my mouth. "I'll tell Mikey he can tell his mom that you did a good job."

"Agreed," Addison said, and with that, Steel's shoulders came down from around his face and he settled back in his chair to enjoy the meal with us.

Since we had been hanging out so much over the past two weeks, we had become familiar with some of the finer details of each other's lives. That was how we all knew that Addison was dealing with a rude and impatient client. Or that Steel's firm had taken on a number of big clients in New York which meant he was considering opening an office there. Or that I was still seriously considering the idea of expanding the bakery and turning it into a coffee shop as well.

"I did some number crunching today," I said as the conversation turned to that very topic. "And the profit margins on coffee are huge. But there is an initial outlay for the coffee machine itself. However, some companies subsidize the cost of the machine in return for exclusively using their coffee."

Addison had stopped eating, while Steel's mouth was gaping wide open.

"What?" I said, returning their weird looks with one of my own. "Why are you both looking at me like that?"

Steel managed to speak first. "I've just never heard you talk business like that before, Nick. It's very...hot."

I shrugged casually. "Yeah, well, I can be full of surprises."

"That you are, baby." Steel's hand met mine and it sent a warm flush through my chest.

"I'm just impressed that you said the word *outlay* without bursting into giggles," Addison joked, placing his hand on top of Steel's.

The three of us sat there, connected by touch, and I could have sworn there were little sparks of love floating around us.

Steel's face turned serious, and I knew this was the moment he would ask Addison to join us in becoming a throuple.

He cleared his throat and we all pulled our hands away.

"Addison, there is something Nick and I would like to talk to you about."

Addison's eyes met mine, and I shot him a warm smile. That seemed to relax him a little as he turned back to look at Steel.

"I think it's becoming clear to all of us that there is something special happening between us. Would you agree with that?"

Addison rocked his head. "Yeah, deffers."

I smiled. As it turned out, I wasn't the only one who could steal catchphrases.

"Good," Steel said. "Because Nick and I have been talking a lot."

"What about?" Addison asked.

"You," I replied. "We kind of can't stop thinking about you..."

"Or talking about you..." Steel added.

"Or fantasizing about you when you're not here."

I grinned at Steel as his cheeks filled with a delicate rosy hue.

"What—what are you guys trying to say?" Addison asked, shuffling in his seat.

"We'd like to ask you, Addison, if you would like to become our—"

"Boyfriend," I blurted out, interrupting Steel, but I just couldn't hold it in any longer.

I'd waited long enough. I didn't want to spend another minute without Addison confirming what I already knew and what Mariah had sung about—that we belonged together.

Steel let out a low chuckle. How he was able to stay so calm and put together, while I was feeling like I was about to explode any second now, was beyond me.

I glanced over at Addison, and my heart stopped.

He didn't look happy or excited. Instead, his face had gone white. He wiped the corners of his mouth with a napkin, before saying what I never ever expected to hear him say.

"I'm sorry, you guys, but no."

CHAPTER TWENTY-SIX

ADDISON

My mind was a foggy haze as I let out my fifth yawn in a row. I guess that was what happened when you didn't get a wink of sleep all night. But how could I have slept after what happened?

I leaned against the wall and stretched my legs out in front of me. The morning air was still, but it had a chill to it. I zipped up my black hoodie and folded my arms across my chest.

The looks on their faces were permanently etched into my memory. Every time I closed my eyes, I could see the tears that fell down Nick's cheeks, or the look of total shock in Steel's eyes as he squinted at me, as if somehow he had misheard my answer.

But he hadn't.

I had been firm and clear. I'd meant it when I said no, even though there were parts of me that were screaming for me to say yes. To accept their offer with open arms and allow myself to have more than I ever dreamed possible—a Daddy and a brother—and a relationship with two of the most amazing men in the world.

The sting of my response stabbed at my heart. I looked down the deserted street and then at the time on my cell phone. He'd be here soon, and I would have a chance to explain my decision. He probably wouldn't like it, but I owed him that much.

Part of what had kept me from sleeping was the thought of Nick blaming himself or thinking that I didn't want to be with him. When I did...so, so badly. It had nothing to do with him. It was all on me—and Steel.

One thing I had learned and seen in so many of my friends' relationships over the years was that the good ones all had an equal balance. With two guys, it was important, but with three, it was more crucial than ever.

A lopsided, uneven threesome relationship just wouldn't work. I'd seen it before, where one person was more into one of the two partners. It only led to fighting, jealousy, and ultimately, the entire relationship dying. And as much as I had been hoping that the lopsidedness between Steel, Nick, and me was getting better, the bitter truth was that it wasn't.

Not once had Steel made love to me. I'd been with Nick, and so had he, but Steel and I? Just us? Never. Even as we'd spent so much time together over the past two weeks—our kissing, hugging, any touch at all—still felt weird and out of place.

I had tried overlooking it. Then I had tried to find any small signals that indicated we were moving in the right direction, and then blindly hoped that they would continue. But we'd reached our peak.

The truth was that Steel wasn't into me. I wasn't his type. Even though that killed me, I couldn't be angry at him for it. Attraction was one of those things that couldn't be controlled. It was something that was either there—or it wasn't.

And for him, it just wasn't there when he looked at me.

I yawned again, and then my eyes flew open at another realization. I was back in the spot where I had been attacked. And I wasn't afraid. Holy hell, I hadn't even given it any thought. See, maybe I didn't need to be with anyone else. Maybe Kymmy was right, I was stronger than I gave myself credit for. I couldn't help but feel a sense of pride at that.

I blew out a heavy breath when the sounds of keys jangling drew my attention.

"Addison?" Nick's voice rang out in surprise. "What——what are you doing here?"

I started to get to my feet. "Hey, Nick."

When we stood face to face, I immediately saw the dark, puffy bags under his eyes. It looked like he hadn't gotten much sleep, either.

"Are you okay?" he asked, taking a half step in toward me, but then stopping himself from coming any closer.

"No," I replied. "I'm not."

A look of anguish spread across his face. He pursed his lips tightly, his jaw was clenched. I had never seen him looking like this before.

He lifted his keys, walked over to the front door of the bakery, and opened it. I followed him inside without saying a word. With a flick of the switch, the lights turned on.

He turned around to face me and said, "Why did you say no, Addison? And why did you leave so quickly?"

I winced. That hadn't been my finest hour, taking off like that so quickly. I'd been in such a hurry to get out of there that I had forgotten to take my backpack. I just couldn't deal with the flood of emotions I was facing, and I knew that if I stayed, I'd probably break down in front of them. That was the last thing I wanted.

"That's what I want to talk to you about, Nick. Can we——can we get some coffee?" I asked. "I didn't get much sleep."

"Me neither," Nick said gloomily, his eyes never leaving my face. "At least this time you're prepared for how bad the coffee's going to be."

We walked down the street in silence, toward the worst coffee in America. Once we'd gotten our cups, I suggested we go back to the park we had sat at once before. Nick nodded and we crossed the road, making our way to the exact same bench as the last time.

"So," he said, his eyes pinning me down with a serious look. "Why did you say no?"

I took a sip of the godawful coffee, letting it scald my tongue. I suddenly felt so exposed, like when he looked at me, he could see into my soul. Did he really have no idea?

"It's not you," I began speaking. "I really like you, Nick. A lot."

His eyes danced with confusion. "I like you too, Addison. That's why I don't get why you said—"

I raised my hand in the air, cutting him off. I needed to say it.

"Your feelings and my feelings are pretty clear. We definitely have something...special. Which is why it hurts me to say this, but I have to." Our tired eyes met. "Steel doesn't want me. He's never kissed me or touched me. He's not attracted to me. That's why I said no, Nick. It would never work between the three of us because, well, Steel's just not into me."

I studied Nick's reaction. He was being unusually still...and quiet, which was throwing me off. His forehead creased as he turned to me.

"I don't get it. Steel likes you, Addison. I know he does."

"But you can feel it, right?" I prodded.

Nick nodded. "Yes. There's something there. A hesitation, as if he's holding back for some reason. I just don't know why."

I let out a deep sigh. "I think I do."

"What? What is it?"

"You remember Britney's song *I'm Not A Girl, Not Yet A Woman*?" I asked.

"Uh, of course," Nick shot back instantly. "Such an underrated song and the music video was utterly gorgeous."

"It was set in the Grand Canyon, wasn't it?"

A small smile escaped Nick's lips. "Close. Antelope Canyon."

"Well, there you go," I said, elbowing him playfully and his smile grew.

God how I loved these little moments between us, and we seemed to have so many of them. We really were such a good match.

"Well, see, I'm like that song. Britney was singing about being at an awkward age where she's too old to be seen as a little girl, but not quite mature enough to be a woman. I'm like that, or at least the boy version of that. I'm...an in-betweener."

Nick's thick eyebrows pulled together. "What do you mean?"

"I'm too old to be a boy. No Daddy wants me. And I'm too young to be a Daddy myself, if I wanted to be one—which I don't. So, I'm stuck here in no person's land."

Nick reached out and slid his hand down around my back.

"That's not fair," he insisted gently.

"It may not be fair, but it's true," I replied. "It's just the way the world is. It's almost like as a boy, you have to find your Daddy before a certain age, because once you're past it, you're locked out. For good. No one wants me now, Nick."

"Hey, that's not true." Nick's voice was louder now, more forceful. "I want you, Addison. And..." He cast me a determined look. "Steel does, too. I'm not just saying that, I know he does."

"I like your youthful optimism," I said, letting out a half-smile.

"It's not optimism," Nick shot back. "It's the truth. Leave it to me, Addison. I am going to get to the bottom of this."

I looked at him and could see the steely resolve in his face. The tiniest glimmer of hope flicked up in my belly, which I proceeded to push away. There was no point in thinking that this would change anything.

Nick might have been a force of nature, but not even he could make Steel want me.

CHAPTER TWENTY-SEVEN

STEEL

Nick stormed into my home office.

"Well, hell——" I began as I turned my attention from the computer screen and swiveled around in my chair. This was a pleasant mid-morning surprise I hadn't been expecting.

"Is it true?" Nick's voice rang out sharply.

Sitting up a little taller, I took him in. He didn't park himself in his usual spot at the corner of my desk that I kept clear especially for him. Instead he stood a few feet away, glaring at me.

Head cocked to the side.

Hand on hip.

Chewing gum...loudly.

"Is it true that I invented a time machine, so I'm looking at the same bratty boy who I met almost two years ago?" I started chuckling at what I thought was a pretty sassy remark, when I was cut short by Nick's words.

"It's not funny, Steel. How can you sit there and make jokes about this when you have ruined everything?"

That wiped the smile off my lips and got me on my feet in no time.

"Whoa, whoa, whoa...baby."

"Don't you *baby* me," Nick said, taking a step back as I moved closer toward him. "I want to know if it's true, and I want you to tell me. Right now."

"Is *what* true, Nick? I have no idea what you are talking about."

"Addison."

A heavy pang hit my chest at the mention of his name.

I guess I was still reeling from the way Addison had responded to my question over dinner last night. I was never as certain as Nick had been that he would say yes, only because as a lawyer, I had learned throughout my career not to make any assumptions.

In particular when it came to people.

And definitely when it came to people in love.

Or trying to find their way to love, at least.

Still, the sting of Addison's flat-out rejection and subsequent hasty departure stung more than ever. I looked at Nick and could see his chest heaving with every breath he was taking. I hadn't seen him this worked up since we had first started dating.

"What exactly about Addison are you referring to, Nick?"

His dark eyes narrowed in on me. "Is it true that you're not attracted to Addison because you think he's too old?"

"What?" I shot back, shaking my head in disbelief. "No, of course that's not true. Why on earth would you even say that?"

"Because that's what Addison thinks."

His words felt like a slap in the face.

"Wait, how do you know that's what Addison thinks?"

"Because he told me, Steel."

"When?"

"Just before. He came by the bakery and told me why he said

no last night. And now," Nick said as he moved in closer, "it all makes sense."

I let out a noisy breath and stretched my hand out. Nick looked down and saw it, hesitated for a moment, before lacing his fingers with mine.

"Let's go sit on the couch. We need to talk, Nick."

As I led Nick into the living room, my mind was racing almost as fast as my pulse.

"Can I get you anything to drink?" I asked as we sat down on the white leather couch. I had to assume that some of Nick's attitude was due to being upset about what had happened with Addison and that some of it was probably due to a lack of caffeine.

Nick gave a casual shrug.

"That would be...nice."

I concealed my smile. I could tell Nick's bratty exterior was melting a little, but he was fighting it, like an exhausted puppy that wanted to sleep but was determined to keep playing.

"The usual?" I asked. Nick nodded and I closed my eyes. "Let me see if I can remember it. A trenta vanilla sweet cream cold brew with two pumps of vanilla, three pumps of caramel syrup, two pumps of cinnamon dolce syrup, two pumps of hazelnut, two pumps of toffee nut syrup, two pumps of mocha, two pumps of white mocha, two pumps of pumpkin spice, three pumps of maple pecan syrup, and five shots of espresso."

I opened my eyes to see Nick's mouth gaping open. He quickly snapped it shut when he noticed me looking at him.

"You forgot *no sugar*," Nick said, desperately trying not to look or sound impressed by my amazing memory skills.

It had taken me close to two years to memorize that goddamn order, and I had finally nailed it. Well, minus the *no sugar* part.

I called the order in to the cafeteria downstairs, and ten minutes later it was delivered to our door. My boy was sipping on his caffeine monstrosity, while my heart was thundering in my chest.

"So," I finally said. "I guess we need to talk about Addison."

Nick was drinking his coffee but kept his big brown eyes plastered to me.

"Go on," he said quietly.

I looked around the room. There was no escaping it. And heck, that wasn't even what I wanted to do. I didn't want to run away from my feelings. That was the shit I had done when I was in my twenties. I had grown as a person and as a man since then. And now I needed to draw on that strength to do the one thing I owed Nick and myself: speak truthfully.

"I'm torn, Nick." I decided to jump right in at the deep end. "I love you. So much. More than anything in the world. More than—more than I ever thought it was even possible for one man to love another."

Nick put his drink down on the coffee table, his gaze leaving mine for a few moments. When he turned to look at me again, his face had lost its hard edge. His eyes were back to being the soft, friendly, gorgeous things I could happily stare into for the rest of my life.

"I love you too, Steel." His words were soft and genuine.

"And then there's Addison," I went on. "I have feelings for him, you have feelings for him—"

"He has feelings for us," Nick reminded me.

I settled farther back into the couch. "Right."

"So, why are you torn, Steel?" Nick probed, his voice thick with yearning and a desire to understand me and where I was coming from.

I blew out a breath.

"Because as much as I want it, Nick, as much as I want the three of us to be together, I'm—I'm...afraid."

"Oh, Steel."

Nick shuffled over until our legs were pressed together. He reached for my arm and began stroking his fingers up and down it.

I took in Nick's gentle touch like a sponge absorbing water.

"For so long, I've been feeling that I haven't been good enough for one boy, so how can I be good enough for two? Addison deserves better. You both do."

I dropped my gaze to the ground, feeling the relief of unburdening myself, but also feeling lost in the cavalcade of emotion it unleashed within me. Now that it was out, now that I had said it, maybe it would prove to be true? Maybe Nick would use this as his chance to get out, leave me, and find a Daddy who could give him everything he wanted? Because I knew one thing for certain—my beautiful boy deserved every single good thing this world had to offer.

I felt Nick's fingers hook under my chin, lifting my head slowly.

"Steel, I'm sorry."

Wait, what?

I snapped my head so fast in his direction that I could have sworn I heard my collarbone crack.

"Sorry? Why—why are *you* saying that?" I asked, confused. Maybe I had misheard. Surely, that had to be it. What on earth could Nick be apologizing for?

"I'm sorry if I made you feel that you weren't good enough for me." His eyes began to well with tears. "Because, Steel, you are the best Daddy, the best man, I have ever met in my whole life. And there isn't a day that goes by when we're lying in bed together with your arms wrapped around me, where I don't think to myself that I am the luckiest boy in the world."

"Oh, baby." I cupped his face in my hands. "*I'm* the luckiest."

"No." Tears streamed down his cheeks. "I am, Steel. And I'm sorry that I've only been thinking that and not saying it to you. I will never do that again. From now on, I'm going to tell you every single day."

Our lips found each other, and if I had ever wondered if a simple kiss could change my life, I had just found my answer.

That kiss was my forgiveness and release.

I forgave myself for everything I had been thinking and for the fears and doubts that I had harbored and that had held me back with Addison. I released myself, opening up to the possibility of what lay before us.

Two magnificent, one-of-a-kind, brilliant, beautiful, and sometimes bratty boys.

With me as their Daddy.

My heart ached with desire for the two of them. Every fiber of my being was telling me this was the thing, the icing on the cake, that would take what was already a precious and sacred thing and elevate it into a realm of an even more majestic and almost unimaginable love.

Desire.

Passion.

Fun and silliness.

Crazy outfits and pop diva puzzles.

Photography and caffeine.

Spontaneous singing and nights spent snuggling on the couch.

I wanted it all.

I wanted my boys with me, where we all belonged. Together.

I was determined to get this, to make it happen. I had to step up and tap into that inner strength I knew I had coursing through my veins. My boys needed me to do it, and so did I.

"We have to get Addison back," Nick said as if he were reading my thoughts.

I brought him in for a hug, holding his warm body close to mine.

"Oh we will, baby, we will." I stroked the back of Nick's head. "And we're not going to wait to do it. I am going to call Addison right now and invite him over for dinner tonight."

Nick pulled away, his eyes filled with hope. "You will?"

I nodded. "Yes. We're going to have a talk. A proper one. Lay it all out on the line. And after we do, I am going to ask him the same question I asked him last night. And this time, baby, I have a feeling his answer will be different."

"Please, Daddy, please make it happen."

Nick crashed into me again. I held him tight as I clenched my jaw. I didn't care what it took, what hurdles I had to climb. Come hell or high water, I was going to make this happen.

CHAPTER TWENTY-EIGHT

NICK

There's another reason why so many sequels don't work. People just can't believe how truly good a happily ever after could really be. It seems unrealistic to think that Prince Charming doesn't have any faults, or it's too depressing to think that the perfect couple have to deal with real-life, dreary, mundane problems.

Or that they'd actually ever have to step up and talk about real shit so that their picture-perfect relationship would stay like that and last forever.

But I was living proof that my Daddy Charming was everything I could have possibly ever hoped and dreamed for, to the power of a thousand. Even if it seemed unrealistic or improbable to anyone else, time after time, Steel showed me that he loved me so much and would do anything for me.

I didn't know what I had been expecting to achieve by barging into Steel's office and giving off major attitude vibes, but I was so upset by what Addison had said, that I didn't know how else to react. The thought of Steel not liking Addison because of his age seemed so unlike the man I knew and loved. But for Addison, it was real. And that hurt me on a level I wasn't expecting.

And then Steel came through in a way I wasn't expecting either. He didn't run or hide from what we were facing. He didn't get defensive or angry about it. And he didn't try shifting the blame to anyone else.

No, he did the most amazing thing any Daddy could do.

He owned it.

And when I sank into his arms and he told me we would have a do-over with Addison—and this time, it would end well—I believed him. With everything I had in me, I knew my Daddy would come through—for all of us.

That didn't stop the rest of the day dragging on forever, though. After Steel had called Addison and arranged for him to come over for what we unofficially dubbed *Dinner Take 2*, I went back to the bakery and Steel returned to his work.

Not that I could think about anything pastry or spreadsheet-related. Instead, I did what any business owner who was on the cusp of having his amazing Daddy invite an incredible guy to become a throuple later that evening would do—I spent all day texting my best friend.

11:20am

Me: *It's happening, it's happening, it's happening!*

Mikey: *What is? Is Britney finally free?*

Me: *Ha, ha. Very funny. No. Tonight we're asking Addison to become our boyfriend.*

Mikey: *Oh wow, that's so awesome! I'll keep my fingers, toes (and everything else) crossed for you.*

11:53am

Me: *Should I wear those cute black shorts we picked up a few* *weekends ago that make my ass look great, or my favorite faded blue jeans that make my ass look great?*

Mikey: *Why cover your ass at all?*

Me: *Hmm, that's a good point.*

Mikey: *OMG, I was kidding! Go with the shorts. You have great calves.*

Me: *Mikey, I knew there was a reason we were best friends. I love how observant you are. Shorts it is!*

1:02pm

Me: *OK, OK, OK, having a slight panic attack here. What if Addison says no...again?*

Mikey: *Again???*

Me: *Yeah, we asked him last night and he said no. But I've spoken to him, and I've spoken to Steel, and I know what the issue is, so we're going to resolve it tonight.*

Mikey: *Well then, if you resolve whatever the issue is, why would he say no?*

Me: *You're the best, Mikey!*

Mikey: *I knew there was a reason we were best friends. I love how observant you are!*

1:34pm

Me: *So, what are you doing?*

Mikey: *Nick! How bored are you right now? Geez...*

Me: *I haven't been this bored since you made me watch 50 Shades of Grey.*

Mikey: *Hey, the books were half ok, but yeah, the movie was pretty bad.*

Mikey: *Why don't you just go home and let Remy close the bakery?*

Me: *Then I'd be bored at home and drive Steel crazy.*

Mikey: *I'm sure he's used to that, LOL*

Me: *Don't you LOL me, Mikey boy.*

Mikey: *I have to go... Talk later.*

2:15pm
Me: *Hello?*

2:32pm
Me: *Mikey, you there?*

2:56pm
Me: *Alright, I am going to go home. I'll talk to you tomorrow.*
Mikey: *Sorry, Stirling forgot something and came home and we had to do something.*
Me: *Lemme guess...you christened your kitchen countertop again?*
Mikey: *Hehe. Yep.*
Mikey: *Twice.*
Mikey: *Good luck tonight! I am sure it will go great.*
Me: *Thanks, I hope so.*
Mikey: *Call me tomorrow?*
Me: *Deffers xo*

Somehow, I managed to not get under Steel's skin as I spent the rest of the afternoon getting ready. First, I took a bubble bath. Then I did a twenty-four carat gold collagen face mask. That was followed by some quiet reading time. I tended to stick to the classics—*Vogue*, *People*, and *GQ*.

Lastly, I ordered another cheeky coffee, so by the time I got dressed—yep, I went with shorts because hiding these calves would have been a crime against humanity—and heard a knock on the door, I was practically jumping out of my skin, buzzing with excitement...and caffeine. So much caffeine.

Steel's steady hands landed on my shoulders as we reached the front door. His light blue eyes shone with the determination of a man who was going after what he wanted.

"Relax, baby. Just breathe. We've got this." He pressed his lips to my forehead. "*I've* got this. You ready?"

I nodded, and Steel opened the door. Addison stood there, looking as deliciously divine as ever. His all-black outfit clung to his body, but his face held an apprehensive expression.

"Hey," I said.

Steel opened the door wider, allowing Addison to step in.

"Hey," Addison replied, looking at both of us.

Steel closed the door.

A silence fell over us before Steel stepped over to Addison and wrapped his arms around his slim waist. He lowered his gaze, meeting Addison's straight on.

"Addison, I'd like to do something that I've wanted to do for a very long time."

Steel's eyes flicked over to me, and I stood there, with my breath caught in my throat, without a clue what he was doing or what would happen next.

Addison looked just as taken aback as I was, but he replied, "And what would that be?"

"Kiss you." Steel's words were as firm as the hardness forming in my pants. "I want to kiss you... Properly."

Addison turned to me, and I nodded without even realizing I was doing it. Fuck, I'd been wanting to see these two kiss for so long.

"Can I?" Steel, being the perfect gentleman, asked Addison.

"Yes," he replied breathlessly.

I knew that seeing Steel kiss Addison would be hot. I was expecting Steel to take his time, begin slowly and then step things up a notch. I didn't for a second think Steel would do what he actually did.

He pulled Addison in nice and close to him, and then in one swoop, leaned in while he rocked Addison back, making it look like a dance move. A tango, or a samba, or something hot and exotic. A moan escaped Addison's mouth, and it was the sexiest sound I had ever heard. Keeping him leaned over, Steel went in for the kiss. It was big.

Dramatic.

Hungry.

Passionate.

And it got me so achingly hard I couldn't believe it. I had front row seats to the hottest show in town.

After what felt like nowhere near long enough, Steel slowly straightened up, gently bringing Addison with him. Both of their lips were swollen, a delectable pink hue breaking out on the delicate skin around their mouths.

I was like a moth to a flame.

"Room for one more?" I asked, stepping in closer to them.

Steel grinned, a wicked look dancing across his beautiful face. "Oh, for sure, baby."

"Deffers," Addison threw in for good measure.

I pressed my face toward theirs and had my first ever threesome kiss. Who knew that adding another person's lips, tongue and mouth into the equation could feel so fucking amazing. There were togues flicking and darting about all over the place, heads moving around, inching ever closer, and breaths mingling in the most wonderful ways.

"Holy hell that was hot," I said as the three of us slowly moved away from each other, like melted cheese being pulled off a pizza.

"Boys," Steel said.

His eyes were alight with sparks of lust and desire, but his voice was firm. He extended his arms and Addison and I placed our hands into his.

"If you would like to follow me, our dinner awaits."

Steel led Addison and me to the outdoor courtyard that overlooked the entire city skyline. The refreshing night air hit my face, but even that wasn't enough to wake me up from this beautiful dream I was living.

"This is incredible," Addison said as he took in the breathtaking view of the city before us. Then his eyes widened as he took in the scene right in front of us.

I had been wondering why Steel had been spending so much time out here during the day. Now I could see what he'd been doing.

A red picnic blanket.

Candles laid out on the ground, fairy lights hanging above.

Two bottles of wine.

And a picnic basket.

"I thought it might be nice to have dinner out in the fresh air," Steel said as he let go of our hands. "Are you boys happy here?"

"Uh, yeah," Addison replied.

"Yeppers," I said as I floated over to the moonlit blanket and sat down, stretching out my legs so that they could both enjoy my spectacular calves.

"I'm starving," I announced.

Hey, the only thing that would make this already incredibly romantic evening any better was sex... and food. Not necessarily in that order.

"Me too."

It made me stupid happy hearing Addison agreeing with me.

"Well, good," Steel said, opening up the basket. "I have come prepared."

My mouth fell open as Steel pulled out two...

"Hot dogs," Addison cried excitedly, clapping his hands with glee.

"Not just any hot dogs. New York City hot dogs," Steel said with a wide smile as he handed them over to us.

The smell of the sauerkraut, onion sauce, and spicy brown mustard hit my nostrils, causing my stomach to growl comically loudly.

"Dig in, boys, there's plenty more where this came from."

He didn't have to tell me twice.

"When did you make these?" I managed to ask in between scarfing down massive mouthfuls.

"Oh, I didn't make them myself," Steel said, looking a little sheepish. Addison and I looked at each other, before Steel continued. "I, er, had them flown in from New York."

"Oh my god," Addison said, genuinely touched by Steel's incredible, over-the-top gesture. I had to admit, it got me too.

"Thank you, Steel," I said as I put the bun down and leaned in to give him a kiss. "You really are the best."

As hungry as I still was, and as delicious as the hot dog was proving to be, I knew this was the moment we had been waiting for. Steel knew it too, judging by the serious look that crossed his face, and clearly Addison knew it, as he put down his hot dog and looked at both of us expectantly.

Steel cleared his throat. "Addison, we need to talk."

"I figured." Addison looked over at me and shot me a warm smile. "I take it Nick told you about our little chat earlier today?"

"He did," Steel said with a resoluteness in his voice I normally only ever heard when he was on business calls. "And I want you to know one thing, Addison. I think you are beautiful. I am incredibly attracted to you. And it has taken every ounce of self-control I have in me not to..." Steel's eyes sparkled in my direction. "Help me out here, Nick."

"Jump your bones and fuck you like the energizer bunny?" I offered.

Their happy laughter settled the nerves in my belly.

Steel turned back to face Addison again. "Yeah, what he said."

Addison swallowed and I could see the tension brewing in his body.

"Really, Steel? Do you *really* mean that? You're not just saying that because Nick told you how badly I was feeling and you're just trying to, I don't know, be a nice guy and make me feel better?"

"I mean it." The force in Steel's voice was like a magnet,

drawing Addison's eyes to meet Steel's heated gaze. "What you were picking up on, Addison, was something else."

"What was it?" Addison asked abruptly. "Sorry, I didn't mean to be so blunt, but I do need to know."

Steel rocked his head. "That's fair enough. You're entitled to know, Addison."

Steel looked over at me and I prayed he was picking up on my silent encouragement. He was doing so, *so* well, my heart was bursting with pride for my Daddy.

"I had some insecurities," Steel started to explain to Addison. "They were all on me. It had nothing to do with either one of you boys. And look, I am happy to talk about it and unpack it in detail with you both. In fact, in the spirit of our agreement to talk about everything, I think that we definitely should do that. But just not right now."

Addison cocked his head. "Oh?"

"Right now..." Steel licked his lips as the flame of desire returned to his face. "Nick and I would like to know just one thing, Addison."

"Uh huh." Addison looked so cute with the whole deer-in-headlights thing he had going on.

"I know this is new. I know we still have a lot to talk about and a lot more getting to know each other to do...but Addison Mark, would you be our boyfriend? Please."

Silence fell between us. And everything else faded away. The lights of the buildings. The noise of the city bustling beneath us. It all evaporated into nothingness. There were only three people in the world. And there was only one word in the entire universe I was hoping against all hope to hear from Addison.

I couldn't take it anymore. I closed my eyes and grimaced, bracing myself for whatever answer he would give.

Thankfully, I didn't have to wait too much longer.

"Yes."

The word rang out like church bells ringing in some country that still had church bells. Possibly Bulgaria.

My eyes shot open. "Really? You really mean it, Addy?"

"You've never called me Addy before," he said, smiling.

"You've never made me the happiest boy in the world before...Addy."

"'I do, I do mean it." Tears fell down his face.

I looked over at Steel and his eyes were misty too.

"Oh my god, stop it, you guys" I said. "You're going to make me cry."

"Looks like it's a little too late for that, baby."

Steel's thumb collected a warm tear from my face. Holy shit. I had started crying without even realizing it.

"This is going to be the best thing ever," I said, wiping at my eyes.

"Deffers," Addison added.

"Yeppers," I shot back with a giggle.

"Oh dear," Steel groaned playfully. "Looks like I'm the only one without a catchphrase."

We all laughed, staring at each other as we did, the candles and fairy lights igniting our faces with a radiant glow.

This was a moment I knew I would remember for the rest of my life.

It was the beginning of a whole new happily ever after.

"Now, back to the hot dogs," I said, eyeing my half-eaten bun, before casually adding, "Food first, and then an almighty all-night sex marathon, yeah?"

CHAPTER TWENTY-NINE

STEEL

How silly of me to think that my two boys would accept my offer of moving inside to get a little more...*comfortable*.

"Nope, not moving." Nick folded his arms across his chest, signalling his defiance.

"You mean, you want me, us, to do it...out here?" I looked around the courtyard.

It was private—hell, it was the penthouse so it wasn't like we had any neighbors around. I looked out at the tops of the skyscrapers that lined the night sky. I seriously doubted there was anyone in them that had binoculars pointed straight at us.

And hey, even if they did...*fuck it*.

"I want to see you two together," Nick said as he pulled out another hot dog from the picnic basket.

"Wait." Addison spoke before I could. "I thought food, then sex. Looks like you're not done yet."

A rascally smile spread over Nick's face. "Why can't I have

both? I'll eat...and watch. Then, when I'm done, I'll join in. Now, go!" He motioned with his free hand for Addison and I to...well, *go*.

So, we did.

Addison turned to face me, his face lit up by moonlight. The look of longing he shot me was unmissable. He wanted this as much as I did, if that was possible. I'd been holding myself back for so long, watching from the sidelines, teetering on the cliff of my desires...always so close, but never going over. Never taking that one extra step.

Until now.

Even though technically Addison was the one crawling along the blanket to where I was sitting, his all-black form making him look like a sleek panther that was about to pounce. When he reached me, I cupped his jaw in my hands. His dark eyes danced a tantalizing dance.

My breath got stuck in my throat momentarily as the hugeness of what was about to happen hit me like a thunderbolt. I was going to have sex with someone other than my boy. I looked over at Nick who looked like he had died and gone to heaven...if heaven included eating New York hot dogs while about to watch your two boyfriends have sex for the first time.

As I observed his strong features, I had no idea what was going through Addison's mind. As it turned out, I didn't have a lot of thinking time left. Addison swooped in, licking along my lower lip while his hand landed on my chest. He nibbled down to my chin, then my neck, swirling his tongue around my Adam's apple, gently biting it. My breathing got heavier in response to the pressure and it felt...insanely good.

Both of his hands were now on my chest, kneading my muscles and pecs like they were Play-Doh. And then his hands reached down...down...until they landed on my cock. He wasn't soft or gentle. No, he grabbed it with full force, causing me to buck.

His eyes flashed me a look of desire, and that was all I needed. I made a grunting noise as I lifted his chin and kissed him with all the passion I had been holding back. I wanted this kiss to make it clear to him, beyond any reasonable doubt, that I wanted him.

"Clothes off," Nick directed from the sidelines, his mouth busily chewing away while his eyes remained glued to Addison and me.

"You're quite the bossy one," Addison said as he giggled in Nick's direction.

Nick shrugged casually. "What can I say? I'm not just a star, I'm also a natural-born director."

I felt a warmth rush through me as my lips stretched into a smile at his words.

Nick pushed the remaining dog into his mouth and began licking his fingers clean.

"Besides," he said with way too much food in his mouth. "The heart wants what the heart wants. And my heart wants to see some hot fucking action."

Addison looked at me and licked his lips. "You heard Nick. Let's give him some hot fucking action."

The words oozed out of him so seductively, I had no choice but to comply. I made light work of our clothes, getting us stripped naked in record time. Addison was straddling me, the moonlight reflecting off the tanned skin on his chest. I ran my fingers softly through his hair. It wasn't a crazy hot gesture, I knew that, but it was something I had been wanting to do for so long. And now, I was. Addison placed his hand over my fingers, before lifting them up and into his mouth.

Desire poured out of him as he swallowed my fingers whole, keeping his eyes on me the whole time.

"You know," I said as my cock twitched in anticipation. "I have something a lot bigger you can suck on."

Without another word, Addison pulled my fingers out of his mouth, and scooted down my body, taking my aching cock in his mouth in one fell swoop. My body bucked against his face, the intensity of the pleasure shooting through my entire body.

"You know what else he really likes..." I heard Nick's voice getting louder as he approached us. "...is this."

I felt Addison's mouth leave my cock. Nick's hand gripped behind my knees and pushed them up toward the night sky. The next thing I knew, a tongue landed on my hole, lapping at it softly.

And then...

Oh, sweet Jesus...

I felt...

...another tongue.

My hole quivered like it never had as my two boys, my two beautiful boys, tongued me with all of their might.

"Fuck," I cried out, losing myself in the noisy, filthy lapping sounds ringing in my ears as the wetness of their probing tongues ignited my entire body.

I felt my hands shaking as I reached down, trying to find their heads. My fingers landed in their hair as I pushed them together, closer to each other and their tongues deeper into me.

I had never felt anything like it before.

CHAPTER THIRTY

NICK

Steel's hand gently pulling on my hair drew me in even closer to Addison, as our tongues lapped at Steel's beautiful pink hole. I always thought there was nothing better than eating Steel's hot ass, but now I could see that there was—eating Steel's hot ass with Addison right next to me, doing the same.

My tongue flicked between Steel's burning flesh and Addison's silky tongue. It felt like my whole world was right here in front of me. A hole and a tongue and the amazing connection it produced between the three of us.

I took one last, long deep slurp before I looked up and said to Steel, "Alright, now I want to see the two of you fuck."

Addison's eyes lit up as Steel nodded. I released his knees and a position change ensued. Addison lying on his back, legs in the air, with me right beside him. Kissing him. Fuck, how I loved kissing him. His lips felt like they were meant for me.

Steel, being Steel, had come prepared. He grabbed condoms

and lube out of the picnic basket. He struggled a bit with the wrapper—I guess he was out of practice—but finally managed to get a condom on. He spread some lube across his fingers to warm Addison up. I could see the exact moment he entered Addison, because his pupils dilated, expanding to take over his eyes.

The three of us were connected again. My tongue in Addison, Steel's fingers inside him. I couldn't tell what Steel was doing, how many fingers he was up to—after all, the man was a gentleman and knew how to prep his bottom—because all I could see, feel, taste was Addison's delicious tongue swirling in my mouth.

That tongue was more than good enough on its own, but now it had something even better: the scent and taste of Steel's ass. I guess mine did too, and it felt like the more Addison and I kissed, the more we exchanged that part of Steel between us. I grabbed my cock and started jerking it, not too hard or fast, but just enough to ride the tide of arousal within me.

"Are you ready, Addy?" Steel asked as a look of recognition swept across Addison's eyes.

It was the first time Steel had called him Addy. And fuck, it sounded ah-mazing.

"I am," Addison managed to get out.

Hey, my tongue wasn't about to take a back seat here. I was enjoying exploring Addison's mouth way too much. Besides, I wanted to be in his mouth as Steel fucked him for the first time. It made it feel like this really was an experience all three of us were having...together.

I saw Addison's chest heave as Steel entered him. I pulled back, remembering the first time Steel's massive cock had entered me. I watched Addison's face contort, with pain at first, until it softened, slowly...slowly...until the torrent of pleasure overtook him.

I kissed into his mouth, fisting my cock, knowing that Steel and I were inside of Addison at the same time.

CHAPTER THIRTY-ONE

ADDISON

I was no slouch as a bottom, but holy fucking hell, Steel's cock was a monster. But of course, being the man that he was, he had prepared me with one, then two, and finally three fingers before entering me with the slow steadiness that he knew I needed.

The burning feeling rushed through me, prickling my skin with a familiar tension. It was a matter of breathing, going with it and trusting that in time, the pain would give way to the most beautiful sensation. It was like waiting for the sun to break through the horizon for the first time. The thought of my favorite time of day relaxed my body and there it was—the breakthrough moment arrived as the tightness dissolved. I lay there with Steel filling me up and sweet, sweet Nick kissing me.

I was on my back but it felt like I was floating through air. Steel's voice stirred me out of my blissful state momentarily.

"Are you alright, Addy?"

"Yeah," I breathed as I started to feel my entire body loosening, opening up.

I'd never felt so beautiful, so desired. Two men feasting on me. Steel calling me Addy, being so gentle with me. Nick being so bossy and forceful with my mouth, as if he controlled it. Who was I kidding? I'd let him control any part of me whenever he wanted. They both could.

They were my boyfriends.

We were joined.

One.

Whole.

Steel picked up the pace, thrusting harder into me. My hole had gotten accustomed to his size and I could take him with a lot more ease now. Nick's lips never left mine and I rocked between the two men. My two boyfriends. I didn't think I would ever get tired of thinking that.

I felt a hand on my cock. I couldn't tell whose it was. I didn't care. It started jacking me off. It was hard and rough, just how I needed it.

My eyes were closed and I was guided only by the rocking of Steel's body against mine, and the swaying of Nick's mouth against me. A breeze tickled my skin as I felt myself coming, spilling out hot ropes of cum onto the cool skin of my stomach. Soon, I felt another release landing across my chest.

I opened my eyes. It was Nick, jerking himself onto me. His face was all contorted, his body writhing as he rode his release. His breathing filled my ears as our lips met again. We were both spent...but we weren't done yet.

"Pull out of me, please," I said to Steel, who immediately did as I asked.

I motioned with Nick to follow my lead as I turned around and peeled the condom off Steel's swollen cock. God, it looked even bigger close up. Nick's head popped up right next to me. I stuck my tongue out as I jerked Steel's dick. Nick's eyes lit up and he did the same, sticking his tongue out too.

We both looked up and for a second, I couldn't tell whether Steel was about to have a heart attack, or if he was just overly excited as it dawned on him that he would be shooting a load over his two boys.

"Give it to us, Daddy."

Nick's voice was all the encouragement Steel needed as the first blast of cum shot out of his cock landing across both of our open, willing mouths. As rope after rope of sticky white cum poured from Steel's cock, Nick and I lapped it all up, our heads gently bumping against each other as we tried not to miss a single, salty drop.

I let the thick liquid collect in the back of my mouth, and once Steel's cock had been completely drained, I leaned over and kissed Nick, the cum overflowing out of my mouth and into his.

Nick had done the same, collecting Steel's precious release in his mouth, and as I kissed into him, his tongue began pushing the cum he had collected back into my mouth.

"Any chance you boys would share that with me?" Steel's face met ours as his smile turned into an open-mouthed invitation.

I lifted my brows for Nick to go first, and he did, leaning over Steel's open mouth and spitting out his own warm cum into it. Then it was my turn to do the same.

Once we had done it, Steel grabbed the backs of our heads and pushed us all in together, lips smashing and cum overflowing out of all our mouths as we hungrily slurped it all up, cum kissing until there was nothing left but saliva, sweat, and the salty remnants of Steel's release.

"Holy shit," I said, wiping the back of my hand against my mouth. "That was the hottest thing ever."

Nick grinned as he took my fingers in his hand. "It was. And just think, Addy.."

I looked down and saw Steel's fingers interlaced with ours.

"...that was only the beginning."

CHAPTER THIRTY-TWO

NICK

I let out a nervous breath as I peered through the curtains of the makeshift stage and out into the packed crowd at Deffers. The audience was buzzing with anticipation. *Daylesford's Most Eligible Daddy* contest was about to start and I could tell everyone was here for it. A '90s jam about pumping up the jam or something was playing, mixing with sounds of laughter and happy chatting. The place was lit.

Unlike me.

"Hey." Liam's hand landed softly on my shoulder. "Are you alright, Nick?"

I turned around to see Liam, Mikey, and Declan gathered around me. If the audience was pumped, the scene behind the curtain was one of frenetic mania. Daddies were rushing around, frantically putting on their outfits, checking their hair, and making sure they were looking their best. It was funny watching men who would otherwise pride themselves on being calm and steadfast being so...well, giddy.

Like me.

Except I had a good reason to be feeling as if I were just about to do the craziest thing in my entire life. Because I was.

All four of us were.

I looked at my friends, their faces a heady combination of excitement and the same spiked level of cortisol that was flowing through my veins. I hadn't been this anxious waiting for something since the four days after the 2020 presidential election.

"I'm okay-ish," I said, replying to Liam's question.

"It's going to be great."

I grinned at Mikey's optimism.

"Besides, Nick. We have both literally been naked, except for a pair of briefs, on our hands and knees at a party full of men. This should be a walk in the park for you."

My mind instantly flashed back to the last time—actually the last two times—I had been for a walk in a park. It had been with him. Addison. I released another anxious exhalation, reminding myself of why I was doing this. Why we were all doing this.

"How are you boys feeling about this?" I asked, my eyes glancing around our huddled mini-mirage in a sea of chaos and occasional cries of, "Has anyone seen my black leather jockstrap?"

"I feel good," Liam said with a firm nod. "There's nothing like living in a van to really make you see whether you are compatible with someone or not."

We let out a round of giggles, easing the tension a bit.

"Besides," Liam continued. "If I have to hear Hudson tell me one more time how this is the first year that neither he nor his friends are eligible to compete in this contest, I swear to God..."

"You'd drive that van off the highway?" I suggested cheekily.

Liam let out a loud laugh. "Yes, exactly."

Declan nodded his head firmly. "Porter has been exactly the

same. It's like it's a big deal for our Daddies that they're not able to be part of the contest anymore."

"I think it's more of a realization," Mikey added somewhat philosophically. "One chapter of their lives is over, and as much as I know they're all happier than ever with us, there's always a little bit of sadness whenever you leave something behind."

"Well said," Liam agreed. "And just think, now, a whole new chapter is about to begin. For them—and for us."

I gulped as I turned my attention to Declan. "What about you? How are you feeling?"

Declan bit down on his lower lip. "Good. Scared. Exuberant. Scared. Excited. Scared. Happy. Lightheaded. Oh, and scared."

"Kinda like me, then," I conceded.

Declan placed his hand in mine. "I think that of the four of us, you and I have the...most unique situations. For entirely different reasons, but I feel like I do know what you're going through. Just know that I am here with you, okay?"

I managed to give a quick nod. It was a relief knowing that he was going through something similar like I was.

"Thanks, Declan. That really helps."

"Remember, though," he went on, "that just because you and I aren't in a conventional situation doesn't mean we can't make this work for us too."

I guessed that was a more diplomatic version of Addison's *fuck rules* mantra.

"You're absolutely right, Declan. We deserve this just as much as anyone else. Even if we have to be a little more...creative in our thinking."

"Exactly."

He shot me a warm smile that reached all the way into my stomach and helped unclench the knot that had formed there and stubbornly refused to leave all day. It had even affected my eating. I'd barely touched food all day, instead making up for it with my usual order of a coffee...or three.

Finally, I turned to my best friend in the whole world. "And what about you, Mikey boy? I bet you're feeling like you've got this in the bag."

His blue eyes shimmered joyfully. "I do feel happy, but I'm not cocky or overconfident."

"I know," I said as I felt waves of pride washing over me as I looked at him.

I'd known him since junior high and my god, how he had changed in the last few years alone. Gone was the scared, timid boy who would run away from bullies and hide from his feelings.

The boy that stood before me realized what he was worth, knew how fab-u-lous he was, and went after what he wanted. Part of me wanted to take at least a little credit for it, but the truth was, it was all him. Mikey Harrison had come into his own and was living his best life, and I couldn't have been happier for him.

"You're confident, Mikey," I said. "And you have every right to be. You and Stirling are the OGs of the group."

"Which reminds me," Declan chipped in. "We haven't discussed the sequence we're doing this in."

"Right. Logistics." This was good. My mind needed something concrete to focus on. "We'll actually do the thing all at the same time, just like we practiced."

"You'll count us in?" Declan asked and I gave a firm nod.

"Yes. So, that just leaves the order we will walk out in." I tapped my fingers against my chin. "I'm thinking, let's go Declan, Liam, Mikey and then me."

"*And then me* what?"

I felt the familiar touch of Steel's fingers interlacing around my waist.

"Me everything," I said, turning around and planting a passionate—and hopefully incredibly distracting—kiss on his beautiful lips.

Shit, I didn't want to ruin the surprise now. We'd made it

through months of secretive planning with no one (and by that, I meant Mikey) caving and telling their Daddy.

When I pulled away, Steel's eyes did that cute dreamy thing they always did when I took him to his happy place. And best of all, he had forgotten what he had asked me about.

"Now, what are you doing here, Mr. Crawford?" I said with an exaggerated finger wag. "I told you I'd come and get you when it was time."

"Time for what exactly, Nick?"

The dreaminess was gone as his eyes narrowed in on me, his smile replaced by a familiar look of suspicion. The man was smart—hey, he was a lawyer after all—so he knew I was up to some shenanigans. He just had no clue as to what they were.

Which was just the way I intended to keep it.

"So, this is where everyone is."

We all turned around at hearing Porter's voice, and saw him, flanked by Stirling and Hudson, approaching us.

"Didn't we tell our Daddies to wait for us until we were ready to receive them?" I asked, putting on what I thought sounded like a faux-British, royal-sounding accent. And a pretty darn good one at that.

Mikey shot me an unimpressed look. "Looks like we have ourselves a case of naughty Daddies who don't listen to their boys, and a best friend who does terrible, terrible accents and refuses to stop doing them."

"The worst," Declan said.

"Totally," Liam piled on.

I raised my hand into the air to get everyone's attention. I paused for dramatic effect, because, yes, I enjoyed being the center of attention for a moment. Sue me.

"Guys. Focus. Please. The contest is about to start anyway, so it's fine that our naughty Daddies are here."

Then my heart stopped. But wait, everyone wasn't here. I

turned to Steel. The knot in my stomach had returned, tighter than ever.

"Where's Addison?"

"It's okay." Steel rubbed my upper arm. "He's running a little late. He said he'd text me when he got here."

And right on cue, Steel's phone vibrated.

"Two minutes until go-time," someone yelled over all the backstage noise, which sent everyone around us into an even more heightened state of overdrive.

"I need my assless chaps," one Daddy yelled out.

"Has anyone seen my cockring?" another cried.

I turned my attention back to Steel who was reading the text message he had received.

"Is it him?" I practically squealed, about to jump out of my skin with nervous anticipation.

"It is." Steel's voice was steady and soothing. "I'll go get him and bring him back here."

"Okay, but hurry. Please."

"I'm hurrying, I'm hurrying," Steel said over his shoulder as he scurried away.

"You've got this, Nick."

I felt Mikey's reassuring grip around my wrist.

"Thanks." I smiled tightly. "We both do."

"Who would have thought we'd ever be doing something like this, right?"

"Tell me about it." But my words were flat. No matter how hard I tried, I just couldn't seem to find a way to access my inner confidence. Something was blocking me.

In some ways, my nerves and inability to settle down made total sense.

Steel was a lock.

I knew him well enough to know what his response would be. And like Mikey, I didn't mean that in a cocky or arrogant way. It was just that we'd been together for so long that I had a deep, soul-level feeling about it.

But Addison?

He was another story entirely. He was unpredictable and could go either way. And it was still all so new with him. We'd only technically been a throuple for a week, but I just knew that it felt right. Like it was destined, meant to be. It was kinda like watching Ryan Gosling on *The Mickey Mouse Club* and just knowing that the guy was going to grow up and be a megastar.

But still, the anxiety within me lingered and it wouldn't let go.

"Hello." Addison's voice came from behind me.

I swung around and immediately threw my arms around his shoulders. Our lips locked for a brief, but fiery, kiss.

Oh, that's right. We were in public.

I quickly introduced Addison to the group, but we really didn't have time. The MC for the evening was already on stage, and by the sounds of things, about to wrap up his introduction and get into the first round of the contest.

Well, after taking a minor, well-planned, almost six-months-in-the-making detour courtesy of the marvellous mind of me!

"Ladies and gentlemen," his voice boomed so loudly it was clearly audible backstage where we were standing. "Before we launch into our first round, we have a special surprise for you this evening."

Liam, Declan, Mikey, and I looked at each other excitedly. This was it. The moment had arrived and holy shit, I was jittery as fuck. But hey, if we pulled this off, it would be the most incredible thing ever.

Think happy thoughts, think happy thoughts, think happy thoughts.

"I'd like to call four very special Daddies to the stage. Stirling Bishop, Steel Crawford, Hudson Madden and Mayor Jones, if you could please make your way up to me."

"What the heck?" I heard Hudson say as Liam pushed him toward the stage.

"I've been telling you our boys were up to something." Porter's words were the last ones I heard as I set Steel off toward the stage with a gentle slap across his ass.

"What—what about me?" Addison asked, his dark eyes filled with uncertainty.

I leaned in and whispered in his ear. "Join them. Stand next to Steel."

The crowd roared with approval as four of the finest Daddies, and one gorgeous boy, made their way to center stage.

"Gentlemen, you have been called here tonight because you each have a very special boy. Or boys, as the case may be. And they have been busy planning a very special surprise for you."

A hush fell over the audience.

"Boys," the host called out, "if you would like to make your way to the stage to join your Daddies please."

"This is it," I breathed out loudly.

"We've got this," Mikey said as we exchanged a round of determined nods.

"Let's do it," Liam said, leading the way onto the stage.

I was sure there was applause, and lights, and even a floor under my feet, but I couldn't hear or see any of that. My heartbeat was thundering in my ears and all I could do was keep reminding myself of all the things I felt when I was with Steel and Addison. How right it was, how I knew that I wanted that feeling more than anything else in the world.

Forever.

All four of us assumed our positions beside our Daddies—with me standing next to a confused Steel and an even more confused-looking Addison—as the host stepped away to the side of the stage.

"On my count," I said, summoning up all my strength, but loud enough so that Mikey, Declan and Liam could clearly hear me.

"One."

I looked at the boys, each of them sending me a warm smile. Good, they were ready. Now all I had to do was join them.

"Two."

I closed my eyes briefly. *You can do anything in the world, Nick. You can do this.*

Sure, it was last minute, but thank fuck that voice inside of me finally spoke up. Where the fuck had it been all day? Nevermind, I'd deal with that later.

"Three."

All four of us dropped to one knee, and we each grabbed the hands of our Daddies.

Or in my case, my Daddy and my older brother.

A series of *aws* and gentle cries flew out of the audience as they realized what was happening in front of them.

Yep.

A quadruple proposal.

"Steel, Addison," I said looking up at them, already feeling the tears ready to fall, even though I'd barely said two words. "What we have is so, so special. I know that it's new and that we have a lot of stuff to figure out, and that I can be a lot sometimes, and that what I'm about to ask you isn't entirely legal but....will the two of you marry me?"

"Oh, baby." Steel looked at me with so much love in his eyes that I thought I would cry.

Oh wait, too late. I already was.

"Yes, of course, baby."

I looked over at Addison. His mouth was gaping half open. His stare was solid, his face frozen.

Oh shit, I'd gone too far.

He wasn't ready.

This wasn't what he wanted.

I was such an idiot for even thinking this stupid idea would—

"Yes."

I blinked and the next time I opened my eyes, the widest smile was filling his face. He and Steel pulled me up into the tightest hug in the history of hugs. Their warm bodies pressed against mine felt like everything I had ever wanted.

Safety.

Acceptance.

Passion.

Love.

So much love that I never wanted to pull myself away from either one of them.

Steel spoke first, while our bodies remained glued together. "I hate to sound like the lawyer here, but you do realize that we can't technically get married, right?"

"Well, not in the legal sense," I replied, not letting go of either one of them.

I could feel Addison's cheeks stretching out against my face as he smiled at my smartass remark.

"But we can have a non-legally binding ceremony. There's no law against that." he said, his grip only getting tighter too.

"We can," I replied. "And, by the way, fuck rules. Right?"

"Exactly. Fuck rules," Addison said defiantly.

"Fuck rules," Steel joined in.

"And while we're fucking rules," I said, not pulling away from either one of them, not even an inch. "There's nothing stopping a certain Daddy from buying his two boys the most expensive, biggest, dazzliest diamond rings in the world."

Steel pulled away, ever so slightly and only far enough to see both of our faces.

"Oh, for sure," he said, his voice thick with emotion. "But baby, there isn't a diamond big enough in this universe—"

"Actually, there are," I interrupted. "And they're all at Tiffany's in New York. I've become addicted to their website."

Steel let out a soft laugh. "Alright, well it looks like I'm taking my two beautiful boys to New York City then."

"Yay," Addison added before leaning in closer. "Is it alright that

I am just as excited about the potential of eating more New York hot dogs as I am about the jewelry?"

I brushed a hair off his forehead and wrapped it around his ear. "Absolutely. That's one of the reasons why...why...I love you, Addison."

His eyes widened and I could see him swallowing hard. "I—I love you too, Nick."

"And I love you, Addison."

We both turned our heads toward Steel. His eyes were locked on Addison.

"I'm sorry I made you wait. I'm sorry my insecurities made you doubt yourself. And I'm sorry I didn't say these words to you sooner. But I do. I love you, Addison Mark. I love both of you. The two of you make me so freaking happy I can't even begin to describe it."

A big tear spilled down Addison's face. Steel wiped it away, but as soon as he did, it was just replaced with another one. And another one. And yet another one after that.

Finally, they stopped, and with his whole body trembling, Addison opened his mouth and said, "I love you too, Steel."

Fireworks started ringing out in my heart. No wait, the fireworks were actually going off on the giant screen at the back of the stage. I'd gotten so wrapped up in the moment I had forgotten I'd planned for that to happen months ago.

I looked around the stage and saw each of the couples in various stages of either kissing or embracing each other.

"Daddies, can we have your answers please?" the MC's voice boomed.

"Yes!" Porter was the first to say it out loudly enough for everyone in the packed club to hear. The crowd erupted in a massive roar.

Hudson smiled and gave two thumbs up.

Stirling nodded his head as he held Mikey by the side of his body. I'd never seen either one of them beaming like that before.

And then it was Steel's turn.

"Fuck yeah," he cried out and the audience stormed to their feet, giving us all a standing ovation.

I closed my eyes and took it all in. The applause buzzed in my ears as my skin tingled with all the love I felt. Not just from Steel and Addison, but all around us. I opened my eyes and could see each of my friends with their Daddies, slowly walking off the stage with an aura of love around them all.

As we joined them, I felt Steel grab my right hand and Addison my left.

Fuck rules.

Hey, I'd been doing it my whole life anyway. I was used to being looked at, judged, sometimes even insulted simply for looking the way I did. And I never let it get to me. I was who I was, and I loved myself. All of me, even the parts that people tried to tell me I should hate or change.

And now, I had the two most unbelievable men I had ever met feeling the same way about me too. I knew they loved me—every single part of me—unconditionally.

I blew out a deep breath. I had no idea what would happen once we stepped off that stage or what our future would look like. Steel was right that throuple marriages weren't a thing, in a legal sense. But in a way, I didn't care. I didn't need legal recognition that may or may not ever eventuate. I wasn't going to wait for some archaic legal system to catch up with what was in my heart.

I'd found the two people I wanted to spend the rest of my life with. And no one could do anything about it.

I had found my Daddy.

I had also found my older brother.

And just as importantly, I had found myself. I was exactly who I was meant to be, where I was meant to be.

This big boy had just found his happily ever after. One that was as special and unique as I was.

One that would be filled with endless laughter on the couch as we snuggled and watched TV...or found more pop diva puzzles to complete.

One that included play dates in the nursery where I could access the freedom I found in being a little.

One that made much better use of a kitchen countertop than just cooking, with Addison and me hungrily lapping at our Daddy's ass.

And one that involved a big-ass diamond ring that I would be incredibly modest about and never flaunt.

Kidding!

I was going to show that bling off to every single man, woman, and child in Daylesford.

I was happy.

Truly happy.

And I wanted everyone in the world to know it.

EPILOGUE 1

Six months later...

ADDISON

I turned the tap off and began drying my hands. Once I was done, I placed the hand towel back over the rail and looked at myself in the bathroom mirror. I could see my brown eyes searching my face. I was looking at myself in a strangely intense manner for some reason. Like I was trying to find something, or like something was missing.

And then it hit me like a bolt of lightning. I covered my mouth as I took half a step back. Then, I took a step forward and leaned in closer to the mirror.

Something *was* missing.

For the first time in who knew how long—forever, maybe?—I didn't have a running monologue of internal hatred and viscous criticism running through my mind.

You're too old.

You're ugly.

Those lines are getting deeper.

Your hair is getting grayer.

No one is ever going to love you.

Nope. There was none of that.

I let out a gasp as the enormity of the realization hit me. For so many years, those voices in my head had criticized the fuck out of me. I was so used to scrutinizing every single last aspect of my appearance with such brutality that now that I wasn't doing that anymore, it almost felt a little weird.

Almost.

I could get over that pretty damn fast. I didn't miss it for a second. Good fucking riddance. I was as glad to get over my internal doubts and fears as I was to have seen the end of 2020, because that year had been a fucking nightmare wrapped in a shitshow inside a trainwreck.

I studied my features in the mirror again. Now that the negative voices in my head were gone, something else was in their place. I wouldn't say *love* exactly, that would have been a bridge too far, but I deffers liked what I was seeing.

I was a good-looking guy. And it felt nice to be able to recognize that and, heck, maybe even enjoy it. And who knew? Maybe one day feelings of liking myself could turn into feelings of loving myself.

Just like my feelings for Nick and Steel had.

I broke out into a wide smile at the thought of my boyfriends. The last six months since Nick's completely unexpected proposal had been a dream. No wait, dreams ended when you woke up. This was a million times better. It kept going and going and going.

I had never met anyone even remotely like Nick in my whole life. I think I could have traveled the world a couple of times over and still never found anyone like him. He was my boyfriend. My little brother. A brat at times. A beautiful boy. *My* beautiful boy.

Well, technically, *our* beautiful boy.

"Hello, Addison?" Steel's voice rang out.

I looked down at the time. Three o'clock, right on the dot. Always on time, like he was every Wednesday afternoon for our weekly date.

"I'm coming," I yelled, shaking my head to let my hair cascade around my shoulders. Just the way my Daddy liked. I opened the door, walked down the short hallway, and out onto the floor of the gallery.

My gallery.

Yeppers, I still couldn't believe it myself sometimes. But with Nick's constant encouragement, and with Steel's incredibly generous down payment—which I had every intention of fully paying back—I was the proud owner of Daylesford's newest photography gallery. And thanks to Declan pulling a few strings at *The Daylesford Times*, the favorable review I got resulted in a ton of interest, sales, and perhaps most importantly for me—acclaim.

Sure, I wanted the gallery to be profitable, but more than that, I wanted people to connect with the work. To be moved by it. To enjoy it. That was why I did it. Being able to bring people into a world that you create, and have them forget about whatever was happening in their own lives, was one of the most powerful things in the world. And it really was so humbling to have the opportunity to live out my dream.

And it was all because of the two ah-mazing men I had in my life.

Steel was standing by a huge twelve-foot, black-and-white print.

"Do you see anything you like, sir?" I said as I stepped up beside him, taking in the beautiful image.

"Oh, I do." Without averting his gaze, his strong arm reached around my waist as he pulled me in against him.

"He's got beautiful eyes," I said, examining the image carefully.

It was up there as being one of my all-time favorites. A super extreme close-up of two men's faces. Sweat lined their foreheads, mouths wide open, clearly in the throes of a very passionate, very intimate experience.

"He does," Steel agreed. "I think that was taken just as I was about to blow a load in his ass."

"Good memory," I replied with a smirk as Steel looked at me and gave me a tender kiss, brushing his fingers gently through my hair.

"And then there's this one," Steel said as he moved over to the next image. Another close-up. Two men. Same situation, making love. Only a different pair of eyes.

Mine.

"That's the second time you made love to me." I smiled, transporting myself back to that sacred moment, with Steel deep inside me and Nick taking the photo. I would never forget it for as long as I lived.

Steel's fingers settled at the small of my back. "It was one of the most magical experiences of my life."

A happy heat settled in my chest. "For me as well."

I rested my head on his solid shoulder, unable to believe how lucky I was. To think I had ever doubted Steel's feelings for me.

The three of us had sat down and talked a lot right after Nick's proposal. Like, *stay up all night until the sun comes up* kinda talking. But we needed to do it. We had to be honest and put it all out there.

Hearing Steel open up and tell me about his insecurities as a Daddy who felt he wasn't good enough for his own boy, much less two, surprised me. I guess it shouldn't have, because hey, Daddies are human too. I suppose I had put him up on an unrealistic pedestal. Well, there was that, and then there was me assuming he wasn't interested in me because I was too old.

I couldn't have been more wrong.

Over the past six months, Steel made me feel like one of the two most beautiful boys in the world. And our weekly Wednesday afternoon date—just him and me—was one of the ways he did that.

The three of us agreed that we needed time as a throuple, but also individual couple time too. Nick and I had our play dates as littles, but we also did things as adults too, like going to the movies together. Nick and Steel decided on a once-a-week dinner out, while Steel and I had our weekly afternoon together.

Despite living in Daylesford for over a decade, I hadn't gone hiking in its beautiful surroundings. Not even once. When Steel heard that, he took it as a challenge and made it his personal mission for us to do every single hike we could.

"I need to get changed," I said, pulling away as I eyed him up and down in his super-tight hiking gear. The shirt cupped his biceps and pecs nicely, but it was his shorts that drew my attention. Navy blue and hugging his meaty round ass so tight that it made me hard on the spot.

Steel noticed the tentpole that had formed in my pants and smiled. "Need help?"

"Sure." His fingers found my crotch. "Let me just close the front door."

"In a minute. There's something I have to do first." Steel's lips found my neck. My head fell back as he delicately bit into me, the sensation unleashing a torrent of desire within me.

"Shouldn't we save ourselves for Nick?" I asked as his tongue swirled around my Adam's apple.

It was another part of our weekly date, that when the two of us were done hiking, we would go home, have dinner with Nick, and then fuck all night. Although that last part was more of a nightly tradition than just a weekly one.

"He and I have already had a play today," I explained.

Steel stopped what he was doing and looked at me, his eyes scorching with arousal. "When?"

"This morning. He left Remy in charge of the bakery and said he just wanted to say hi... to my dick."

A low chuckle fell out of Steel's mouth. "Seems he's been a busy boy."

I lifted an eyebrow. "What do you mean?"

"He stopped by the office right after lunch. He said he just wanted to say hi...to my ass."

My cheeks heated. "He rimmed you at the office?"

"He did."

"That naughty boy."

Steel's lips crashed into mine. "He's so naughty."

"The naughtiest," I agreed before our tongues tangled together. "Door first, then dicks. Okay?"

Somehow, I managed to free myself from the magnetic pull of Steel's body, closed the door, and moved us toward the back of the studio, out of sight of any pesky passersby.

He dropped to his knees as soon as he could and began wrestling with my belt buckle.

"No, no," I said, hooking my fingers under his chin and tilting his head up to meet my gaze. "You mentioned Nick gave you a rimming today?"

Steel nodded.

"Well, I want to see if I can still taste him on you."

A wide grin stretched his pink lips. "Go ahead then."

In no time, Steel had peeled off his practically skin-tight hiking shorts and assumed the position. Ah, the position. I savored it for a delicious, mouth watering few moments. The sexy silver fox on his back, his legs up in the air, his light blue eyes filled with need and...vulnerability.

Fuck, that got me hard.

I lay down on the floor, right at ass level. I gripped his solid flesh with my fingers, before pulling his cheeks apart. His puckered hole tantalized me. I leaned in and smiled.

"Yep, I can tell that he's been here. He's left his scent on you."

"Strawberries," we both said at the same time and laughed.

Just when I thought rimming Steel couldn't get any better, Nick had found a way to do just that. I leaned in and devoured his hole with my tongue as the swirl of a light strawberry scent gently swam in the air around us.

I grabbed Steel's granite cock and began to jack him off, my tongue burying deeper into him. He started moaning—low, deep, and needy. His heavy balls slapped noisily against his skin...and my forehead.

"I'm gonna come, I'm gonna come."

His body rocked and spasmed with every rope of release that erupted out of his cock. I stopped lapping at his hole, but kept my tongue still against his bucking body.

When he was done, I looked at his cum-covered abs, then farther up to his cum-covered chest, before finally seeing his cum-covered chin and face. Holy shit, Steel had completely covered himself.

"Looks like you've made quite the mess here," I said as I ran my tongue along the pearly white release that had settled in the groove between his abs.

"What can I say?" he said as he ran his hand over his face, wiping some of the cum away. "You get me off like only one other boy can."

I reached for his hand and brought his sticky fingers to my mouth and hungrily slurped at them, tasting his thick release on my tongue before swallowing it down. His saltiness always tasted so good, so fucking manly.

When I was done cleaning his fingers, as well as licking up and down the length of his entire torso until not a single droplet of cum remained, I looked into his eyes and said, "Well, it's a good thing I'm one of your two boys, and you're my...Daddy."

His lips twitched in that way they always did whenever Nick or I called him that.

His eyes twinkled. "I love you so much, Addison."

"I love you, too." I smiled as I knew there was no way in hell we were going hiking. "Now, maybe we should go see whether you can taste Nick on my cock?"

EPILOGUE 2

Nine months later...

NICK

Steel's and Addison's eyes were glued to me. I had their full and undivided attention.

Just the way I liked it.

"I've called you both here," I said, trying to keep my face straight and tone even. "Because I have three things I would like to discuss with you."

They exchanged a quick look with one another, and so far, I had them right where I wanted them. I'd called this mid-afternoon meeting for three reasons, that part was true. But only two of the reasons were serious, so my plan was to start with the fun thing first before moving to the other stuff. I mean, what was wrong with eating dessert and then having dinner, right?

"What is it, Nick? Is everything alright?" Addison reached his hand across the dining table. His touch ignited my insides...as it always did. Despite his pensive look, he did his best to flash me a smile.

"Why don't you tell me?" And with those last serious words, I got up and stood on the chair in front of them both. "Do these Daisy Duke shorts make my ass look big?"

I looked down at the two surprised faces of the men I loved more than anyone else in the world. Their facial expressions flitted from disbelief to confusion to happiness.

Again, just the way I liked it.

Steel was the first to speak. "I think there's only one correct answer to that question."

I saw him grip Addison's hand as they both let out a resounding, "Yes!"

I was beaming with pride as I made my way back down into the chair.

"Good." I basked in the glory of their response for a few moments longer. "You shall both have the pleasure of ripping them off me at some stage in the not-too-distant future."

The edges of Steel's lips rose in amusement. "Oh, will we now?"

"I can't wait," Addison added, rubbing his hands together gleefully.

"Good." I sat up a little straighter and placed my palms on the table, all professional-like. "Now that that's taken care of, we can move on to the next item on my agenda."

"There's an agenda?" Steel teased playfully.

I gave a quick—professional—nod. "Yes, this next item relates to business matters, so I would appreciate your seriousness. Thank you very much."

Addison started giggling but covered his mouth to try and hide it. God, he was so utterly gorgeous. He pulled a strand of loose hair behind his ears and turned to face me. What I would have given to reach across the table, mess his hair up, and plunge my tongue into that sweet mouth of his.

Focus, Nick. Focus.

I cleared my throat. "It's about the bakery."

Steel frowned. "Is everything okay, baby?"

"Yes, it is. In fact, it's more than just okay." I turned my head, scanning the room as if I were looking for something I had lost. "I actually have something to give you, Steel. But where oh where did I put it?"

I glanced over and saw Steel and Addison looking just as confused as they had been before. I tried not to smile, but I was enjoying this too much.

I'd finally found not one, but two people who could handle me. All of me. Even when I was unfiltered.

Loud.

Weird.

Bratty.

Bold.

Beautiful.

Young.

Restless.

And any other daytime soap opera title that was appropriate.

They both loved all of me. *All of me.* And *that* was the best feeling in the world.

"Ah, there it is." I pretended I had spotted what I was looking for as I stood up.

Slowly.

Seductively.

Letting their eyes feast on my massive ass, more than half of which was hanging out of these ridiculously short shorts. And my thighs. Geez Louise, my thighs could literally save lives (another line I was borrowing from Lizzo). And boy oh boy, did my two men like what they were seeing as I strutted over to the far side of the dining room. Their eyes never left me—or my butt—for even a second.

"Oh dear." I clutched my chest for dramatic effect as I looked down at the envelope that lay on the carpeted floor. "How did that get here?"

I bent over to pick it up. Yep, you guessed it.

Slowly.

Seductively.

Making my booty pop as if I were back in my go-go dancing days and needing to make money to cover rent.

The air in the room was thick with anticipation. Steel was practically drooling as I walked back to the table, envelope in hand, while Addison had that look on his face that he always did whenever I whispered something wildly inappropriate in his ear when we were in public, and he popped a boner. Which happened a lot. Like, *a lot* a lot.

"What—" Steel's voice cracked as if he were going through a second puberty. He stiffened before continuing. "What have you got there, baby?"

"It's for you," I said, sliding the envelope across the smooth oak table.

He did a quick side glance over to Addison who shrugged his shoulders. Steel picked the envelope up and tore it open. A thin piece of paper fell out, landing on the table. He grabbed it and then his eyes went wide.

He looked up at me with disbelief and pride and amazement in his eyes. Just the combination I was going for.

"Nick, you really didn't have to do this." His voice was choked up with emotion.

"What is it?" Addison asked, and Steel slid the cheque over for him to see.

"I know I didn't have to, Steel. But I wanted to. I promised you when you bought the bakery for me that somehow, someday, I would pay you back. So, here we are. Somehow, someday has arrived, and I'm paying you back."

"Wow, that's incredible, Nick." I could see the pride written all over Addison's face as well.

"Well, actually, it's largely due to you," I said, returning his loving gaze. "You were the one who kept pushing me to rectify the terrible coffee situation in America...so I did. And it's been going..." I started clicking my fingers, hoping the Aussie word he had taught me last night would come back to me.

"Gangbusters," he said, totally picking up what I was trying to put down.

"Yeah, gangbusters," I said happily.

"Gangbusters?" Steel asked.

"It means *awesome* in Australian," Addison explained, playfully bumping Steel.

"Ah, I see. Well, Nick, this is beyond incredible."

"Did you expect anything less from me?" I asked cockily.

Steel's response was instant and firm. "Never...God, how did I get so lucky?"

His eyes moved between the two of us and I felt a surge of warmth fill the room.

Steel's question was one I asked myself every day as well. I still couldn't believe it. After the rocky start he and I had had, to the awful way that Addison and I had met, to all of the talking the three of us had to do to get to where we were now. If I had gone to a clairvoyant three years ago and they had told me that this was my future, I would have told them to stop smoking whatever incense they were inhaling.

But here I was, having the best experience of my life. Sharing myself—all of me—with the two most beautiful men in the world. My Daddy and my older brother.

"Which brings me to my third and final item."

I chewed on my lower lip, batted my eyelids, and looked all-round adorable. I could practically hear their hearts melting at my display, but there was an element of genuine seriousness behind it.

"I owe you an apology, Steel, and you a thank you, Addison."

"Oh." Steel sat up a little straighter.

"Yeah, I don't know if you remember a conversation we had a

while ago. A long while ago, actually. One where I said I would tell you every day how lucky I felt to be with you."

"I remember," Steel said softly.

"Yeah, well, then you'll know that I let that slide. A bit...okay, a lot. I guess life just got in the way. I proposed, things got busy for me at the bakery, Addison opened up his gallery... Anyway, those are all pathetic excuses, so I am recommitting to tell you every day, starting right now, how lucky I am to be your boy. Well, one of your boys."

I shot a smile at Addison, whose eyes sparkled back at me warmly.

But it was Steel's eyes that got me right in the heart. They were filled to the brim with tears.

"Thank you, baby," he whispered. "That means the world to me."

"You both mean the world to me," I said, fighting back my own tears. But I wasn't done yet. I could cry after I said what I needed to say to Addison. I needed to be strong and do that first.

"And Addison," I began as I turned to face him. "I owe you a big-ass thank you."

"Why?"

"Because of you, I've found the thing that was missing in my life, and the thing that was holding me back from really and truly letting go and becoming a little."

It had been dawning on me over the past few months. But in the same way I hadn't been able to tell Steel how lucky I was to have him every day, something had kept me from sharing my true feelings with Addison as well. But that stopped right now.

"I've never had a brother or a sister, and I never truly appreciated how much I missed that growing up. When we become littles, it's like I get to go back and relive that part of my childhood that was missing..."

I suddenly stopped, feeling super self-conscious...and stupid. Was that the dumbest reason in the world or what?

And then Addison said the words that made everything right in my world.

"That's so beautiful, Nick. I'm honored that I'm able to do that for you."

"Really?" I asked timidly. "You don't think it's weird or dumb?"

"Not at all." His voice was definitive. "Everyone has their own reasons for and their own ways of being a little. Nothing is right, nothing is wrong, there's only what works for you...and us."

His words felt like a warm bath, soothing every muscle and joint in my body.

"Hey, Nick," he asked softly. "Would you like to be a little now?"

I felt like I was floating as I nodded my head. We all got up and walked to the nursery, holding hands. Steel and Addison undressed me, carefully putting aside the short denim shorts and black shirt I was wearing as they worked together to slip me into my favorite orange onesie.

My breathing slowed as I became hyper-aware of every little movement and sound around me. Steel paced around the room, turning on every single lamp to soften the lighting.

I felt like I was riding a bike downhill, the wind hitting my smiling face. My stomach was light, my hair was messy, and I was freefalling into the most wonderful, blissful feeling in the world.

I was ready.

I was free.

I was finally a little.

EPILOGUE 3

Twelve months later...

STEEL

"We're here. We're finally here."

Nick's joyous words rang out in my ears as I smiled. He and Addison were having one of their moments, and I could totally see it. This was one of those movie-magic moments they both seemed to love so much.

"Now I know what people who reach the top of Mount Everest must feel like," Addison said.

I managed to suppress a chuckle. "Really? We flew first class and have walked two blocks from our luxury hotel to get here."

"He means the wonder of it all, Steel," Nick said, instantly knowing what Addison was referring to and translating it for me. There had been a lot of that over the past twelve months with my two boys...and I'd loved every second of it.

I looked at their smiling happy faces and my heart glowed.

Whatever doubts I had had about not being able to be a good Daddy for two boys were well and truly behind me now.

Were things always smooth sailing? No.

But was I certain that through talking and loving each other with everything we had in us, we'd get through it? Yeppers!

Okay, so maybe I still didn't have my own catchphrase, but that was okay. I was perfectly content to occasionally borrow one from my two boys. They were up to their clackers with new Aussie-isms and catchphrases.

Wait. Clacker? Well, there you go. I had picked up an Aussie-ism without even realizing it.

"I can't believe it's been almost a year since the night of the epic quadruple wedding proposal at Deffers and we're only getting around to this now."

I felt Nick's hand giving my ass a playful pinch right in the middle of Fifth Avenue.

"And before you say it, Steel," Addison jumped in. "Yes, we know we can't legally get married."

"But we can legally get jewelry," Nick added, and the two boys laughed.

I looked up at the iconic *Tiffany & Co* sign. "Well, these rings aren't going to buy themselves. Are you boys ready?"

Nick shot me a cheeky grin. "I feel like my whole life has been leading up to this moment. I am in the mood for something...expensive."

"Ooh, and sparkly," Addison said with a wide smile.

"Deffers." Nick wrapped his arms around Addison's shoulder. I took his other hand in mine as we walked into the store.

We were met by a lovely attendant who introduced herself as Sarah. She looked to be in her mid-twenties, with a friendly face and short-cropped blonde hair.

"We're looking for engagement rings," I said.

"Sparkly ones."

"Expensive ones."

Of course my two boys would say that. God, how I loved how unfiltered and real they were. Even in one of the fanciest stores in the world, Nick and Addison were...Nick and Addison.

Sarah's bright blue eyes glanced between the three of us before she opened her mouth and let out a delighted little squeal.

"Oh my gosh, for the three of you?" We all nodded. "Oh, you guys, that is so beautiful. Follow me, please."

We followed her to a pristine counter filled with the most exquisite jewelry I had seen in my life. She walked away to grab us an extra stool, and we proceeded to plonk ourselves down as she walked around to the other side of the counter. Nick and Addison had their faces glued to all the expensive, sparkling jewelry contained underneath the polished glass countertop.

"See anything you like, boys?"

Nick let out a gasp as he pressed his index finger into the glass. "There it is."

"Excellent choice," Sarah remarked as she moved to open the cabinet and pulled out the piece of jewelry that had clearly made an impression on Nick.

"Ooh, I like it," Addison cooed as Sarah laid it out for all three of us to see.

"This is an excellent choice," she began as I leaned in closer to inspect it for myself. "This is a Tiffany T, True Wide Ring. It's eighteen-karat gold with round brilliant diamonds. And the best thing...?"

We all looked up at her at the same time. A smile stretched her lips as she moved in closer as if to whisper what she was about to say next.

"...Is that it comes in three different versions. White gold, rose gold, and classic."

"Three?" Addison asked, and then started nodding his head as it began to make sense to him.

"Three," Nick affirmed. His brown eyes shot up at me, a look of pure joy radiated from his every pore.

"Three." I cupped my hands over my boys'. "Could we see them all, please?" I asked Sarah and she obliged.

"Rose gold looks a little like...orange," Nick said, casting a knowing look at Addison and me. I smiled as memories of Nick in his favorite orange onesie came flooding back.

"And classic gold looks like yellow," Addison said, looking at both of us.

"That's your favorite color," I pointed out as he grinned crazy wide.

"And white gold," Addison said, "Looks a lot like the color of..."

"Steel." Hearing both boys say my name at the same time sealed the deal for me. We had found the perfect symbol of our love.

I didn't even really care that our union wouldn't be legally recognized. There was no one on the face of this earth who could tell me that what we had wasn't as real or valid as the love between two people, or five people, or fifteen people for that matter.

We lived in a world where love was so fragile that when people stumbled upon it and somehow, despite the odds, managed to make it work, that deserved to be celebrated. In all its forms.

"These rings are perfect," I told Sarah. "We'll take them please."

"Thank you, Daddy," Addison said.

"Yes, thank you, Daddy. I'm the luckiest boy in the world. Well, one of the two luckiest boys in the world," Nick corrected himself, smiling at Addison.

A happiness settled in my belly. It never got old, hearing my boys call me *Daddy,* and it always sent a tingle down my spine when Nick told me how lucky he was...every single day. Just like he had committed to doing.

After Sarah took our finger measurements, my two boys and I walked out of that store as changed men. We now had a symbol of our love that we would wear every single day for the rest of our lives.

Maybe the bustling Fifth Avenue wasn't the best place to say it or do it, but I couldn't hold it in any longer. I stepped in toward my boys and brought them in to a tight bear hug even Hudson would have been proud of.

"I love you boys so much," I said as I stroked the backs of their heads, my eyes fixed on the ring on my right hand. Yes, I knew that engagement rings technically belong on the left hand, but hey...*fuck rules*.

"We love you too, Daddy," my boys chimed back, and given that I couldn't feel their arms around me, I got the distinct impression that all three of us were hugging each other in the middle of Manhattan...while checking out the newly purchased bling we were all rocking.

Our mutual jewelry appreciation moment was interrupted by my phone vibrating in my pants pocket. I peeled myself off my boys, took it out, and let out a loud sigh.

"What is it?" Addison asked.

"It's Porter. I'm late."

"Which means we're late too," Nick added.

Yep, what had started out as our little private weekend away in NYC had become a whole family affair. All four Daddies and all five boys.

"Where do you boys have to be?" I asked.

"Times Square," Nick said with an eye roll that could have been seen from space. "Mikey wants to do the whole tourist thing. He said he would literally die if we didn't take a fivesome selfie in the middle of New York. What about you?"

I momentarily considered doing my own version of Nick's eye roll but decided against it. Public humiliation wasn't really my jam.

"Must be something in the water. Porter's booked us a...er, bus tour."

"Bus tour?" Nick and Addison asked in unison.

Hmpf. I didn't think they'd let it go that easy.

"Uh, yeah. It's meant to be pretty popular. Totally touristy, of course."

"What kind of tour is it, Steel?" Addison asked, his dark eyes narrowing.

"Yeah, Steel, what kind of tour is it?" Nick parroted, and I could have sworn my boys were enjoying this way more than they should have been.

I scratched the back of my neck.

"It's the *Sex and the City* tour. Not my idea," I added quickly.

The boys laughed.

"You'll have fun," Nick said, running his hand across my chest. "Let's both order Ubers, and then Addison and I will meet you back at the hotel once we're all done."

"Yeah, Daddy," Addison breathed into my ear. "We might have a surprise for you. Did you happen to notice the really nice countertop in the kitchen of our suite?"

A surge of heat tore through me and brought my cock to life. I looked around and reminded myself that we were in public. I gave them both a soft kiss to the lips, all of a sudden feeling like I would have been happy to skip the tour part and go straight to the hotel.

"Sounds like a plan," I said. "Oh, but if I call you at three in the morning and tell you I'm having a great time in a sex dungeon that Porter dragged us all to, you'll know what that means?"

Both boys frowned at me.

I continued, "It means Porter has officially kidnapped all of us and I need help. Call the police to get me outta there."

We all laughed as two Ubers pulled up at the same time. I gave each boy one more kiss—because why the fuck would I ever give up an opportunity to give them one more kiss?—and then got whisked away.

As the driver made his way up Fifth Avenue and past Central Park, my mind drifted, thinking about how incredible the past twelve months had been. And to think, I had come *this close* to throwing it all away because of some internal fears that hadn't even turned out to be true anyway.

Loving two people had taught me an important lesson: love really was limitless. I'd always thought that my feelings for Addison were wrong because they signalled that my feelings for Nick had diminished. Even though I could feel in my heart that it wasn't true, my head had tried to overrule me and convince me otherwise.

The car stopped and the driver turned and said, "Here we are."

"Great, thanks." I stepped out onto the busy sidewalk.

"Steel." I heard Stirling's deep voice over the hustle and bustle of the street.

Ah, there they were. My three closest friends standing slightly apart from what looked like a way too overexcited group of tourists. I saw sun visors and fanny packs, as well as some very sharply dressed women with exquisite shoes, and more than a few campy-looking guys wearing *SATC* shirts.

After a round of quick hugs, we were escorted into a bright pink bus emblazoned with *SATC* in glittery gold writing across the side. There went my *no humiliation in public* policy.

"Who's idea was this?" I asked as the four of us sat bunched together in the back row, our knees knocking against each other.

"Porter booked it," Stirling said, looking about as happy as I felt.

"Only because Hudson conveniently was out of Wi-Fi range and begged me to do it," Porter shot back.

"Guilty as charged," Hudson said with a shit-eating grin on his face as he tried to wrap his hands around his neck, only to realize there wasn't enough space for such a manoeuvre.

"Smooth moves, man," I teased, and we all chuckled.

Porter shuffled in his seat. "At least we have proper back support."

He had a point. Hudson leaned in closer. "At least I booked the two-hour tour and not the seven-hour one. You guys should be thanking me."

"Jesus," Stirling exclaimed. "People willingly sign up to do this for seven hours?"

Hudson's grin wasn't leaving his face. "They sure do. Look, you guys, I was killing Liam with my repeated viewings of *Romy and Michele's High School Reunion,* so he put me onto this show. And OMG..."

I burst out laughing, watching my massive, tatted friend acting like an excited school boy.

"It's so, *so* good. You guys have to watch it."

"Pass."

"Pass."

"Pass. I spent way too fucking long being called the Samantha of the group. I think I'm still traumatized by it."

Stirling looked at me and smiled. We were both thinking the same thing. These guys—these crazy, stupid, amazing, brilliant, sometimes infuriating but always loyal, loving, and supportive guys—were our brothers.

And they would be forever.

"Hey, isn't *Daylesford's Most Eligible Daddy Contest* taking place this weekend at Deffers?" Porter asked.

"Yeppers," I said with a broad smile. "It sure is."

"Do you miss not being there for it?"

"Not even for a split second."

The four of us sat in silence for a minute. Or at least as much silence as we could expect to find on a bus with overeager tourists-slash-fans screaming with delight every time the announcer mentioned something like *"That's the restaurant where Miranda and Charlotte had brunch,"* or *"That's the street corner where Carrie had a fight with Mr. Big in the rain."*

Who the hell was Mr. Big?

"It feels like the end of an era, you guys," Hudson remarked wistfully, while still managing to pay attention to everything the announcer was saying, his head twisting and his cellphone snapping photos of every last detail.

In a way, he was right. There was a feeling of things ending, or at the very least, changing.

"Hey, did I tell you guys what Declan and I did last night in the hotel room? It involves—"

"Someone make him stop," Stirling cried out.

And then...some things would never change. My head hit the back of the seat as I smiled.

"It feels good to be moving on with our lives," Hudson said, looking at us.

"It does," I agreed.

"We've all found our special boy...or boys in your case, Steel," Porter said as he flashed me a sincere smile. "Who needs things like Daddy contests or nonstop sex marathons that last all weekend? What we've all found is so much more special and amazing."

We all nodded our heads dreamily, each one of us absorbed by thoughts of the incredible boys we had the privilege of loving. We really were the four luckiest Daddies in the universe.

"Maybe things aren't necessarily ending," I said, picking up on Hudson's earlier comment. "Maybe it's time for us to hand the keys over to a new generation, you know?"

My question was met with more nodding.

"After all, there are plenty more Daddies in the sea..."

THE END

ABOUT CASEY COX

Contemporary/New Adult MM Romance Author

Casey Cox is devoted to delighting readers with sassy, sweet and sometimes steamy MM gay romance tales of gorgeous, good-hearted and complex men chasing that thing we all love: a guaranteed HEA.

Casey lives on the east coast of Australia, loves the beach and is a proud fur-parent to two utterly adorable, perfectly-perfect French Bulldogs named Ralphie and Lilly.

For more information, please visit
www.caseycoxbooks.com

www.ingramcontent.com/pod-product-compliance
Lightning Source LLC
Chambersburg PA
CBHW020546020726
47494CB00006B/1948